I Saw
THREE SHIPS

Also by Bill Richardson

FOR CHILDREN

After Hamelin

The Alphabet Thief (with Roxanna Bikadoroff)

The Aunts Come Marching (with Cynthia Nugent)

The Bunny Band (with Roxanna Bikadoroff)

But If They Do (with Marc Mongeau)

The Promise Basket (with Slavka Kolesar)

Sally Dog Little (with Céline Malépart)

Sally Dog Little, Undercover Agent (with Céline Malépart)

NOT PRIMARILY INTENDED FOR CHILDREN

Bachelor Brothers' Bed & Breakfast

Bachelor Brothers' Bed & Breakfast Pillow Book

Scorned and Beloved: Dead of Winter Meetings with Canadian Eccentrics

Waiting for Gertrude: A Graveyard Gothic

ABSOLUTELY NOT FOR CHILDREN

The First Little Bastard to Call Me Gramps: Poems of the Late Middle Ages

I Saw THREE SHIPS

WEST END STORIES

Bill Richardson

Talonbooks

Talonbooks
9259 Shaughnessy Street, Vancouver, British Columbia, Canada V6P 6R4
talonbooks.com

Talonbooks is located on xʷməθkʷəy̓əm, S<u>k</u>w<u>x</u>wú7mesh, and səl̓ilwətaʔɬ Lands.

First printing: 2019

Typeset in Minion
Printed and bound in Canada on 100% post-consumer recycled paper

Cover and interior design by andrea bennett

Talonbooks acknowledges the financial support of the Canada Council for the Arts, the Government of Canada through the Canada Book Fund, and the Province of British Columbia through the British Columbia Arts Council and the Book Publishing Tax Credit.

LIBRARY AND ARCHIVES CANADA CATALOGUING IN PUBLICATION

Title: I saw three ships : West End stories / Bill Richardson.
Names: Richardson, Bill, 1955– author.
Identifiers: Canadiana 20190084987 | ISBN 9781772012330 (softcover)
Classification: LCC PS8585.I186 I83 2019 | DDC C813/.54—dc23

For Jean McKay, writer, musician, self-acknowledged ship counter

I play not marches for accepted victors only, I play marches for conquer'd and slain persons.

...

Vivas to those who have fail'd!

—WALT WHITMAN, "SONG OF MYSELF," SECTION 18 (1855)

Contents

FA, LA, LA, LA, LA

Of the thirty-two addresses where I've received mail in the last forty years – I'm restless, I move – twenty-four have been in Vancouver, most in the West End. That's a downtown neighbourhood. Start walking west from any given point, and you'll soon come to the modified forest that's Stanley Park. Head either north – that's towards the mountains – or south, and you'll get to salt water, to Coal Harbour or English Bay. Go east to get to the city's business district. Shopping galore. Whee.

West Enders are apartment dwellers. A few of the big old Edwardian piles that were usual before the war remain, but most of the housing stock is multi-family: three-storey wood-frame walk-ups or mid-rise concrete buildings or high-rise towers with spectacular views from their upper reaches. In the sixties, the West End was a swinger's paradise, the place to be if you wanted to visit an exciting club or rock a bikini or flip your hair in a convertible. By the time I arrived, in the fall of 1978, neighbourhood demographics favoured old people, queer people, and sex-trade workers. It was heaven.

Condos were rare. We had fun in cheap rented quarters. In the spring of '79, I secured a small apartment – my fourth in less than a year – in the Elcho, on Davie Street, a pebble toss from the fabled playground of the Garden Baths. I paid $165 a month for a funky one-bedroom above a bakery and a television repair joint and an antique store where I bought the embroidered kimono I used to wear when I went out dancing. The Gandy! The Luv-A-Fair! The Shaggy Horse! The Elcho was among the first to fall when the present long wave of demolition and construction began. The kimono suffered the fate of all such garments when carelessly laundered with beer and sweat. All known photos have been destroyed.

Sometime after the end of the Elcho and before the Garden Baths burned to the ground – sayonara, Sodom! – queer became more brandable than transgressive. The West End, especially Davie between Burrard and Jervis, roughly speaking, was transformed into Davie Village, a city-sanctioned LGBTQ+ theme park, with signage and banners and hashtags and pedestrian crossings painted like rainbows. This was social progress, no doubt, even though I sometimes hanker after the renegade days when it felt like you were violating community standards just by getting up in the morning and going out into the world and being yourself.

Cultures change and economies change; you'd need to be my age (b. 1955) or older to remember a $165 apartment. Cities and their neighbourhoods change. It's what they do best. When Vancouver's creative class began to migrate east and congregate in the neighbourhoods proximate to Commercial Drive, drawn by the lights of the trendsetting lesbians who went there first, the cool kids followed. While young queers remain a visible presence in the downtown precincts, they don't require the ghetto reassurances we oldsters found and cultivated in the years right after Stonewall. The imperative to claim queer space, physical space, while vital, is maybe now less urgent, more dilute. The Village feels – this is wholly subjective and no doubt many would dispute this – less evolving than historic; less needful, perhaps, than was once so.

This shift, if that's what it is, is morally neutral. I don't judge it, nor do I lament it. What would be the point? I continue to live in the West End. I don't feel like a stranger here, despite the now-and-again twinge of dislocation that comes when old, familiar streetscapes are altered when buildings one has known for decades are bulldozed and tower after tower goes up, all built on podiums of commercial space no small independent businesses or young entrepreneurs can afford. The past is far too precious to waste on something as cheap as nostalgia, but I confess I have it in me to regret – "mourn" would be overstating the case – the loss of a society that sufficiently and collectively values a little apartment over an antique store and bakery and TV repair shop enough that it makes the necessary allowances to accommodate such a possibility. I see my own ghost, young and on the make and trailing a ridiculous kimono, whenever I pass by where the Elcho was, ditto the Garden Baths. The cockroaches, it's true, I could have done without. Ditto the crabs.

The stories in this book are, by and large, West End stories. "Sin Error Pining" is set in Brandon, Manitoba, but is informed by a West End past; "Snow on Snow on Snow on Snow" is more Gastown / Downtown Eastside, but intersects the West End. All the stories – the earliest, "With Man to Dwell," is from 1996 and the most recent, "Since We've No Place to Go," is from 2014 – were written at Christmastime for *The Georgia Straight* or *Reader's Digest* or for CBC Radio.

The stories fit the season of their writing in that they respect mystery. They're about secular people who undergo epiphanic moments of revelation or transcendence, experiences for which faith offers a custom-built cabinet with lots of tidy drawers, but that leave the religiously unpersuaded feeling like the fuselage has depressurized and they're gasping for breath, praying to forces unnamed for the mask to fall. Otherwise, Christmas in these pages is mostly an environmental condition, a prop; it would be a mistake to think of this as a collection of "Christmas stories." "Christmas stories" suggests something wholesome and family-friendly. Whatever else these stories might be, wholesome they ain't. I hope not, anyway; if they're wholesome, I've failed.

These are reworkings of shorter pieces. I wrote the originals quickly, then forgot about them. They languished on hard drives. When I brought them together in the same room – there were about twenty all told at that first meeting – I anticipated an awkward reunion, and I wasn't wrong. There was a lot of unproductive coughing, embarrassed looking away. One by one they stepped outside for a smoke and didn't come back. As I spent time with those who remained, I was struck by how the class of '96 found something to say to more recent graduates. They matched, somehow; their edges were cut to fit. They made plausible claims to kinship.

Unwholesome Christmas stories require unwholesome magi, more stumbling than steady, and my trio of fools emerged in the imperfect persons of Bonnie (Nicola Harwood) and Philip (Davie Denman) and his not entirely loveable, nickname-averse boyfriend, Gary. I was embarrassed, a mite, at an absence of invention, at the degree to which their preoccupations and peccadilloes were my own: aimless adults in late middle age, childless, but clinging to a kind of childhood through their absorption in the lives and requirements of their geriatric parents – their mothers, more exactly. To any reader who wonders if I harbour unresolved daddy issues, I say: I totally understand why you might think so. Vehicular mishaps (road and air!), cardiac collapse, aneurysms, desertion, transmigration into the body of a wolf: apparently I'll resort to anything, no matter how gothic or cheap or convenient, just to excise the paterfamilias so the story can carry on with whatever its business. For the record, no matter how dastardly, bastardly, and cardboard one-dimensional my fictional fathers, Stan Richardson (1926–2014) was a mensch. What's tested here is something less Freudian than writerly, and I wouldn't dispute a simple diagnosis of laziness, my barnacled familiar and long-time bane.

I was interested to see that the stories – incidentally, not deliberately or analytically – compose a casual, informal portrait of the evolving West End; also that they're an unintended Journal of the Plague Years. Vancouver is a port city, and ports are where epidemics traditionally find their first foothold. I've never known a time when the news here wasn't dominated by the fretful reporting of one plague or another. The AIDS pandemic, as eventually we came to call it, was the most tragic and affecting; also, galvanizing. Latterly, the opioid epidemic has cut a horrible swath. Not all our plagues have mortal consequences or play out epidemiologically. Anyone who was here in the mid-nineties will remember the Leaky Condo Plague. Everywhere were residential buildings draped in blue plastic shrouds, carping tarps flapping in the wind like flags signalling shoddy construction, absence of accountability, homeowners on the line, financial ruin.

We've endured, or haven't, the concomitant plagues of speculation, of construction cranes, of displacement. Real estate provokes fever wherever you go, but in few places on the planet does it leech so maniacal, so sweaty a febrility as in Vancouver. (At this moment of writing, I should say, a "correction" is brewing in the market that, by the time of publication, might have become a wholesale bust. Whatever. Ongoing volatility is as safe a prediction as predictions can be.) Scarce accommodation, unaffordable accommodation, the chaos, the disruption of gentrification, the spawning of class divisions, the uncertainty, the suspicion, the envy, the fear, the guilt, the gloating: no one can find its trace elements in blood or saliva or semen, but real estate, broadly speaking, is its own pathology, its own infection. It's too big for one metaphor. It's a mighty ark. There's not enough room to accommodate everyone who wants to clamber on. Tickets are pricey. Lifeboats are few. Who's out there in the frothy wake, drowning, not waving? That would be the homeless, who are legion, and homelessness is our most visible, shameful, needless plague.

But enough, already. Too much, already. Story collections shouldn't need forewords to sustain them. Typically, me, I never read them; forewords, I mean. The only reason I hope anyone has had the patience to have endured this far is so she/he/they will know how truly thankful I am to Talonbooks, a venerable Vancouver publisher, for giving these stories a second chance at life. To Kevin and Vicki Williams, to andrea bennett, both for her editorial and graphic acumen, to Charles "Eagle Eye" Simard, and to all and sundry at the house, my gratitude. I acknowledge my late agent, Esther Poundcake (?–2018) who never did anything during our years together to get me a big advance or tout my name in London or Frankfurt but was one hell of a poodle. I loved her and I miss her and I will fulfill the promise I made during her last hours on Earth, when she was unable to rise from the floor and the vet was on her way, that I would allocate her 15 percent cut of whatever the proceeds from sales to the purchase of meat.

There are some beautiful words in this book and they're all Walt Whitman's. The epigraph and envoi, as well as the quotations that appear in "Everybody Knows a Turkey" and in "Snow on Snow on Snow on Snow," are from a 1915 edition of *Leaves of Grass* (London: George G. Harrap and Co.). Thanks to Holmfield and Crystal City and the dish pit at Whole Foods, Robson, and most especially to William Joel Ze'ev Pechet, who knows all the reasons why. I neither applied for nor received grants from publicly funded agencies during the writing of this book, so, like, you know, relax. Finally, I salute Charles Campbell and John Burns (*The Georgia Straight*); Mary Aikins (*Reader's Digest*); and Sheila Peacock and Sheryl MacKay (CBC Radio) for taking in the hideous, squalling babies I abandoned on their various stoops. Here they are, all grown up. These are those who survived.

—B.R.
December 18, 2018

I Saw
THREE SHIPS

THE Santa Maria

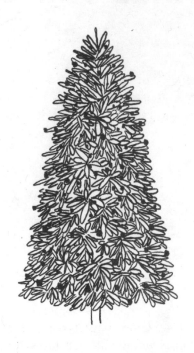

SINCE WE'VE NO PLACE TO GO

On Christmas Eve –

Dishes done, stocking hung, spiced wine mulling. Kitchen-counter radio tuned to the all-carol station. Sing, Bing, sing.

Rosellen's ready. Set to go. As soon as J.C. deigns to appear, they'll begin. It's hard to say when that might be; consistency has never been the cornerstone of his charm. Rosellen doesn't mind, just as long as he turns up before eleven. That's when "quiet time" starts at the Santa Maria. It's right there, in black and white, written in the agreement everyone signs but nobody reads when they move in; all anyone cares about is whether they get their damage deposit back with interest. Also, whether pythons count as pets.

Quiet time is from 11 p.m. to 7 a.m. Repsect your neighbours.

Rosellen's knack for flagging typographic missteps revealed itself in the earliest days of her literacy. It was a savant's gift, freakish, lavishly praised by her convent school English teachers, nuns who encouraged her to repay her debt to God – how else to explain it? – by taking up a career as a proofreader or copy editor.

Rosellen's demurral confounded them, as though she'd been blessed with perfect pitch but had no interest in pursuing a musical vocation. A holy waste. Rosellen shrugged off the righteous inquiries of whoever the Sister – Sola or Perduta or Abbandonata – when they pressed her on this stubborn impiety. She delighted in error's detection, but didn't give a good goddamn about its correction. Digging for the taproot of this obstinacy would take her into sulphurous substrata, deeper than she cared to go. Some cans of wroms were best left unopened. *Repsect your neighbours.* Rosellen honed in on "repsect" right away, wondered if she ought to have the page redrafted. Might some tenant – disgruntled, litigious – be able to make legal hay from so slight a cock-up? Rosellen embarked on a study, a rogue experiment undertaken with no protocol or control or hypothesis in mind, just a hunch about human fallibility that it would please her to prove. She opted to look away, to respect repsect. She allowed the error its life, left it unexpurgated, free to range, to spread its blameful stain on page, on time, on space.

Over the ensuing years – December 1984 through December 2018 – Rosellen knowingly, flagrantly presented this flawed document to hundreds of incoming Santa Maria novices. She watched them inscribe their names – sometimes ploddingly, sometimes with a flourish – then appended her own witnessing signature in the adjacent space. Not once in all that time did anyone arch a critical brow, *tsk tsk*, or otherwise call out repsect.

Rosellen allows that it might not speak well of her, the surge of stupid glee that washes over her gunwales every time she gets away with it; this shabby, enduring alliance she's forged with a minor orthographic stumble on a contract no one ever troubles to read, let alone challenge; a contract that has, in any case, now run the course of its earthly usefulness, for which there will never again be a requirement; a contract that is nothing, now, but blue-bin fodder.

For the Santa Maria's days are numbered. For the gangplank is on the rise. For the manifest is sealed. For repsect will go down with the ship. Rosellen will mourn it, privately. To whom could she unburden herself? J.C., perhaps; J.C., expected, but unaccounted for. The asshole. She gives the mulling wine a stir, licks the whisk, makes it her microphone.

R-E-P-S-E-C-T.
Find out what it means to me.

In unholy counterpoint, Bing and Rosellen make the welkin ring.

Fa, la, la, la, la – Sock it to me – la, la, la, la!

On Christmas Eve –

Clementines for wine, and clemency for J.C. He's late. So? If anyone should be allowed latitude with the 11 p.m. rule, it's J.C.; Rosellen, too, for so many years the curfew's staunch enforcer. Who's going to tell her she can't kick up a fuss? The building's half-empty, it's been that way for months, and it's not as if they're planning to tear up the floorboards or pull all the fire alarms. Shenanigans unlikely. Not at her age. Not at his. However old he is. She could find out, nothing's secret anymore, not with the internet. Rosellen was a late adopter; now, Google has her in its thrall. She could search his name, try out that Boolean wizardry they told her about at the Apple store. Jean-Christophe + Christmas Eve + late. Which he's not, not really, how can he be late when there's no appointed time of arrival, when there's only decency as the gatekeeper? When did he get here last year? Just after eight. What time is it now? 8:15 according to the clock on the stove, so 7:15, in fact.

Rosellen hates that bloody clock, a Satanic timepiece that can't be persuaded to jettison Daylight Savings. She's wiggled this knob, waggled that button, begged, sworn, importuned. Pointless. The clock won't budge. She's managed only to vex awake the automated oven timer, which, once stirred, couldn't be deterred. Night after night, at 10:47 – now masquerading as 11:47 – it springs to life, starts galloping, hard, in the direction of Fahrenheit 350. Rosellen does a lot of midnight roasting. She tells herself this enforced act of subtraction-by-one, for six months of the year, will keep her sharp. Arithmetic is another brick in the barricade against dementia; it can be, at least, or so she's read, when properly stacked and mortared alongside Sudoku, crosswords, jigsaws. So far, so good. There's the odd grasping after a word but, on balance, she's fine. Competent. No kettles in the freezer, no ice-cube trays under the broiler. Holding steady, with only minor tremors.

She'll do whatever it takes to ensure she doesn't end up like her mother, known to one and all, long before the advent of Lady Gaga, as Lady Gaga; her mother, dead + burned + scattered, but still celebrated by some of the long-term housekeeping staff at her care facility for her gift of gin acquisition and concealment. Tonic? She didn't care for it. Rosellen intends, come the unlikely day she can afford such an indulgence, to shell out for one of those "in memorial" benches that line the seawall. She'll have the brass plaque inscribed with her mother's name, along with the epitaph:

> *This much cannot be disputed:*
> *She liked liquor undiluted.*

It's pointless to try but she'll give the clock another whirl, this being the season of miracles. The nail of her right index finger whitens with the pressure. She leans into the reset button, channelling all her inquisitorial will: submit, repent. No change. What does it matter? You choose your battles. Soon, this will all be over. Soon, the range, the clock will be toast. The Santa Maria will be toast.

"Think I'll make some toast," she says.

On Christmas Eve –
  Wham, wham, wham.
  "Rosie?"
  Wham, whammity, wham.
  "You there?"
  Had it been anyone other than Bonnie, Rosellen would have feigned absence, maybe hollered, "Go away, I've gone to mass!" She's accustomed to being on call 24-7, that goes with the territory, but there are limits. Christmas Eve. J.C. due. Her bagel, compliantly crisping, now on the smoking cusp of ejaculation. Sometimes, you have to put your foot down. Had it been anyone but Bonnie, she wouldn't answer. Or she would. Bend the ear of whoever the petitioner. Let out the dogs of angry contradiction. Let 'em howl.

No, you didn't see a goddamn mouse, 'tis the night before Christmas, none is stirring, haven't you been paying attention?

No, dumbass, I don't happen to have a baster or a tool that would also work as a baster.

What do you mean you have movers coming tomorrow, it's Christmas day, who the hell moves on Christmas day? Two Dumb Elves with Stupid Hearts?

Wham.

Had it been anyone but Bonnie, whom she's known all these years.

Wham.

Bonnie, whose brimming, appalling toilet she's plunged, whose hair-clogged drain she's snaked.

Wham.

But it is Bonnie.

"Rosie, I'm so sorry to bug you. I just need a minute."

So much for peace on earth.

Rosellen (b. 1949) comes from a generation raised to believe in the power of a good credential. When it became clear that her marriage was running on fumes, that the time for the digging of foxholes was upon her, she signed up for a correspondence course in property management. Her husband – ex-husband … could be late husband, for all she knows – Bryan, excelled at infidelity, porn-watching, returning empties, air guitar. What else? Nothing else. It fell to Rosellen to tend to the changing of washers, the hanging of fixtures, the plastering of fissures. She didn't feel put upon; she appreciated this evidence of susceptibility to repair, the demonstration that not everything around her was immune to mending. When the world was too much with her, she'd take the bus to Canadian Tire, just for the pleasure of smelling the vulcanized air.

The correspondence course wasn't cheap, but the fee included all instructional materials, plus a tool belt of unimpeachable quality. The manuals – there were eight – contained only one typo. Rosellen considered sending a note but decided against it; whoever was stupid enough to mix ammonia with beach had it coming. She passed with distinction in half as long as it took most other candidates. She was motivated.

The same day she received her exam results and accreditation in the mail, she answered an ad in the paper – where once such postings were published, O Best Beloved – for a caretaker/manager at the Santa Maria, a small residential building on Harwood Street, in the West End. "Must start immediately." The imperative appealed. It was late November. Daylight was in short supply, likewise cheer. She didn't have the wherewithal to endure another pretending-to-be-merry Christmas in Ladysmith with Bryan's family of redneck rye drinkers, everyone waxing nostalgic about the killing cold of Saskatchewan, his adenoidal brother, a retired rancher, forever illuminating the darker side of binder twine, his pathetic sister-in-law with her crafts addiction and illustrated dictionaries of symptoms and their petulant, entitled, clamorous children. Jesus. No. Never again. The salary wasn't anything to write home about, but there was the compensating perk of a fully furnished studio apartment. "Small but bright," the ad said, which proved half-true. She jumped without leaving a note.

Rosellen arrived at the Santa Maria with a yellow plastic dairy crate into which she'd folded some hastily culled clothes. One bulky sweater was wrapped protectively around a Royal Doulton shepherdess that had been her mother's, the delicate crook long ago broken, badly glued. She brought the tool belt, too, as well as a calligraphed faux-vellum certificate attesting to her expertise as a Property Manager; the course administrator described it as "suitable for farming," which provoked a welcome spike in Rosellen's serotonin. Early in the morning of December 1, 1984, she moved into the caretaker's suite on the main floor of the Santa Maria, apartment 101, its view of the street obscured by a holly hedge. A few hours later, demonstrating a more marked devotion to material accumulation, Bonnie arrived. It took four movers three hours to haul her sundries and notions up the stairs, into the little penthouse atop the building's third floor.

Bonnie's apartment, with its commanding alley outlook and jangly soundtrack provided by the city-employed trash collectors and the volunteer Guild of Binners, is innocent of whatever glamour "penthouse" might conjure. Its single amenity is a Juliet balcony, deep enough to accommodate one outward "Mother, May I?" baby step. Unusually – to Bonnie's mind, appealingly – a resident Romeo, unadvertised, was part of the package.

"What fresh Hellenic is this?" Bonnie wondered on her first sighting of Vidal Papadopoulos. This was the morning of December 2, scant hours after her Santa Maria embarkation, the shoreline of the recent past still visible, swimmable if she cared to throw herself overboard. Semi-comatose from a night of unpacking, her cuticles a ragged disaster after so much rending of cardboard, she'd taken her coffee onto the Juliet, thinking only to escape the jumble of cartons, to survey the scene.

Across the alley from the Santa Maria's hindquarters was – still is – the Pacific Colonnade, a twelve-storey mid-rise, a building unremarkable in design, substandard in execution. Bonnie gave it a critical once-over, noted the rust stains left by rainwater trickling from downspouts, noted the cracks in the cladding, noted that most of the tenants – conventionally modest, covetous of privacy – kept their blinds lowered. Not Vidal. Her aerie was on a parallel plane with his fourth-floor flat. To look ahead was to look into his unobstructed living room. There he stood, perhaps twelve metres distant, assuming the wide-legged stance of a Colossus astride, swaddled in a plush white terrycloth bathrobe, his hands-on-hips posture suggesting impatient, yet amused, expectancy: a burlier, more hirsute Mrs. Danvers, waiting for the second Mrs. de Winter, eager to find out just how much she could take. Eye met eye. There was no doubting the mutuality of their regard, but neither gave a wave or nod or wink.

Neither looked away, not until Vidal pivoted on his heel, spun in the direction of the adjacent sideboard.

"What are you up to, funny man?"

Vidal bent over a turntable. Did he give his butt a Br'er Rabbit wiggle, this way to the briar patch? He set the stylus on an LP – already in place, primed for this moment – then turned to his audience of one. The vinyl spun. Vidal danced, a shy little shimmy that evolved into what Bonnie described to her best friend Philip as "Zorba Night with the Chippendales."

This was no one-off. For twenty-five years, more or less, from December 2, 1984, until well into the present millennium, morning after morning, barring those short spans of time when one or the other might have been out of town or flu-ridden or hungover, Vidal vamped and Bonnie observed. For a quarter century Bonnie saw her neighbour age, watched his cock shrivel like a slug slow-roasted on a tanning bed, saw hernias emerge, the scars of their correction, saw the lavish bath mat of his chest hair whiten, the Yeti of Naxos. Others must surely have benefited from Vidal's terpsichorean contortions – they were visible to anyone with a north-facing view – but Bonnie was persuaded he had her uppermost in mind as the ideal audience for his signature moves. The Tumescent Trot. The Priapic Preen. She was his first reader. His Muse.

Leafing through a magazine at the grocery checkout, Rosellen noted a spacing error, or so she supposed; "The penis mightier than the sword" surely wasn't the writer's intention. She was intent on buying pork chops and onions, was undefended, unprepared for molten joy to pour down from the parapets. She thought she might wet herself. Nothing had ever roused in her such happiness. The penis mightier than the sword became her dulling mantra on those mercifully rare occasions when Bryan called her up from the audience to assist with the dick trick that took no time at all to perform. It was the penis mightier than the sword that came to mind when Rosellen saw, for the first and only time, Vidal in full flight: an experience that reinforced her conviction that external genitalia evolved for reasons that were at least as comedic as generative.

"You don't mean it," she said to Bonnie.

It was a chance collision in the storage room. Rosellen – new to her supervisory duties in the building, anxious to prove herself, perhaps more rule-bound and doctrinaire than necessity required – was on a get-acquainted inspection tour, alert to evidence of vermin, sniffing to determine if anyone had been smoking, which was forbidden in public areas.

"Can I give you a hand?"

She helped Bonnie force shut the door of her locker, its interior a study in tortured complexity. They talked, compared notes. Bonnie's included Vidal.

"You don't mean it."

"I do."

"No."

"Yes."

"No."

"Come see for yourself," said Bonnie. "Tomorrow morning. Be there by eight, curtain's at quarter past."

"Should I bring anything?"

"No need. I've got coffee. He'll bring buns."

"And a weenie," said Rosellen.

They fell about. Sophomoric indulgence. Transgressive giddiness. Next morning, she was there on the dot; Bonnie's mother, Gloria, was the other guest.

"I have binoculars," she said.

"I don't think they'll be necessary," said Bonnie.

"You're pretty close to the action," said Rosellen, whose tool belt contained an advanced tape measure she might have used to ascertain the exact span.

Bonnie said, "Spitting distance."

"Maybe you should," said Gloria, raising her glasses, optimizing the magnification. "Wait. I see movement. Definitely not an eggplant."

Gloria, Gloria. *Gloria in excelsis.*

Bonnie never misses her more than at Christmas, a season neither could abide. It was the only time of year her mother, etiquette's standard bearer, allowed herself one hearty, loud "Fuck." It would fly from her lips – seemingly unprovoked, at some random moment – with the merry, pent-up power of a champagne cork orbiting the room on New Year's Eve.

Gloria, Gloria. *Sic transit Gloria.*

On Christmas Eve –

Not any Christmas Eve, either, but Christmas Eve, 2018, the Santa Maria's last Christmas Eve on Earth. In 101, Rosellen mulls wine and waits for J.C. In the penthouse, Philip is at the window, looking across the alley to the Pacific Colonnade. Vidal Papadopoulos is decorating his tree.

"He has nice balls."

"You had a choice," Bonnie says, "yet you went there. God. Look at this."

She holds up a cocktail apron, 1950s vintage, apricot-coloured, unfathomably sheer, with satin ties. Did postwar hostesses really favour such impractical apparel when passing around celery sticks slathered with Cheez Whiz? Bonnie ties it on, essays a model's sashay, winces. Her hips are no longer runway limber. Never were.

"That was Gloria's?"

"It was," says Bonnie. She unfastens it, holds it up to her face like a veil: the Salome of Nicola and Harwood. "Yes or no?"

"No," says Philip.

"Oh, come on."

"No."

Philip is firm.

"Asshole," she says, tosses it into a box, locates a felt marker, prints "Sally Anne."

"It doesn't take an *e*."

"Does."

"Doesn't."

"Does, bitch."

"Doesn't, faggot."

"Fuck you, Nicola Harwood."

"Fuck you right back, Davie Denman."

They love each other, so this is how they talk. On and on they'll go, on and on for longer than is appropriate for two people well into middle age on what is advertised as a silent night; old friends feinting and sparring at the corner of Heathen and Holy.

Philip is helping Bonnie sort through her stuff, winnowing grain (not much) from chaff (a lot), preparatory to her move from the Santa Maria. She's agreed to let him be the final arbiter of what stays, what's turfed. No court of appeal. Thirty-five years of needless materiality emerge from box after box after box. Why? For what? How has Bonnie, a lifelong freelancer, as impecunious a person as ever he's met, managed to accumulate so much dross? It seems to seek her out as though on a current, like that growing gyre of discarded plastic in the Pacific.

"What about these?"

Bonnie shows off binoculars.

"Gloria's?"

"She had a brief flirtation with ornithology."

"Truly?"

"She heard some persuasive birders on the CBC and got all enthused. She bought the field glasses, bought a *Peterson Field Guide*, got up early one Saturday, hooked up with some club. Never went back. She said, 'Oh, Bonnie. They caused such a commotion when I wanted a cigarette. I mean, why? Out there in the open, I was perfectly happy to go stand farther away in the swamp, but no, they just couldn't abide it. It wasn't the smoke, it wasn't the smell, it wasn't the dire prospect of wind-born carcinogens, it was just the nerve. Like they'd all decided I'd be the one who'd leap up from a blind in a fright wig, bellowing *booga-booga-booga*, scaring off the great tit. And the shoes. Oh, darling, their shoes. Did I ever tell you that I was all set to go into nursing, but I just couldn't go through with it, not because of the blood or bedpans, but because of the shoes? Birdwatchers wear nurse shoes. Horrible. Maybe I'm better suited to philately. Or numismatics.'"

Philip laughs. He misses Gloria, misses her almost as much as he'll miss his own mother, Frances, who says this will be her last Christmas. Her only regret is that she waited so long to learn how to text; she wants to stay alive long enough to avail herself of every available emoji.

Philip passes the binoculars from hand to hand, gauges their weight, their substance.

"Expensive?"

"Count on it. You remember how she was. If ever a little problem came along, she figured God created it so she could throw money at it."

Philip raises them to his eyes, turns back to the window, notes that Vidal has finished draping the tree with fairy lights, plugged them in. He hums "Twinkle, twinkle." He considers the apartment's decor.

"I spy, with my little eye, icons upon the wall."

"Our Lady of the Perpetual Boner?"

Philip gasps.

"Holy Peloponnesian War, Batgirl. Is that his mother?"

"There's a picture of his mother?"

"No picture. In person. In the flesh. Wrinkly, but warmish."

"Gimme."

Bonnie applies the binoculars to a purpose unsanctioned by the Audubon Society.

"His mother or some relation. She's a hundred, at least."

"Twin triumphs of the Mediterranean diet," Philip says. "Do you think she knows?"

"About the morning sausage show? No. Maybe. Consider the source. The land that gave us Oedipus."

"Find out where she lives, send her the pictures."

"Diabolical," says Bonnie. "Maybe I will."

Bonnie, a documentary filmmaker and photographer, documented Vidal's morning burlesques for twenty-five years. She stopped when Gloria became ill; when, of necessity, she shifted focus.

Philip says, "Why was he so compliant?"

"He wanted to be seen. I was as brazen as he was. He respected that."

Times change. Would Bonnie be so sanguine now, so laissez-faire about the quandaries of consent? Well. There was no question they were both willing parties. Bonnie was no innocent and Vidal was like a squirrel that comes to the same park bench, habituated to a daily offering of nuts.

"Will you miss him?" Philip asks.

"Things cooled between us so long ago."

"Where are those photos?"

"Basement. Storage locker. Lockers. I've got two."

"Two! Golly. Penthouse lady is special."

Into this short phrase, Philip, famous for his impersonations, folds an encyclopedia of camp inflections, from Carol Channing to Jim Nabors to Ru Paul, with a dozen stops between. Virtuoso work.

"Boxes, boxes, still more boxes. Everything in them needs digitizing. Maybe I'll get a grant, hire someone."

There have been years, more than a few, when Bonnie subsisted entirely on cash awards from federally funded agencies, all for projects that rarely made it beyond the proposal stage. No one, not even Philip, suspects her of praying, but she does, every night, and never forgets to ask God's blessing on the Canadian taxpayer, the munificent saver of her maple-smoked bacon.

She says, "It's not just money shots of the Cretan cretin. God knows what's down there."

"God might know, but Nicola Harwood must care."

"Feel like tackling it?"

"Can I wear that apron?"

"Shut up. Grab some bubbly from the fridge, okay?"

On Christmas Eve –

"You look fab, Rosellen."

It's Philip who says so. Rosellen wasn't expecting him, but here he is, Bonnie's reliable sidekick. Her wingman.

"Super sweater, Rosie," Bonnie says.

"Holiday spruce-up," says Rosellen, fingering one of the eight felt reindeer that prance across Poitrine Plain. Denim coveralls from Mark's are her signature look, and the tool belt.

"Expecting company?"

"Santa. You know."

Tepid chuckles.

"I'd ask you in, but –"

"No, no, Rosie, I'm sorry to bother you, terrible of me to come knocking like this, you know I wouldn't unless I had to, especially not on Christmas Eve, but all this packing, packing, my God, it's endless. I don't even know what's in my storage locker anymore, it's been so long, and I was hoping you'd remember the combination."

"Or maybe you have some bolt cutters?" Philip blurts, a sudden inspiration. He's never used bolt cutters. He's not sure how he knows bolt cutters are a thing in the world. He couldn't tell a bolt cutter from a mascara wand. Bonnie gives him a levelling look.

"First time for everything," he says.

"In fact, that is not so."

These two. Their act. This routine they've been performing since the earth cooled. How can they not know how shopworn it is?

Thirty-five years – half a Biblical lifespan – that's how long ago they came aboard the Santa Maria, Bonnie staggering under the weight of her excess freight, Rosellen like a Buddhist with a bean can for a begging bowl. Bonnie was twenty-two, newly graduated from Emily Carr when they first met in the storage room, the younger woman pressing the whole of her bodyweight into the door of the kennel-like cage she'd been assigned to store her overflow. Laws of physics would have to be more broken than bent for containment to be achieved.

"Mine's empty," Rosellen said.

"You can't mean it," said Bonnie. "You are the woman I aspire to be. You are the mother I should have had. You must have stuff to come."

"Nope. Brought everything over in a cab. Back seat. Didn't even need the trunk."

"You're kidding."

"Have it if you want. The locker. I don't need it."

"Really?"

"Sure."

"You'd actually rent it to me?"

"No need. It's yours. I have power. I can make it so. Keep the lock, too, if you want."

Rosellen had clapped her high-school locker relic on the door, a pro forma gesture; there was nothing she needed to secure. She ripped a page from her notebook, wrote down the combination. Bonnie read it aloud.

"13-31-55."

To Rosellen it sounded like a mangled incantation. For so long, she'd been the only other person on the planet to whom it meant anything. It was inexplicably unnerving, giving it away, as if she'd siphoned vital fuel into the tank of a total stranger.

On Christmas Eve –

Bonnie and Philip in Rosellen's doorway, Bonnie clutching a bottle of something sparkling, as though there were a ship to christen rather than the Santa Maria to bury. To set aflame, set adrift, Viking-style.

"I remember it started with 13, right? Lucky 13."

Rosellen nods, takes a sheet of scrap paper, an estimate from a roofing contractor that dates from when the Santa Maria merited maintenance beyond the merely palliative. Earlier that day Rosellen had clutched at the empty air, grabbing at the free-floating, forgotten word "guacamole" – she'd had to google "avocado + garlic + dip" to retrieve it – but this necessary, talismanic sequence, for so many years part of her proprioceptive arsenal, rises to the fore. She writes it down.

"There you go."

"Thanks, Rosie."

"Merry Christmas."

"You, too. Oh," she says, remembering the wine, "here, Rosie. For you."

"Prosecco," says Philip. An operatic roll of the *r*.

"You've got a long night ahead of you," says Rosellen. "You'll need it more than I will."

"You sure?"

"Sure."

They're off, giggling down the hall. Unappealing sound coming from anyone over forty. Silence settles. Of J.C., no sign. Maybe he won't come. Worse things have happened. He's not the only game in town. She's discovered Netflix. If he's not here by 9:30, she'll move on. *The Crown. Stranger Things.*

"Last chance," she says, at 9:29.

The air unresponsive; then, not. It's nothing gradual. It's as though a lever is pulled, a dam opens, a flood rushes in, changing all before it. The atmosphere, re-atomized. His telltale scent. His olfactory calling card.

"Oh."

Rosellen is vibrantly awake.

"Oh, oh."

She feels a relief so profound it should be tangible, something she could gather, burn, warm her hands over.

"Oh, oh, oh."

Here come the tears, creatures of water, salt, evolving out of the corners of her eyes. From a remote province of her brain the chemical signal "Make snot now" is telegraphed to the appropriate worker.

"You're here."

She's choking on happiness. She's never been so glad to be breathless.

From her mother, in addition to the Royal Doulton shepherdess, Rosellen inherited a keen sense of smell. Even so, it took her a long while to decode the tripartite layerings of J.C.'s giveaway scent. She easily tagged the citrusy, cloying assault of Armani's eau pour homme; it was one Bryan tried before committing himself to Inebriate, by Johnnie Walker. She could readily name the particular pungency of Gauloises; she'd smoked them when she was toying with *la vie de bohème*, then came to her senses. But what else? Something chemical.

Antiseptic. It made the nostrils pucker. It was when she evicted a trio of party boys – standing in their doorway, pointing to the quiet time clause, *Can't you read, have you got no repsect?* – that she got it. In their freezer, along with the dregs of a pint of Ben and Jerry's Chunky Monkey, and a zip-lock bag containing what appeared to be used condoms but which she convinced herself were fishing lures, plus a family-sized bag of corn + pea + carrot medley, were row upon row of tiny bottles, medicinal-looking. "Locker Room," the labels said.

Rosellen consulted Bonnie.

"Poppers!"

Thrill of unanticipated recognition. Happy exclamation of one who, say, opens the door to discover the cat, three months absent and presumed dead, has now returned. As in, "Poppers! Where have you been? Are those your kittens?"

Bonnie's disquisition on the deployment of these nightlife accessories struck Rosellen as more empirical than breezily anecdotal. Rosellen, daring a tentative whiff, recoiled. She feared she might be jolted out of menopause where she'd been securely buckled for years. It was worth it. Mystery solved. Picture made whole. Armani + Gauloises + Poppers. This was the equation that, when correctly calculated, worked out to J.C. So what if they added up to something that lacked the gravitas, the burnished historicity of frankincense + gold + myrrh? Rosellen didn't care. She knew it was possible to do good work with simple tools. It impressed her that J.C. managed as well as he did, considering his situation, his liabilities, what he had to work with. Which was nothing. Unless invisibility counts as something. Which, maybe, it does.

Rosellen would like to find a J.C. confidant, an informant, some neighbour who remembers him, could clear a few things up. Stealthy inquiry has revealed a handful of likely candidates; Google has been helpful. Under what pretext would she accost them, whether on the street, or at the Tim Hortons, or at the No Frills? She couldn't keep up a pretence of detachment, or explain her more-than-passing interest in her Santa Maria predecessor, long gone but not gone, who manifests out of the ether every Christmas Eve, exuding the potent aroma peculiar to pretty much any gay bar back in the days when disco ruled the earth. Longing + desperation + 2 a.m. Age lines already visible in your face in the mirror behind the bar at the Shaggy Horse, the Central, the Royal, the Gandy Dancer, the Luv-A-Fair. At Celebrities. At Numbers. The smell of 1984. The year J.C. capsized. The year she was launched.

On Christmas Eve –
Rosellen ladles mulled wine into the punch glass she picked up for a quarter at the Denman Mall thrift shop. It once belonged to a set: bowl, dipper, goblets. She lifts the orphan to her lips, avoids the chip in the rim.
"To you. To us. To the Santa Maria, too. Bless this ship and all who sailed on her."
She can tell by her visitor's impatient radiance, by the thickening perfume and the unaccustomed current in the room, that J.C. would rather forego the speeches. If he had a foot, he'd stamp it. He wants what he's come for. He wants their game. He wants Hunt the Angel.
"Hold your horses, Mr. Pushy-Pants."
She takes a long, slow sip.
"I waited long enough for you."
This strained foreplay precedes the wide-ranging probe that will be their main business. They'll start, as traditions dictates, in 101, not that Rosellen has any thought of finding it there. It's 422 square feet, with no surfeit of angel-sized hidey-holes. Also, she's been "decrapifying." Everyone in the building – those few who still remain – has been similarly engaged. The Santa Maria's end is nigh, ditto the Nina and the Pinta on either side: three-storey walk-ups, stucco-clad, ordinary structures that for sixty years have

given ordinary shelter to ordinary people leading lives that are as ordinary as any life is allowed to be.

It's not as though they haven't all seen it coming. They've been waiting on death row for the last eighteen months, ever since a developer scooped them up, all three, as though in a game of jacks. The Nina, the Pinta, the Santa Maria, taking up all that space, three minutes from the park, three minutes from the beach, three sisters past their prime, arm in arm in arm, waiting for the streetcar named Expire.

Now, passersby study the promissory eyesore of a billboard besmirching the little lawn outside the building. It depicts a fanciful rendering of a brave new world, populated by happy, young, hand-holding couples – all combinations/permutations of genders and races – walking cheek-by-jowl with smiling oldsters who are similarly diverse in their depictions, on whom has been conferred a range of physical abilities, some supporting themselves on walkers, some on scooters, some jogging with unseemly avidity, while all around are rainbow-coloured children clutching balloons or holding leashes attached to well-mannered puppies with Frisbees in the clench of their drool-free jaws: these are the blessed, the well-contented, the eventual inhabitants of the 150 units – some market rate, some subsidized – that will comprise "Three Ships," as the new edifice is to be called. Occupancy by late fall 2020. Move in in time for the holidays. Come home to Three Ships, your Utopia-by-the-Bay.

On Christmas Eve –

"In here?" asks Rosellen, teasingly; J.C. is beginning to jostle.

She opens a closet, opens the small wooden box where she keeps paper clips, eraser nubs, opens a cutlery drawer, the freezer compartment of her fridge; a fridge so old it needs weekly defrosting. Rosellen thinks she won't miss the fridge. She will miss the fridge.

"Or here, or here, or here? Where can it be?"

J.C. tolerates this foolishness, barely. Once, a wine glass fell, seemingly of its own accord; toppled from the counter for no good reason, shattered on the hard tile floor. A month later she was still finding tiny shards. Rosellen took note. This was how it was. Unpredictable when riled. Men were, in her experience. Well. She understands his reluctance to linger. 101 was where he cut the tie. That much Rosellen knows about J.C., knows for sure.

Brigitte Hensel found him. Brigitte lived in 102. She thought to look in because it had snowed and the walk hadn't been cleared. That was unlike J.C., always quick off the mark with a shovel and a broom and salt. Brigitte knocked. No reply. She yoo-hooed. Silence from the other side. Her third eye opened. A sixth sense warmed. She happened to have a key for the apartment, a spare given her by J.C.'s predecessor, Keith, a nice enough man, but careless, prone to locking himself out. Brigitte kept the key in a safe place, in the left shoe of a pair she no longer wore – they were stylish but bothered her bunions.

Brigitte shared all this with Rosellen her first day on the job, sought her out within hours of her arrival, recounted how she'd held her breath, had steadied herself, had feared the worst. She turned the key. Brigitte told Rosellen – who put the kettle on, for it was clear this would not be a brief visit – what she saw when she stood in the doorway, saw too vividly even though the blinds were drawn, the room was dim, told her about the silence, eerie and dense, about a suffusing clamminess she wasn't just imagining, told her how she debated whether to call the police or an ambulance, then summoned both, the fire department came too, there were emergency service vehicles lined up all down the block, told her all about what J.C. had done, told her in more procedural detail, with more causal and casual speculation than Rosellen thought necessary.

Brigitte had lived in the Santa Maria since 1954. She was the last of the original tenants, had outlasted Sandra Healey by a full ten years. Sandra was a loner, moody, no friends in the building, no friends anywhere, really, no family in the city, a niece somewhere in the interior, Revelstoke perhaps, maybe Trail, also a sister in Edmonton from whom she was known to be estranged. It wasn't unusual for weeks to go by without a Sandra sighting. She bought in bulk, didn't subscribe to any magazines or newspapers, never seemed to receive any mail, so of course no one thought anything of it, why would they? Brigitte didn't have a key to Sandra's apartment. No one had a key to Sandra's apartment. An axe was deployed to enter Sandra's apartment.

"Can you guess how we knew she was gone?"

"I'm sorry I don't have any biscuits," said Rosellen.

"J.C. always had Digestives."

Brigitte, the Santa Maria's living memory and conscience, was anxious to impress upon Rosellen that she, the new janitor – Rosellen, a certified property manager, bristled silently – cleave to the high bar established by her predecessors in the custodial arts, of whom there had been but two, both men. At stake was the honour of not just the building but also her sex. Brigitte made it known, with force, that the Nina, and the Pinta, and the Santa Maria were famous in the neighbourhood for the quality and quantity of their seasonal decorations. The Nina laid claim to Halloween, the Pinta to Valentine's Day. It fell to the Santa Maria to go all out at Christmas. There had never been a time when this order of high holy day precedence was not observed. Never. For a few years, a fellow named O'Rourke had tried, for obvious reasons, to whip up some froth around St. Patrick's Day, but it never took. He grew bitter. He moved. Good riddance.

There was one storage unit, Brigitte explained, the largest of them, in which building supplies were located: cleaning equipment, fire-exit replacement bulbs, the Suite for Rent sign, etc. Also, there were several packing crates containing everything ornamental required to make the season bright. Rosellen would find grade-A plastic greenery, holly and cedar boughs and frosted pine cones, also foil garlands that blared out festive wishes: "GOOD WILL TO MEN!" "PEACE ON EARTH!" There was an inflatable St. Nicholas that glowed with an inner light. There was a darling crèche cobbled together entirely out of sponges and pipe cleaners, handcrafted by Mr. Parker, who had lived in 301, who perished from snake bite while visiting the Grand Canyon. Travel was fraught; Brigitte herself preferred to be at home. There were elves with a workbench. There were reindeer made of woven branches and nutcracker dolls and felt stockings, appropriately appliquéd, to hang from the wrought-iron stair railings, twenty-nine of them, one for every suite in the Santa Maria. There were strings and strings of lights which, annoyingly, irrationally, wouldn't work at all if one bulb was deficient, it was as if they belonged to a union. There was a piece of colourful gift wrap that had been cut to fit the door in such a way that the painted sign "Santa Maria" became "Santa" for the length of the season. That same pattern of wrap – a Boxing Day bulk buy from London Drugs – was applied to empty boxes of varying dimensions, all done up with paper and ribbon, props for placement under the Christmas tree, which was nice, very nice, even though artificial. Plus there were eight boxes of decorations to hang upon it: frosted balls, tear drops, snowmen, the Magi, elves, candy canes, tinsel. There were any number of Santas, a multitude of reindeer, but there was only one angel, the angel intended to perch atop the tree, from which vantage she surveyed the lobby through which there was very little room to pass by the time everything was in place. Brigitte had much to say about the angel, her harp, her halo, her wings made of real feathers, she wasn't sure from what bird. She'd been purchased years ago by Brigitte's late sister in Victoria, bought from a sweet little store that long ago went out of business. The angel was irreplaceable. The angel must be treated with care. It was only when she saw the angel that Brigitte felt all the weight, the warmth of Christmas settle upon her. Jean-Christophe, Brigitte stressed, underscoring the point with many jabs of rheumatic fingers, had been a genius, no, really, she meant it, a *genius*, at arranging all the festive miscellany into a more-than-palatable whole; of course, he'd been a window dresser back in Montréal, employed by some big fancy store, so he was at an advantage. Even so, Brigitte knew she spoke for the whole building in saying she hoped Rosellen would make an effort, would do her level best to match his exquisite hall-decking.

"The second Sunday in December. That's when they go up."

"That's soon."

"That's right."

"That's a week away."

"That's correct."

Rosellen was half-hoping she'd self-destruct, or that Brigitte might, when she happened upon Bonnie at the lockers, the first of many unplanned meetings. Bonnie stood by while Rosellen disinterred the boxes of decorating supplies. They were in excellent order. About them was the aura of sanctity, of ceremony. Of expectation.

"I'm not sure how I'll manage this," said Rosellen, possessed by the creeping certainty that she was unequipped, constitutionally as much as experientially, to take the helm of the Santa Maria. What difference did her summa cum laude standing in the correspondence course make? It was as though she'd read every available book on mothering but had no idea what to do once the baby was hungry and howling and failing to latch.

Bonnie said, "Why not make it fun? Have a party."

"A party?"

"A big get-together. Dainties. Punch. Get everyone involved, maybe a little tipsy. Whoop-dee-doo. Let the good times roll. You know. A party."

When had Rosellen last been at a party? The annual trial by tedium in Ladysmith didn't qualify. Who would have asked her to a party? Who would she have asked? How small her life had grown.

"I'll give that some serious thought."

"Leave the punch to me," said Bonnie.

Rosellen found Brigitte waiting when she returned from the storage room to 101; waiting on what Rosellen, at least, considered the wrong side of the door. She was stretched out in the La-Z-Boy. It was among the supplied furnishings, wasn't a chair for which Rosellen cared.

"I let myself in."

"Ah."

"I still have the key."

"Oh."

"Best I should hold onto it."

"I see."

"Just in case."

Rosellen made a mental note to call the locksmith first thing in the morning.

Brigitte said, "Anything new?"

Rosellen explained the party plan. What did Brigitte think?

"Not a good idea. Jean-Christophe knew just where it all should go, everything in its place. If you ask everyone to help out, it'll be a dog's breakfast. Also, it would be a change. Change is hard. We've been through a lot of change. Jean-Christophe. What happened. All that. You know. Change."

Rosellen murmured sympathetically, but her resolve was welling, stiffening. Directly Brigitte was out the door – a long goodbye – she set to work making a poster. Rosellen, no artist, could still manage a few red-berried holly leaves, a crude Santa. She added a scattering of cookies that might easily be mistaken for reindeer droppings, which was also true of the shortbreads she'd made year after year for the last two decades, never adequately, following the recipe passed on to her by Bryan's sainted mother.

HOLIDAY DECORATING PARTY

DECMEMBER 9

MEET IN THE LOBBY

2 P.M.

COME ONE, COME ALL

Rosellen was like a raku master, folding a flaw into a tea bowl. "Decmember" was neither accidental nor glib. It was Rosellen's intention to bestow the La-Z-Boy on whoever was first to call the flub to her attention. Having the party and getting rid of the rocker might, she hoped, help exorcise her control-freak predecessor. In the name of all that's wholesome, J.C., I cast you out! Begone!

She pinned her handiwork to the lobby bulletin board.

Santa Marians who were not Brigitte complimented her on her initiative, welcomed her to the building, said how much they were looking forward to the party, and oh, by the way, could they bring some chips, some crab dip, a flagon of something reviving? If "Decmember" was remarked, it went unmentioned; Rosellen was fated to remain the chair's long-term guardian.

To Brigitte alone fell the burden of qualm. For one thing, why not "Christmas Decorating Party"? In "Holiday" she read the erosion of all she held dear, the decline of the west, hell's handcart poised on a downward incline, wheels well greased. Rosellen lashed herself to the mast, withstood the old woman's sirocco of ire. Brigitte bitched, Rosellen beamed. Brigitte groused, Rosellen glowed. Her charm offensive worked. Brigitte thawed. On Decmember 9, she was in the lobby with her Marks & Spencer fruitcake platter, the first to arrive. Her icicle earrings were magnificent. She couldn't stop saying, not in the moment, nor for weeks to come, that she'd had a lovely time, just lovely, couldn't understand why no one had thought of this before. The only tarnish on her tine was that the treetop angel, the angel given her by her sister and that she in turn bestowed upon the Santa Maria for its use and enjoyment in perpetuity, was nowhere to be found.

"Where can it be?" Brigitte persisted in asking. She looked everywhere, even unwrapped the purely decorative boxes. No angel.

"Let's just make do," said Bonnie, none too patiently. She'd appointed herself Rosellen's party lieutenant.

"Make do with what?" was Brigitte's sharp retort.

Brigitte, who grew up poor, held in practised disregard la-di-da penthouse people. Her antipathy was further provoked by the near visibility of the new tenant's labia; Bonnie had come upon a thrift-store cache of vintage micro-skirts and delighted not only in wearing them but in telling everyone what a bargain they'd been.

"Sure they were cheap, there's nothing to them," Brigitte sniffed to Rosellen, who smiled, rerouted the conversation.

"Hey, Nicola Harwood, let's take this jolly Santa and stick him on the tip-tip-tippy top," said Philip, who did not live in the Santa Maria. Why was he at the party? Why was he butting in? What did Bonnie think she was doing? No one else had invited a friend along. Why had he brought that fizzy wine, why did he insist on talking like Bette Davis?

"Good idea, Davie Denman," said Bonnie, who clambered on a chair to reach the highest branch. This was foolish, everyone knew it was dangerous, how accidents happen; also, it afforded anyone who cared to look an even closer glimpse of her lady parts.

"Santa Baby," sang Philip.

As Eartha Kitt impersonations went, it wasn't bad, as even Brigitte had to admit.

Christmas advanced, a quickening march. The missing angel proved a bone Brigitte could neither swallow nor bury. She pestered Rosellen with phone calls, notes under the door. Any sign? Any luck? Any clues? Finally, on Christmas Eve afternoon, Rosellen made an eleventh-hour trip to Canadian Tire, hoping that among the picked-over remnants of seasonal decor she could locate a reasonable facsimile, something Brigitte would find more satisfactory than the Santa Bonnie had rigged to the treetop using a combination of a paper clip and the wire ribbing from the cork of Philip's Henkell Trocken.

Rosellen needed a restorative cup of Murchie's Christmas Blend before hauling out the stepladder and crowning the tree with the new recruit, who was Black, who held to her lips a herald trumpet. Brigitte would look askance, but Rosellen thought she was snazzy. She boiled the kettle, lifted the lid of the Brown Betty. Slack-jaw wonder. There she was, the AWOL object of so much fretful concern, the pale-faced original, beaming beatifically, halo, feathers, tiny harp intact, if ever so slightly moistened. How? Rosellen had used the teapot the day prior. It was innocent of angel. Who? When? Why on earth – then she whiffed, for the first of many times, the mélange of what she came to know as "Eau de J.C." What she eventually identified as the formula of Armani + Gauloises + Poppers. The La-Z-Boy squeaked, rocked gently, as if someone had risen from its embrace. As if the seat might still be warm. She checked. It was not. She thought, How strange. She thought no more about it.

Brigitte had a stroke that next spring. She managed to call 911 herself, was able to wave with her right hand from the stretcher as they carried her off to St. Paul's; in her left she clutched the little overnight bag she kept packed with just such an emergency in mind. Rosellen went to see her in Extended Care. Patient visiting had not been covered in her property management course. The author of those correspondence materials had never imagined unlocking the combination of Santa Maria + West End Vancouver + 1985. Rosellen took up her position just as the plague years were gathering strength, amassing arms, sighting young men in the crosshairs. John from 201, Brandon from 304, Trevor from 206, both James and Robert from 109, and half a dozen others she could still name if she put her mind to it, all struck down. She went to check in on them, also at St. Paul's, went at first because she wanted to, and then because she felt she must. She went to the funerals, too, until they became too frequent, too much to bear, desultory, often sparsely attended, and the inevitable, dispiriting, yet somehow admirable appearance of one elderly drag queen done up in dowager's weeds who always arrived five minutes into the proceedings and made a show of taking a place in the front row of mourners. Better to stay home. Better to light a single candle and wait by the phone. Someone might call. When there was a funeral, there was a vacancy. The show must go on.

"Keep an eye on my place," Brigitte would say, whenever Rosellen dropped by. "I want it to look just like I left it, not a spoon out of place, when I come back."

Which she never did. Rosellen watched her weaken, watched the waning of her will. She was gone before Victoria Day. Suite for rent.

Summer passed. Days dwindled. Rosellen grew accustomed to, if not fond of, the La-Z-Boy. Her poster – for which Letraset and photocopied clip art from the public library had been employed – was blameless.

"Where's Philip?" she inquired of Bonnie at the Second Annual Holiday Decorating Party, December 8, 1985.

"With Gary."

"Gary?"

"His new boyfriend."

Rosellen took note of the exaggerated eye roll, didn't inquire. She had lots on her mind. She was puzzled. It was that damned angel again. She herself had taken down last year's decorations; there was not the same communal enthusiasm for the dismantling as there had been for the assembly. She waited until Twelfth Night had passed, as Brigitte had directed she must. Anxious to avoid any future kerfuffle, Rosellen took great, great care to put the angel, the Brigitte-approved model, mummified in tissue paper, in a box, alongside some red and silver balls and a whole flock of partridges. She took the trouble to write "Treetop Angel" on the outside of the box. She remembered saying, "There you go, you rascal. See you next year."

The one person who would truly have cared was no longer there to raise a fuss; still, it was maddening for Rosellen that Brigitte's angel was, once again, not where she'd been so carefully placed. It was maddening that, once again, she resisted all efforts at discovery until, on Christmas Eve afternoon, she turned up in the breadbox. The mysterious waft. The creak of decompressed springs. The La-Z-Boy in motion.

"Jean-Christophe?"

Fragrant zephyr.

"J.C.?"

Tropical billow, damp and warm.

"Ah."

It took several Christmases for the game to develop rules, for Rosellen to intuit the "You're getting warm / You're getting cold" olfactory protocol of Hunt the Angel. One year in the crisper, one year in a box of Cheerios, one year wrapped in a fitted sheet among her linens. In 1993, the range of search expanded beyond the apartment, into the Santa Maria's common areas. In the storage room, or tucked behind the framed forest-scene prints in the lobby, or in one of the long-dormant cubbies outside each apartment where bottles were left in the days of milk delivery: there were many places an enterprising spirit could conceal an angel. In 2006, for whatever reason, J.C. failed to manifest. Rosellen's relief when he renewed their covenant a year later was deep and abiding.

"Where the hell were you, Puerto Vallarta?" she asked. From the bathroom she heard the toilet heave, belch.

⚓ ⚓ ⚓

"Do you know how he did it?" Bonnie asked.

"No."

She'd called by to inquire if Rosellen could look in on her place while she travelled. She'd be gone for two weeks, out-of-town assignment, good money.

"Will I have to watch the Vidal Show?"

"I think he's in Greece. On the Island of Hiatus."

"So much the better."

Bonnie looked around the room, appraising.

"This place was furnished when you moved in, right?"

"It was."

"Was that recliner here?"

Philip was planning to open a second-hand store over in Gastown. Bonnie was on the lookout for stock. She had an eye for all things vintage; every so often one of the scandalous micro-skirts still made an appearance. Brigitte would part the veil, would whisper in Rosellen's ear, "Mutton dressed as lamb." Rosellen was amused to discern how, in her gathering old age, she didn't disagree.

"It's always been here. It was Jean-Christophe's," Rosellen said, then felt the ice thin under her feet.

"Philip knew him, just a little. From the bars. I gather he was a big old leather queen."

"Oh," said Rosellen.

Her heart felt swamped. She looked at her watch.

"He was one of the first to get sick. Took care of himself before it got bad. Do you know how he did it?"

(Frank in 203. Kurt, who was the first to move into Brigitte's place and who came to the party a few months later looking unwell and didn't last out the year. Janice in 310, who begged Rosellen to tell anyone who asked that it was because of a transfusion. No one ever asked. More than twenty years later, her L.L. Bean catalogues are still delivered.)

"No."

There were places Rosellen would go with Bonnie. Not there, though. Not there.

"If you ever want to get rid of it – the chair, I mean – Philip would be interested. People like that kind of crap now. Hygge. You know."

Rosellen nodded. She wouldn't be getting rid of the chair. She knew it was crap, but it offended her to hear someone else name it such.

"I'm on my way out, Bonnie. I'll look in, get the mail."

"Don't water the plant, I'm desperate for it to die."

"Bon voyage."

"So long."

"So long."

So long ago.

On Christmas Eve –

Bonnie and Philip are in the Santa Maria storage room. It has about it the look of civil unrest, toppled towers in gross disarray. They've found the Vidal cache. It's more extensive than Philip imagined or Bonnie remembered.

"It pains me to say so," Philip says, "but in the summer of '89, he was a hunk. I mean, totally."

"No question."

"He was in his prime," says Philip, executing a perfect Maggie Smith as Jean Brodie, just as he did to frequent, hilarious effect at oh-so-many big old gay brunches, back when big old gay brunch was a thing, back when everyone was afraid or angry or both and he spent most of his Sundays and half his income at Delilah's, drinking mimosas, and coyly resisting the importuning of the throng that he do Tallulah, just one more time.

"If I go down on a man it chokes me and if I go down on a woman it gags me. If I get buggered it hurts like hell and if I get fucked it gives me acute claustrophobia. So I've just gone back to reading, love!"

"Oh, Jesus," says Bonnie. "What do you call that look?"

"Deborah Kerr on the beach in *From Here to Eternity* meets Susan Hayward in *I Want to Live* meets Nana Mouskouri on *The Hollywood Palace*. A little bit death. A little bit transfiguration. A little bit 'Look ma, no hands.'"

"His poor mother."

"His poor mother."

Snorting, whooping, carrying on. Rosellen passes by with J.C., does nothing to intervene, even though they're out of control, even though it's 11:20 p.m. She couldn't care less. It's too damn late for caring. Too late in the year. Too late for the Santa Maria. Too late on Christmas Eve. Over and soon. Over and out.

"In here?" she asks J.C. as they navigate the hallways, shabbier and shabbier, the carpets frayed and stained. "In here? Or in here?" she inquires, opening the glass-fronted case that contains the fire hose, or peering up for a tell-tale shadow in the scallop-shaped wall sconces, on sale at Rona, that went up ten years ago, the last time the building had a makeover. No and no and no. J.C.'s ambrosial essence wavers and dwindles. Getting cold. Getting cold.

On Christmas Eve –

Rosellen, now closer to seventy than sixty, takes a breather in the boiler room. She sits on a plastic dairy crate, the same one into which she'd packed her few belongings at the time of the Great Marriage Bolt of 1984. "Where will you go?" she says out loud, voicing the question everyone in the Nina and the Pinta and the Santa Maria has been asking, whenever, wherever they meet. It pleases her to think that J.C. might remain, that he'll outlast the wrecking ball, that he'll float among the carpenters, welders, plumbers; that he'll come to roost somewhere on one of the twenty-seven storeys of Three Ships. What if the developers knew? Would they fold him into their marketing plan? Comes with parking, also ghost.

"I will miss you," says Rosellen.

She rises – God, her joints are stiff – stretches. The light flickers. The furnace heaves, gutters, kicks into action. It's old, too. Its days of labour will soon be done. Absurd, this wash of sympathy for the inanimate, but that's what she feels for the furnace, for the lights, for the stucco, for all the human contrivances that have combined to give her, and so many others, shelter from the storm. In the hallway, there's a near smash-up with Bonnie and Philip, running for the back door, sprinting for the alley like grab-and-dash pranksters; running with surprising agility, surprising because neither is young, lord, look at them go, as if they don't feel the weight of those boxes they're carrying, three each, God knows what's in them, something from Bonnie's abundant hoard.

"I tell you, Nicola Harwood, we mustn't."

"You are right, Davie Denman, we would be fools to engage in such foolery."

"But fools we are, and foolery is our game," they crow, in perfect unison, as though they've rehearsed this moment for hours. For years, more likely.

They're out the door, into the alley. They're no longer her responsibility. Whatever juvenile scheme they've hatched, she need never know. She's not their mother, has never been anyone's mother, which causes no pang. All those years of needless egg production, a service from which she would have gladly unsubscribed. She sniffs: smell of mildew, smell of mouse, smell of something very possibly dead in some overlooked corner. Smell of J.C., too. Faint. Very faint. She smiles.

"I'm ready if you are," she says.

Bonnie will be gone in a week, will say her last goodbye on New Year's Eve as four exhausted men and two vans pull away from the building. Tears. Thank yous. Promises. They won't see each other again until they meet by accident on the seawall, three years hence, in 2021. Bonnie will be walking with a friend. Rosellen, who will have mastered Facebook during the time it took her to recover from her hip replacement, will be feeling more herself than she has in a long, long time. During a fumbling moment in the introductions Rosellen will realize Bonnie has forgotten her last name, will wonder if perhaps, after thirty-five years, she ever knew it. The die-cut sticker on her mailbox identified her only as "MANGER." Few could wring thirty-five years of enduring delight from an absent vowel. Rosellen Sweete can; blessed is she among women.

"Let's get together soon," Bonnie will say when the conversation has run its two-minute course.

"Sure," Rosellen will reply, as one does, even though of all the stupid, frivolous things conventionally intelligent people say, "Let's get together soon" is surely the stupidest. The frivolousest. Bonnie and her friend will proceed in the direction of the Lions Gate Bridge and the garish rise of the heritage sulphur heaps. Rosellen will settle onto the bench that bears the plaque she quit chocolate to afford.

"I remember the Snata Maria, 1954–2019. R.S."

Rosellen will stay as long as she's allowed – January 15 is the last possible day of occupancy – the captain doing what the captain must for the ship she loves. Shortly before noon, she'll shut the door to 101. The active decision not to lock will set her synapses chatting. She will remember what she's forgotten, will make a final pass through the basement. Bonnie will not have completed the job she began on Christmas Eve. In both her lockers, one assigned and one gifted, will remain a sordid miscellany. Rosellen will have tried calling her, will have left messages. No response. Too late. Whatever's there belongs to cranes, backhoes, diggers. She'll find her lock, closed tight, pondering whatever secrets it contains in its tempered heart. For the first time in thirty-five years, she'll whisper its "Open Sesame."

Hello, old friend.

We have places to go.

Let's get the hell out.

Dead bulb in an Emergency Exit sign. Permits expired on the fire extinguishers. Not a moment too soon. She'll go out the front door for the last time. She'll have promised herself she won't give the place so much as an over-the-shoulder glance. She won't be that strong. She'll do a Lot's wife turn, will walk away backwards, eyes glued to the place she loved, the ship that came in the nick of time. That saved her.

Of J.C. there will be no sign. Who knows – perhaps he'll watch her quit the building, then move right back, make peace with his own lost past, revel in sole, if short-term, proprietorship of 101, of the whole damn place. Maybe, as Rosellen is making her way to her new apartment – she'll have found one, at the last minute, two blocks north, one block west – he'll be rolling about in the La-Z-Boy, may he lounge in peace. Never, not once, in thirty-five years did Rosellen sit in the bloody thing.

Will they meet again, Rosellen and J.C.? Rosellen suspects not. She can reasonably forecast occasional bouts of nostalgia, but has no reason to expect paralyzing gales of grief. To endings, she's no stranger. About them, she's cultivated a level-headed serenity. One never knows. If next Christmas Eve she were to discover the angel in her popcorn maker, if she were to whiff in the air the unholy trinity of J.C.'s signature scent, she wouldn't be so very surprised. For that to happen, however, he himself will have to find the angel. On her last night in the Santa Maria, before she shuts off the breaker for the stove, before the troublesome clock dims forever, Rosellen will spend a long time meditating on where best to leave her. About that concealment, she will be very very very very very very very very very very very cunning. So, good luck, J.C. Good luck to us all.

On Christmas Eve –

Passing through the basement, J.C. beside, behind, all around her, Rosellen checks the washers, the dryers, checks the high ledges, checks the small hole in the drywall left when someone bashed into it moving out last month; she makes a note to repair it, even though no one will be left to notice or mind. She feels a familiar, welcome warmth as Jean-Christophe leads her up the stairs, leads her to the lobby – that last Decorating Party was a humdinger – leads her to where the tree stands, there in the corner, where it has always stood. Up, up. She looks up. That is where, for the first, for the last time, she finds the angel, hiding in plain sight, just where God, just where the Holy Ghost, just where J.C., too, intend her to be, beaming from the highest artificial branch, blameless, immaculate, radiant, her mouth a perfect O, wide open in silent hallelujah, there, in her rightful, proper place; there, right there, exactly where, in this time, in that place, she belongs.

On Christmas Eve.

EVERYBODY KNOWS A TURKEY

(Has any one supposed it lucky to be born?
I hasten to inform him or her it is just as lucky to die, and I
know it.)

You can fortify your house against burglary, bad weather. You can
launder your hands against colds, flus. You can know your escape
routes, predetermine a mustering point, stay inside until the shaking
stops. A little anticipation, a modicum of common sense, a boy-
scout dash of preparedness will go a long way to smooth the road.
There will be unforeseen potholes but there's nothing to be gained
by gnashing your molars into pulpy nubbins ruminating on all the
terrible tricks fate might have stashed away up its billowing kimono
sleeve: the rogue meteorite inscribed with your name that enters the
atmosphere as you step onto your balcony under cover of darkness
with only a covert cigarette in mind; the truck that takes you out
when it jumps the curb at Robson and Bute as you're leaving Muji
in a state of tepid dudgeon, bereft of purchase, freighted only with
irrational, guilt-edged annoyance at the Japanese, at the diminu-
tiveness to which they are heir, which makes them unsympathetic
to the king-size bedding requirements of corn-fed Caucasians, of
which you are one; the microbial cluster of *E. coli* that's established
its secret terrorist cell on a leaf of thrice-washed romaine, that's made
its furtive way into your faded cotton carryall, that's accompanying
you home from Whole Foods intent on the imposition of intestinal
anarchy. My God, you could recharge your Tesla with the needless
energy you'd generate if you ceded the sacred kingdom of the mind
to the hegemony of such absurdities. There's no more need to take

them into account than one might the possibility that a skunk, which has no business being abroad on Christmas Eve, nonetheless is; that a skunk – a creature which, at this time of year, should properly be curled up in its den, applying cosmetic stripe whiteners and catching up on correspondence – happens to be not only animate but also lying in wait under the 1988 Honda Civic which has been parked near Comox and Gilford for the better part of a month now, mere steps from the building which has no plaque acknowledging that once, in distant times, Malcolm Lowry lived there; the Honda Civic cum Petri dish for the cultivation of rust that has somehow evaded the rancorous scrutiny of the very city employees who manage always to lie in wait adjacent to your own vehicle, ticket in hand, attending the exact second the meter turns over; the Honda Civic that's registered to some careless miscreant who's gone away for the holidays, taken off for Maui or the Turks and Caicos, never giving a thought to how that eyesore would afford the aforementioned skunk a place of concealment from which to ambush Minnie when she did what any dog would do; when, obedient to instinct, she tested the limits of her leash, when she went snuffling after the scent of something fragrant near the oil pan.

Conrad, whatever his flaws, however many his failings, has never been averse to acknowledging culpability. On the contrary, about blame he is irrationally proprietary. "My fault!" he frequently says, his customized version of the more usual Canadian rejoinder, "Sorry!"

"My fault!" Conrad is primed to chime, "Mine, mine, mine!" with the ready alacrity of a birthday boy who, having blown out his candles, sets his sights on the largest slice of cake.

Conrad needs no convincing that his is the flag to plant in the stinking mound of blame to be claimed. Rudimentary vigilance would have been sufficient prophylaxis against the predicament in which they're mired, Conrad and Minnie, Minnie and Conrad. Conrad could so easily have been practising mindfulness, but Conrad was distracted, was communing with his phone, his angled head charmingly up-lit, haloed by the Android's Fra Angelico (ca. 1395–1455) glow. Quite why he was overtaken by an intemperate need to settle an argument he was having with no one but himself about the lyrics for "The Little Drummer Boy," he could not say. A resolution could easily have waited, but he gave in to the urge to know the number and placement of rums and pums. He let down his guard. Minnie went snuffling.

"Pa-fuckity-rum-fuckity-pum-fuckity-pum-fuckity-pum," says Conrad, when Minnie is assailed by the force of Hell's own tire fire. Then, "My fault."

The dog's retreat, backwards, on three legs, is remarkably agile, considering. How Minnie ended up a tripod is anyone's guess; she was missing the limb – right, front – when Conrad found her in the shelter, a conspicuous absence indicative of a trauma that would have been both a biographical linchpin, and a predictor of possible behavioural issues: irrational refusal to pass through revolving doors, or an otherwise inexplicable aversion to escalators, or the compulsive need to hide under the bed whenever the peasants pass by on their way to the fields, swinging their scythes and whistling tunes from *My Fair Lady*. None of the shelter employees would speculate concerning the circumstances of the leg's removal or even acknowledge that such a deficit warranted consideration. They didn't want the dog to be defined by her disability. All that mattered was her temperamental equilibrium, the preternatural sweetness of her personality, not to forget her kindly regard for cats. For children, not so much. Did Conrad have children? No? Good. Perfect. Problem solved.

Squat and sturdy, Minnie reminded Conrad of a coffee table he'd acquired at a yard sale, back in his college days. It also had three legs where four were required, and it stirred in him an affection both immediate and inexplicable. He'd hauled it from city to city, from apartment to apartment, along with the six bricks that were required to keep it on a level plane. Minnie and the wonky coffee table were among the few possessions to make the transfer from his marital home to his bachelor pad. His decision to (a) unilaterally acquire a damaged rescue dog and (b) attempt to mitigate the offence by naming the creature after his spouse, explains, at least partially, why

Minnie is now his ex-wife and why Conrad has sole, uncontested custody of Minnie. She's a basset hound / Welsh corgi / German shepherd / northern beagle cross. For woman Minnie there was, in fact, a last straw, and it was the charge, in U.S. dollars, on their shared credit card, for the genetic testing that determined so specifically dog Minnie's antecedents.

(*I think I could turn and live with animals, they are so placid and self-contain'd;*
I stand and look at them long and long.)

Tomato juice is the remedy that comes to Conrad's mind as the skunk ambles into the night, already rearming. Minnie yelps, whines, whacks at her face with the one front paw that's still in her keeping. Tomato juice. Isn't that what they always recommend, tomato juice, plenty of it? But where, on Christmas Eve, can he find tomato juice? The supermarkets once nearby on Davie have all been bulldozed, along with all the gas stations, to make way for condo towers. The one remaining convenience store is, inconveniently, closed until Boxing Day.

What to do? He dials the landline he ceded in the divorce, along with just about everything else.

"Minnie?"

The pungent dog whines.

"Not you."

"Conrad?"

"Merry Christmas, Minnie."

"Same to you. What's up?"

"Not much. Sorry for the intrusion."

"It's no intrusion," says Minnie, but of course it is. It's Christmas Eve. She has things to do, fussing to attend to, a husband to mind. Minnie hadn't let the dust settle. She moved on.

"What are you up to?"

"I'm just here with Conrad."

That Conrad's successor was also named Conrad had been much remarked by friends and family members, as well as by Conrad. Also by Conrad.

"Merry, Merry, Conrad," Conrad carols from somewhere in the background. No doubt Minnie has been plying him with eggnog, her family's special recipe, the ingredients and method of assembly guarded with a fervour approaching the Masonic. Conrad has fallen out of touch with Minnie's clan, save for her sister, Regina, in Regina, who still thinks to send him her annual newsletter, rich with details pertaining to knitting projects, gutter cleaning, her husband Mert's colonoscopy results.

Conrad, out in the cold on Christmas Eve with Minnie, imagines Minnie and Conrad, halfway across town, in MacKenzie Heights, in the Arts & Crafts house where Conrad once lived with Minnie; lived also, for a short time, with Minnie. Stockings will be hung from the mantel. A stack of Pres-to-Logs, guaranteed to burn blue and green and more reliable than cord wood, will be stacked on the hearth. The fire will be glowing. He imagines the tree, its familiar decorations – some had been in his family for generations; imagines the table, quadrupled in length with all its leaves inserted, the very table his parents had given them as a wedding gift, the table his well-organized ex would already have set for the next day's feast: the china, the flatware that had once been theirs, the patterns he'd had half a hand in choosing – he was one of the rare straight men who genuinely cared about that sort of domestic detail – all laid out in regimental array. There would be a centrepiece: pine boughs, holly, frosted cones, all sprayed with fire retardant, then arranged around a vanilla-scented candle, specifically manufactured to be strong enough to soften the edges of unwanted pet odours. Minnie, who had the bluntest palate in all of Christendom, and on whom subtler fragrances were wasted, would have sourced it from the nearby veterinary clinic where they were displayed on a shelf adjacent to remedies for mange, heart worm, coprophagia. Minnie, with her circumscribed olfactory range, would have been the ideal companion in this, his present fetid circumstance. She would scarcely have blinked at the chemical mix that is skunk squelch, would have pulled a mitigating votive from her purse, where she always had a lighter, along with a roll of scotch tape, also a multi-head screwdriver. Conrad blinks hard. He consigns the past to the past, puts what might have been from his mind. He gulps acrid air, splutters to the point.

"Minnie, do you have any tomato juice?"

Minnie, who maintains a larder full enough to outlast any catastrophe, however prolonged, is an inveterate bulk buyer whose eventual site of ash scattering could easily be Costco. For Christmases past she had caseloads of tomato juice, enough to baptize a whole pack of skunked bassets.

"Tomato juice?"

He says "to-may-to," she says "to-mah-to." Conrad smiles, ruefully, at exactly the same time he rues, smilingly: an act of unanticipated simultaneity that causes temporary facial paralysis and would have provoked him to query Siri about Bell's palsy, had his phone not been in use as a phone.

"I don't, Conrad. I had oceans of the stuff, but I took it to the food bank. Conrad's allergic. He has a problem with all nightshades, as it turns out. Eggplant could be the death of him."

"Oh," says Conrad, shamefully buoyed by the certainty that Conrad the Second will never enjoy, as had he and Minnie, the prize-winning ratatouille she would make in volume every summer, would put up in jars for winter use in the pantry with the earthquake-stabilized shelves. To him alone belonged that little piece of history. That morsel of her treacherous, stony heart.

"Why are you asking about tomato juice?"

"Just wondering."

"Funny thing to just wonder about."

"Funny time of year."

"It is," says Minnie. She chokes back a giggle, says, "Stop that!"

Conrad the Usurper, who could stand to lose thirty pounds, make that forty, must have winched himself up from the sofa, must have slouched towards Bethlehem to join her at the phone. He'd be making obscene gestures, would be aiming them down the line at his predecessor, arranging his ruddy features into sophomoric masks of contempt, all the while nuzzling Minnie's neck, groping her withers, subjecting her to a thorough pat-down – he's a customs officer, recently retired. At frisking, he's adept.

"Pa-rum-pum-pum-pum," says Conrad, through gritted teeth.

"Pardon?"

"Nothing. Sorry for calling out of the blue, Minnie."

"You okay, Conrad?"

He's the furthest thing from okay, but he's also years removed from any expectation that Minnie will prove his provisioner of succour. Or even tomato juice.

"Fine. Merry Christmas, Minnie."

"You, too. Take care. Happy New Year."

Click. Gone.

(Listen! I will be honest with you,
I do not offer the old smooth prizes, but offer rough new prizes,
These are the days that must happen to you ...)

Too dejected to take into account the imminence of piles, Conrad sits on the cold curb. Minnie collapses next to him, leans in. The vacant space where her leg should have been allows her to conform to Conrad's contours.

"Let us acknowledge," says Conrad – he's well into his cups, no point pretending otherwise – "that we are on the unceded Territories of the Coast Salish Peoples, including the Musqueam, the Squamish, the Stó:lō, and the Tsleil-Waututh First Nations. Sorry, guys. Bad deal. Shitty, shitty. Pa-rum-pum-pum-pum."

Minnie moans. He puts his arm around her, remembers daring to do the same thing with biped Minnie on their first movie date, *Gallipoli*, at the Denman Cinemas, long gone, now a dollar store. How long ago? No. This is no night for higher mathematics. This is a night to be with those you love. This is a night for wine, for music, for warm companionship. For truth and reconciliation, why the hell not? Conrad, suddenly desperate for contact that isn't canine, reaches for his phone, launches a probe to explore its outer rings of omniscience.

"Why does skunk spray smell so bad?"

For reasons mostly whimsical, but also owing to his irascible and long-term and highly confidential erotic regard for Nicole Kidman, Conrad requires his phone to answer all queries in an Australian accent, also to address him as "mate."

"Skunk spray" – the voice is chummy, confiding, goofy in its Antipodeanity – "is composed of mercaptans, a bonding of hydrogen with sulphur atoms, mate. Hence, the odour, mate."

"Mercaptans? As in 'O Captain! Mercaptan!'?"

Conrad wrote his master's thesis on Walt Whitman. Once, an M.A. was all you needed to land a job-for-life teaching English at a community college. That was where he met Minnie, on the picket line, during one of the many labour disruptions that enlivened their early careers, in the palmy days when unions were muscular and management trembled. Oh, the eighties!

"Pardon me, mate?"

"'O heart! heart! heart!'" says Conrad, feelingly,

"'O the bleeding drops of red,

Where on the deck Mercaptan lies,

Fallen cold and dead.'"

"I'm afraid I don't know what you mean, mate."

"Then you weren't paying attention in class," says Conrad, "along with everybody else. My fault, I'm sure."

"Do you have another question, mate?"

"Can you say 'shrimps on the barbie, mate'?"

"Shrimps on the barbie, mate, mate."

Conrad snorts his pleasure, is about to request his digital PA ransack YouTube to locate the jauntiest version of "Six White Boomers," lyrics included, but Minnie's distress pulls him back from the

Down-Under rabbit hole. She pulses with stink, by now they both do, it rolls from them in noxious waves. There's a pineapple express making its way in from the South Pacific, and the night is turning mild, moist; the atmosphere's warmed molecules are an assembly line passing the mercaptans from hand to nimble hand, spreading the joy hither and yon. It takes no time at all for the whole neighbourhood to share in their tragedy.

(*What are the mountains call'd that rise so high in the mists?*
What myriad of dwellings are they fill'd with dwellers?)

"Holy Jesus," spits the offended tenant of a nearby apartment, not in the cultivated tones of one rehearsing his lines for an upcoming pageant. All around him, Conrad hears the bang-on-a-can report of windows slamming shut. Vibrations jar another verse from memory's filthy ledge.

"*Away to the window he flew like a flash,*
Tore open the shutters and threw up the sash."

One day, when his vulnerabilities are more subcutaneous, Conrad will ask Minnie if he can fetch from her basement the box containing his childhood books. Some are heirlooms, first editions of more-than-just-sentimental value. There's *Treasure Island*, with the N.C. Wyeth illustrations, and the Ella Dolbear Lee *Mother Goose*, circa 1918, and the six-volume set of *My Book House*, edited (astonishing he can remember this) by Olive Beaupré Miller. Also awaiting repatriation is *A Child's Garden of Verses*, with the illustrations by Jessie Willcox Smith, the same artist who provided the decorations for his family's cherished edition of Clement Clarke Moore's *A Visit from St. Nicholas*. That book was kept under wraps, quite literally, in a chamois shroud; was only exhumed on Christmas Eve. Everyone would gather near the tree while Conrad's father read it aloud – not that he required the prompt of the text, he had it by heart. He delivered it with many histrionic gestures, with elocutionary flourish.

"Now, Dasher! now, Dancer! now Prancer and Vixen!
On, Comet! on, Cupid! on, Donner and Blitzen!
To the top of the porch! to the top of the wall!
Now dash away! dash away! dash away all!"

Conrad feels a hot surge of shame when he remembers the year he and his brother, John Christopher, couldn't stifle their giggles at the lines

The moon on the breast of the new-fallen snow,
Gave a lustre of midday to objects below...

"I think we'll end this now," said their father.

He closed the book, rewrapped and restored it to its special place on the shelf.

"Perhaps we'll try again next year."

But the following November, one day after receiving a clean bill of health from his doctor – which detail his widow made sure to include when she told the story, as she often did – he rose up from his chair at work, as if to greet a visitor, clutched his left chest in the discomfited, offended way of one just pickpocketed, then fell face forward onto his blotter, narrowly missing the message spike.

(O how shall I warble myself for the dead one there I loved?
And how shall I deck my song for the large sweet soul that has gone?
And what shall my perfume be for the grave of him I love?)

"What books do you want?" Conrad asked John Christopher.

It was one of their rare intentional meetings; rare as grown men, at least. The divvying imperative brought them together after their mother died in a small plane crash: "Of all things," she would have said. It was an aberrantly rock-'n'-roll exit for a woman averse to showiness.

Post-mortem claim-laying can be rancorous: when chattels are lowing, then rabies awakes. But the brothers met on a plateau of resigned bemusement.

"Was ever a melon balled in this house?" asked John Christopher, surveying a cutlery tray devoted entirely to implements intended for that purpose. "Even once?"

"Not that I recall. What books do you want?"

"You take them. Take whatever you want, Conrad. It can all go to auction as far as I'm concerned."

Which was, in the main, the fate it found.

On John Christopher, as on so many people and decisions and events, Conrad pins the tail of regret: John Christopher who left for Montréal the day after he finished high school, who didn't come home or even send a gift when their mother remarried; John Christopher, who changed his name to Jean-Christophe, who returned to the West Coast five years later speaking a weirdly accented English, who didn't deign to utter a cautionary word before he came to Sunday dinner with Marc-André, of whom no one had heard. Marc-André claimed to speak no English at all, which they later learned was a complete fabrication; these were the late seventies, it was a separatist provocation. His camp affectations required no translation. They were calculated to pierce the flimsy Anglo armour of his appalled but unflinchingly courteous hosts at their first and only meeting; Marc-André, whom John Christopher introduced, blithely, as his lover, which engendered a visible rising of bile in Harrison, their stepfather, a seasoned pilot, a decorated veteran of the RCAF who flew dozens of bombing missions over Germany, sustaining not so much as a scratch; Harrison, who managed, inexplicably, to pilot his Cessna, their mother his only passenger, into a Howe Sound mountainside on a perfectly clear day, leaving the boys with a great many melon ballers, to say nothing of unanswered questions. Accident? Murder? Suicide pact? WTF?

"Fruitcakes," said Harrison when the ashes of the evening were cooling, when all that remained of the prodigal and his companion was the stubborn lingering whiff of their colognes, their cigarettes.

"Queer as the strike of thirteen," he said, settling himself into the La-Z-Boy that had been their father's end-of-the-day refuge, the "amen" in amenity. It galled Conrad to watch the interloper exorcise his predecessor's ergonomic ghost, the way he adjusted its repertoire of angles and tilts with droit de seigneur bravado. Long-buried passages from *Hamlet* surfaced, glowing like polished skulls.

"You're welcome to it," he said, when John Christopher put in his spoke for the recliner, nothing else.

"You're sure?"

"Very."

Why that, of all things? Conrad didn't ask. There was much about John Christopher that resisted understanding.

(*What is a man anyhow? what am I? what are you?*)

They kept in touch casually, cordially. Now and again, one would think to call the other. They'd meet for dinner, catch up on each other's news. Conrad had secured his teaching job, tenure track. He'd been out with Minnie a couple of times, thought there might be potential for something long-term. John Christopher and Marc-André had parted company but remained friends; they were both involved in the leather community, as John Christopher called it. He'd started managing a small apartment building, just a few blocks from where the skunk launched its devastating Christmas Eve salvo. It was a dead-end job, but it allowed him to devote his time and energy to all things leather and to the Dogwood Monarchist Society (DMS), a sort of queer benevolent services agency: the Shriners, but with more stylish headgear.

In the early days of their courtship, perhaps to bolster his Bohemian street cred – needlessly, for he would soon learn how thickly conservative was Minnie's marbling – Conrad took her to the DMS Coronation Ball, a gala celebration where drag queens and leather men vied for the hotly contested titles of Empress and Emperor. John Christopher was one of the aspirants to the throne that year. It was a big deal; he'd been campaigning hard for months as the consort of a glorious confection known as the Presumptive Empress Amber Flashing.

"Really?" said Minnie, when Conrad pointed out his brother, working the Coronation crowd at the Commodore Ballroom. He wore leather boots, a leather jockstrap, a feather boa, and was throwing carnival beads with the wild abandon of a cocaine-powered flower girl.

Minnie asked, "Is he supposed to be something?"

"Sorry?"

"In that getup. Is it like a costume? Is he supposed to, you know, be something?"

"Why don't I get us some beer?" said Conrad.

"I'm really hating this," said Minnie when he returned from the bar; she'd been twice mistaken for a drag queen channelling Jane Fonda in *9 to 5*.

"You want to go?"

She nodded.

Their exit – unannounced, furtive – was observed by Marc-André, who ratted them out. When Conrad didn't get in touch to offer excuses, or to inquire about the outcome of John Christopher's candidacy – failed – a chill settled. A gap widened.

Marc-André called from Montréal – he'd moved back, Conrad had no idea – to report that John Christopher had died by his own hand, died in his apartment, died alone. None of his friends knew enough to understand there was family to contact. Nor did the police, after their careful sweep of the place, after interviewing his neighbours, have any clue. Not even his address book made it possible to connect the dots; the page where those particulars would have been recorded had been removed.

"Look," said Conrad, showing the tattered gutter edge of the missing leaf to the grief counsellor he saw, at Minnie's urging, courtesy of the college.

"I see."

"Doesn't it look like it's been torn? Ripped out? In anger?"

The counsellor, not adept at forensic analysis, said nothing.

"My fault. I keep asking, 'What if, what if?'"

"'What if' is not a productive line of inquiry. 'What if' is a country that will absorb you if you wander too far in. It's nowhere you want to get lost. Nothing grows in the land of 'What-If.'"

She looked pleased at this coining, made a note. Conrad imagined her a few years hence, on the talk-show circuit, touting her new bestseller, *The Land of What-If.*

> (*Pensive and faltering,*
> *The words* the Dead *I write,*
> *For living are the Dead ...*)

It's getting on for midnight. There's a church nearby, no belfry, no chimes, but with a decorative steeple in which are concealed speakers. They broadcast carols played on a digital carillon, tinny and indistinct, but not so murky that Conrad fails to recognize "The Little Drummer Boy" when it comes along. Minnie, sensitive to his moods and with her own reasons for howling, howls.

"Now what?" says Conrad. "Now where?"

Minnie is without idea or resource.

Conrad, ironically, lives nearby, a five-minute walk, but he can't possibly go back to his building, not to where Minnie's legality – she is three kilos heavier than the strata regulations allow a dog to be – has been the subject of an ongoing dispute and enforced Weight Watchers sessions with the council, a clutch of fat-shaming autocrats whose anuses have all won the Employee of the Month award from the firm of Clenched & Puckered. The advent of a staggering stink bomb on a night when everyone is mixing champagne cocktails and listening to Perry Como would seal her fate; his, too. It had perhaps been imprudent, after his last chance confrontation in the lobby with the board president, to deploy the phrase "dumb cunt" before the elevator door had fully closed.

There's a marked uptick in the volume of pedestrian flow. The faithful, the curious, perhaps even the bored are making their way to the service. Within half a block of Conrad and Minnie, they stop, scent the air, compose their features in a moue of disgust, cross the street. Tolerance for someone in such a predicament is bound to be at a premium. Maybe Conrad should force the issue, join the parade of mass attenders, put their Christian charity to the test by seeing if they'd be welcomed in. Perhaps Minnie could earn her keep by taking part in the pageant, could take on the cameo role of Dog in the Manger. Conrad could corner the pastor, try to put a theological spin on the situation, find out how Noah dealt with skunks on the ark.

Are skunks present in the Bible? Did God send the Pharaoh a plague of polecats? Seems unlikely. Woman Minnie would know, or could quickly find out. She's still head of the Reference Department at the College Library. Many authoritative concordances, online or bound, are at her ready disposal. Minnie's mind is as well stocked as her shelves or hard drive. Had Conrad confessed the reason for his call, she could have told him that tomato juice is useless for neutralizing mercaptans. She could have told him that's an old wives' tale. Who better to relay such news than your old wife? Former wife. Whatever. But Conrad had not let on. The yoke of his ignorance is not easy, his burden is not light. It's raining, no refreshing sprinkle but vast and ample drops, ripe, imported from Hawai'i.

(*Dearest comrades! all is over and long gone;*
But love is not over – and what love, O comrades!
Perfume from battle-fields rising – up from the foetor arising.)

Contrary to the preponderant flow of traffic – east, towards the church – comes a pair of travellers heading in the direction of the park. The percussive clatter of wheels alerts Conrad to their imminence. More than a block away, they're sufficiently specific in their persons and presentation, even in the dark and the rain, that some deductions can be reasonably made. They are, no doubt, members of the legion of the homeless. What are they pushing that makes such a din? Not the usual supermarket trolleys. No, they've adapted to their purposes, in one case, a battered baby carriage, and in the other a wheel-mounted gas barbecue. They're merry gentlemen.

"Too fuckin' much, man. Can you fuckin' believe it?"

That much he can make out, but no other particulars of whatever story prompts such hilarity. They're rehashing – you can know this, even if Conrad can't – their meeting with a pair of Christmas Eve inebriates, a man and a woman, who'd given the travellers what remained of a bottle of fizzy wine.

"It's better when it's cold," the woman said.

"It was cold when we opened it," said the man, sad and disbelieving, as though the dispersal of its frostiness was an act of betrayal.

"Also it was full. Once it was full and once it was cold, but it's neither of those things now."

"It's still Prosecco, though," said the man, as if this compensated for its shortcomings. "What's left of it is still what it was, which is Prosecco."

They all chortled at how he fluttered the *r*, an affected trill. ·

"Beggars can't be choosers," said Grill, which was the street name he'd claimed for himself, for self-evident reasons, a bit of whimsy that, much to his surprise, awakened superpowers he had so far chosen not to use, and which he would never divulge or show off to strangers. He was from a prosperous family; groaning Christmas boards, fine New Year's wines, Palm Springs for the season. Did he miss his old life, its material perks? Typically, no, or so he would claim. At this time of year, though, maybe a smidge; he'd be glad to have something more festive with which to toast the season than a tin of Sterno strained though a sock of dubious provenance.

"If wishes were horses then beggars would ride," said Pram, and chuckled along with the others, even though that had been a favourite proverb of his cruellest abuser at the school he'd been compelled to attend, where kindness was in short supply. He lasted it out as long as he could, ran away, got back to Gods Lake, to his family, but nothing was as it had been and nothing was ever going to be the same, he could tell, and so he hit the road, hitchhiked to the coast, made it out west in three days, and stayed. That was twenty years ago. Since then, he's been nowhere. Since then, there's nothing he hasn't seen.

"Hark, hark, the dogs do bark, the beggars are coming to town," said the woman, pleased to contribute this morsel to their thematic potluck. As though her Mother Goose recollection was prescriptive, an incantation, there arose from a street or alley nearby a baying of such deep urgency – Hound of the Baskervilles! – they could only stand in silence to marvel at the moment.

"Holy shit," said the *R*-roller when the tsunami of skunk washed over them, seconds later. "Anyone mind if I take a leak?"

Without waiting for a reply he turned his back, loosed a voluminous stream, admirable in a man of his years.

"By the way, you guys," the woman said, "there's a pile of boxes stacked by a dumpster just down the lane. There might be something interesting there. A treasure!"

"Thanks for the tip," said Grill.

"Yeah," said Pram. "Merry Christmas."

"Happy New Year," the woman said.

The man gave himself a few more shakes than a sober man might have found strictly necessary, zipped up, said "You guys look after yourselves."

They made to go their separate ways.

"Hang on!"

They paused, turned. The woman was reaching under her coat, unknotting something tied behind her waist.

"Another present. Maybe you can use this."

It was an apron, flimsy, of uncertain utility, nothing to wear when getting in and out of dumpsters, or fending off intruders, or cooking over fires. They thanked her, nonetheless.

"'Tis the season to be *joli*," said the man.

"Try it on!"

"Not right now," said Grill, but Pram did, gamely, a good sport, angling his leg like a runway model.

"Hilarious," she said. "Can I take a picture?"

"We should get going," said Grill, whose Spidey senses signalled something untoward.

"One little picture, just one," she protested, waving her phone. Pram shrugged. Sure. Whatever.

"Do that model thing again, that cute little knee bend."

He complied.

"Oh yeah, that's what I'm talking about. Work with me, baby."

"Lady, we should get going," said Grill, who shot her friend a silent plea for intervention. He didn't want to incinerate them with his laser eyes, but he would if there were no other option. If he was backed into a corner and there was no way out.

"Come on, Bonnie. Let them get on with their night."

"Sure, sure. Thanks, fellas. Good luck. And check out those boxes."

"Okay."

They resumed their westward leading.

"And that apron looks good on you. Take care of it. It was my mother's!"

(*Do you take it I would astonish?*
Does the daylight astonish? does the early redstart
twittering through the woods?
Do I astonish more than they?

This hour I tell things in confidence,
I might not tell everybody, but I will tell you.)

So the two travellers walk, pushing pram, guiding grill, loaded with the boxes to which they'd been alerted. One carton has been inexpertly closed; it contains photographs, of what or of whom they can't say. This wasn't what they were expecting or necessarily hoping for. So what? It will be good to have, in the absence of aftershave or neckties or subscriptions to the *National Geographic*, something useless, like art, to dig into on Christmas morning.

They pass a man splayed on the curb, his dog beside him, the misbegotten pair who were prophesied by the passing mercaptans. Both are in distress. Big deal. Everyone they know is in distress. Pram and Grill don't offer sympathy and they have no advice, not on this Christmas Eve, navigating the trails of this shut-down town where the miracle unguent of tomato juice can be hard to find for ready money, but flat Prosecco and see-through aprons are delivered by strangers. It is, indeed, a city of miracles. It is, indeed, a night of wonders.

Conrad watches them pass, benighted Conrad who, if only he thought to ask, would have known that hydrogen peroxide, baking soda, and Dawn dishwashing detergent are all the potion ingredients he requires. It remains tomato juice in which he mistakenly invests his hope; it's tomato juice in which he believes on a night when it's good to have faith, have somewhere to pin it, however thin and frangible that place or that faith might be.

"What's the time?"

"It's 12:07 a.m. (Pacific Standard Time) on December 25, mate."

"What time does that make it in Melbourne?"

"7:07 p.m. (Australian Eastern Daylight Time) on December 25, mate."

"Bottom line," says Conrad, this time to Minnie, "is that it's time we were going."

He stands too quickly; there's a surge in the current of his blood, he thinks he might faint, his vision blurs, he sees John Christopher, healthy and whole, pass by on the other side of the street, walking hand in hand with Walt Whitman. They're speaking French. Fog of tears. Blink away. Nothing.

(This now is too lamentable a face for a man,
Some abject louse asking leave to be, cringing for it,
Some milk-nosed maggot blessing what lets it wrig to its hole.

This face is a dog's snout ...)

"Come, Minnie."

She struggles to rise. Conrad's phone is still on the curb.

"What should I do?" he shouts in its direction.

"Pa-rum-pum-pum-pum," answers the voice that sounds less like Nicole Kidman than Mel Gibson with his nuts in a vice.

"Pa-rum-pum-pum-pum what?"

"Pa-rum-pum-pum-pum, mate."

For the first time in his long life as a man, Conrad resorts to violence. He brings his heel down, brings it down hard, again, again, again.

"My fault! My fault! My fault!"

When he's done, he feels filthy. He feels satisfied and whole, he's Stanley Kowalski with a graduate degree.

"Are you still there? Is anyone fucking there?"

Silent night.

"Not so smart now, are you, mate? Let's go, Minnie."

They walk with no purpose in mind, no specific plan, no destination other than, maybe, the great wide barrens of "What-If." They don't need much, just to find some place they can settle, if only for the night; some place where they won't hear "The Little Drummer Boy." Or "Waltzing Matilda." Where Conrad can say, "O Captain! my Captain! our fearful trip is done ..."

At a discreet distance they follow in the clattering wake of Pram and Grill who stop to look up at the sky, pointing to where they know the stars to hang, however inscrutably, behind the clouds, the veiling rain. Stars for wishing. Stars for falling. One star – where? – for following. Soon enough, Minnie and Conrad, five legs between them, will catch them up. They will be three beggars walking, one in rags, one in tags, one in a silken apron. They'll be walking on Christmas Eve, walking and walking on parallel paths, with no real where in mind, no real certainty about what they'll find when they get there. Wherever there might be. They'll know it when they find it. It will be nearby. Chances are, it will be nothing like what they expect.

(Camerado, I give you my hand!
I give you my love more precious than money,
I give you myself before preaching or law;
Will you give me yourself? will you come travel with me?
Shall we stick by each other as long as we live?)

SNOW ON SNOW ON SNOW ON SNOW

(From the clasp of the knitted locks, from the keep of the
well-closed doors,
Let me be wafted.

Let me glide noiselessly forth;
With the key of softness unlock the locks ...)

Saint Zita of Lucca (ca. 1212–1272), the patroness of bakers and of
domestic workers – including housemaids, butlers, manservants, and
ladies-in-waiting – is no policy wonk. In Heaven, as it was on Earth,
her eye is on the unadorned, the numinous; she has scant regard for
systems theory, or administrative cunning, or the gimme/gotcha shell
games of power brokers. She misses the good old days when she was
more reliant on saintly intuition than on gadgetry. Ever since the
ballyhooed rapprochement with the Fallen Angels, ever since the
importation of all that Hades-built circuitry from Serpent Industries,
ever since the advent of the Eternal Plug-In, her life has been, well,
Hell. That first pager was bad enough, but this new generation of
infernal devices is insufferable; not just the gizmos themselves but
the confounded seminars they have to endure every damn time a
new program or app comes along. *Oddio!* it's like being martyred all
over again; so says her best friend, Saint Sebastian, and he should
know. Zita wishes her work was less quota-driven, less surveilled
and charted; surely it's enough that God knows her every move, why
should middle management stick their oar in?
  "where r u"

Thus texts Saint Isidore of Seville, the killjoy technocrat managing the Christmas Eve shift. Zita requested the 24th off fully a year ago – she always does – and now, plainly, something's come up, she's about to be assigned. Okay, fair enough: when you're a patron saint, you're always on call. But oh, how she longs for the days when such a summons was radiant with formality, when it would fall, rose-scented and in perfectly pitched Latin plainsong, from the bow-shaped lips of a herald angel. Izzy, Lord, what a bore – the Barbarian of Seville they call him behind his back – overweening and impatient, too; he'll expect an immediate response. Zita replies, slowly, with one finger, tsking every time she makes an error, holding her device at the furthest possible remove from her face, squinting; she's forgotten her cheaters. Again.

"By way of approved prior arrangement, I am in my hometown of Lucca, thank you for asking, and praise the Lord."

She wonders if the intended tartness is too subtle; Izzy is a blunt instrument. Zita's not given to sarcasm but it's not as though this is some novel move on her part: that Lucca is where Zita travels every Christmas Eve is well and widely understood. She likes to look in on her own incorruptible remains, on display under glass since 1696 in the Basilica of San Frediano, open daily, from 9:00 a.m. to 6:30 p.m. In repose, as she herself will readily acknowledge, mortal Zita, what's left of her, looks like a chestnut roasting on an open fire.

"911 need u asap"

In other circumstances, in other hands, this might have been an instance of what Zita understands is called "sexting."

"May I be so bold as to inquire why I am so urgently required?"

"411 coming soon get back now"

"I rejoice in compliance. May the light of the Lord shine upon you and bring you peace. Asshole."

Zita purges the vulgarity before hitting send, then summons her rideshare. She allows herself the five available seconds before the driver's arrival to regret the dashing of her plans. She had intended, on her return from Lucca, to spend a quiet but merry evening at home watching all 154 episodes of *Hazel*, which was the thoughtful gift chosen for her by Saint Clare of Assisi, patron saint of television; Clare, who had not respected the thirty-dollar upper limit, had picked Zita's name from the Holy Grail in this year's Secret Santa draw. Hazel and her madcap adventures with the Baxters remind Zita so vividly of all those years she spent working for the Fatinelli family in thirteenth-century Lucca. It wasn't always easy and they weren't always kind, but she won them over in the end, despite her habit of taking food from their pantry and distributing it among the poor. "Zita the Commie" they would have called her a few centuries later.

"Hey, Z," says Saint Christopher, appearing out of nowhere in his witchy way, manifesting on the Via Fillungo in a Fiat 124 Spider. It's the 2037 model; he's taking it out for a test spin.

"Hey, C."

"Going to the office?"

"Affirmative. ETA?"

"Hard to say. Lots of sobriety stops, cherubim partying, the usual. Maybe ten secs."

"Seven would be better. Izzy's in a tizzy."

"I'll try."

"*Andiamo*."

Zita buckles up. A harp glissando from her phone announces the arrival of Izzy's promised link with the details of her assignment. What constituent needs her intervention? A baker who's burned the panettone? A maid who's applied the wrong polish to a dining room table and lifted the shine from the surface mere hours before twenty guests arrive for Christmas dinner? A valet in a lather because he can find but one of the master's diamond cufflinks? She clicks on the attachment, casts her line, is puzzled when she reels in a nondescript, passport-style photo of an average-looking man, Caucasian, middle-aged, along with this brief descriptor:

Leonard Cohen, small business owner, born in Winnipeg, Manitoba, Canada, 1959. Son of Morley Cohen and Zita Cohen (née Frankl).

Present coordinates: 49° 17′ 02.5″ N, 123° 05′ 43.0″ W. Recommended search term(s): "Wedding gown, used." Please make assessment, take appropriate action, and file your report by 8 a.m. On behalf of the Father, the Son, and the Holy Ghost, I remain, Saint Isidore of Seville, Acting Director of Digital Intercessionary Procedures.

"Pompous twit," says Zita, taking care to activate her anagram filter lest Izzy be listening in. He is, and we can leave him at this point, puzzling over "I'm two to pups."

Zita is annoyed but also intrigued. A first quick glance is typically sufficient to suggest why she should have been buddied up with whoever the needy case; not here, though. She shares a name with the subject's mother – Hungarian, probably, as Zitas tend now to be – but that's a charming coincidence, and surely not the reason she was chosen when so many other saints might have come marching in. Why not Homobonus, the patron saint of business people, with whose name Saint Sebastian has had so much irreverent fun? "I'm just heading off to the Via del Corso to spend my homo bonus," he says, reliably, each and every payday. It never gets tired. Or why not Saint Teresa Benedicta of the Cross (1891–1942), born Edith Stein? She would surely be a better match should an innate grasp of the subtler mechanisms of faith be required to set things right. Not that Zita minds a bit of crossover, understand; she's big-hearted, brimming with the spirit of ecumenism. Who you are, what you do, whatever your external signifiers – yarmulke, turban, hijab, Easter bonnet – it's all the same to her. Disraeli, Einstein, Joan Rivers, Jake Gyllenhaal: these are but a few of the names on her roster of clients successfully assisted. What they shared in common, apart from the fundamentals of creed, was a lost key. It is Saint Anthony of Padua (1195–1231) who is called upon to assist with the retrieval of lost things in general, but Zita of Lucca's special gift is locating mislaid keys.

"Here we are," says Saint Christopher, as they turn up the winding drive that leads to the Celestial Surveillance Centre (CSC). "Six point five seconds."

"Thanks, C."

"Five for five?"

"You bet."

Zita takes a handful of the Perugina bonbons offered her by Saint Michael at the security desk. She hurries to her cubicle, anxious to avail herself of the mainframe searching capabilities of the CSC. She plies her desktop computer with the required password – "ilovelucca99" – and then tests the mettle of optical fibre by entering the provided geographical pinpoints and the search term, "Wedding gown, used."

"Gotcha."

❄ ❄ ❄

Used, yes, but gently. Barely, even. Leonard Cohen, walking home through the falling snow on this Christmas Eve, making his way down a Gastown alley, the brick walls of the surrounding buildings vibrant with graffiti and gang tags, is the second person to wear that gown. Grace Rainier (née Thatcher) was the first, a long time ago, way back in the spring of 1952. It was Grace's best friend, Shelagh, who made the modifications – tasteful, yet daring – to Simplicity Pattern 3958. The work of it! So many hours of designing, of stitching the frothy, .multilayered confection of ivory, tulle, taffeta, of amply adorning the frosty bodice with guipure lace, with seed pearls.

Shelagh and her husband, Hammer – they married in 1954, Grace was the matron of honour – have enjoyed a long, happy retirement near Qualicum Beach. It's a nice place to be at home, even though home is rarely where they are; they have an RV and they travel far and wide attending square-dance conventions. They've done this for years now, they have friends everywhere. Shelagh, still nimble with a needle, is forever lending a hand with sequin attachment or making a quick repair to a frayed crinoline, more often someone else's than her own. She's the sort of person who takes good care of her things, and of her friends, too. At church – Shelagh goes alone, Hammer's not a believer – she adds Grace's name to the list of those for whom prayers of healing should be offered; not that healing is even a remote possibility. Poor Grace. Her memory has been shattered beyond repair. Not even Shelagh floats among the fragments. Grace no more remembers Shelagh than she remembers her sons (Trevor, James), her cats (there were seventeen all told, and as many as five at a time in the house, so muddling them is a forgivable lapse), her late husband (Buddy), or the date of her anniversary (April 27, the feast day, consider the irony, of Saint Zita). Grace no more remembers Shelagh than she remembers the gown, or all those late nights they spent together in the spring of 1952, Grace admiring herself in the mirror; she'd been dieting, sort of, since Christmas. She loved watching her ceremonial robe take shape on her not-quite-slender person, Shelagh on her knees, trimming, tucking, lacing the hem, lacing the coffee with rum. Grace brought the rum. It made them giggly, confessional. Shelagh was the only person – well, other than Buddy – who knew that, pursuant to the events of April 15, Grace would not be intact when she sailed down the aisle. Shelagh remembers, as Grace does not, how the bride-elect summed up her experience of maidenhood sacrifice: "About as painful as getting a wisdom tooth pulled, but only half as bloody." Shelagh remembers her mouth full of pins, how she almost choked them down from the shock, almost spit them out from the laughing. It would give Grace such pleasure to recall that time, that dress, if only she could. The sweetheart neckline, the inverted basque waist, the long fitted sleeves, not to forget the chapel train, the very train that, on Christmas Eve, drags through the accruing snow, carving a shallow wake behind Leonard Cohen.

Grace can't remember the gown, nor her wedding day, nor the flowers she carried – red roses, feathery ferns, baby's breath – nor the knowing wink she gave her friend and seamstress when it was Shelagh who caught the bouquet. Grace can't remember Leonard

Cohen, which is proper since she never laid eyes on him. Oddly, though, in the ineffable (but not random) way of these things, she remembers Leonard's father. She remembers him even though they collided but once, ever so briefly. She remembers his face, but not the reason for their meeting; she could never tell you that it was to Morley Cohen himself, the founder of Loving You Always Wedding Gown Storage, that she entrusted the care of her nuptial swathing, the intricate ensemble on which Shelagh had worked so long, so hard. It was Grace's mother, Margaret, who insisted on this consigning.

"You can't leave it hanging in the closet, dear," Margaret chided. "That ivory will yellow. That would be a shame."

"Six dollars a month," Grace countered. A new bride, she was already a shrewd shopper with a keen eye for the cheaper cuts of meat. She knew all about the pleasing elasticity of six dollars.

"I'll help out if money's a concern," Margaret told her. "It's an investment in the future."

"How?" asked Grace, who came into the world trailing clouds of stubborn practicality. "I'm never going to wear it again."

"But your daughter might," said Margaret, who could not foresee that there would be grandsons only, who had no way of knowing that Trevor would prefer boys, that James would die at thirteen of leukemia.

"Maybe she won't."

"Maybe she will. Something old to go along with the borrowed, the blue, the new. Keep it, Grace. I wish I'd taken better care of mine."

Grace knew this to be so. She also knew her mother's misgivings had nothing to do with how those robes hadn't been preserved with Grace's eventual nuptials in mind. Margaret would have so relished travelling down to dangerous Gastown, reclaiming her gown, bringing it home, laying it out on the bed, taking her sewing shears, and cutting the thing into ribbons – take that, take that, take that. That's what she would have done after her husband left her for a stewardess. A stewardess, my God! One rung up from secretary, maybe, but only just one. What was more humiliating? The betrayal or being implicated in so shopworn a cliché? Margaret was blindsided. She'd been so supportive, so happy for Bob's boss to have accorded him the chance to travel out of town on behalf of the company. It was a sign his hard work was paying off. He was all nerves the night before. She pressed his suit, matched his tie, made sure his shoes were buffed. He'd never so much as buckled a seatbelt, but didn't he just cotton on to the finer points, the perks of air travel, as if he were born to it? He was a natural. Bastard. Bastard. Margaret would have loved to have laid out that wedding gown, unleashed her inner Medea. But no. After the honeymoon, she'd merely hung it in the closet in the upstairs hall, hung it in a cut-rate garment bag. Her rage redoubled when she hauled it out, fully intent on reducing it to kitty litter, only to find that the moths had gotten to it first.

"Just take care of it, Grace," said Margaret.

Grace gave in.

❄ ❄ ❄

A mere hover and click on the gown was all Saint Zita required to divine its story and provenance. But how and why, on this snowy Christmas Eve, it adorns the person of Leonard Cohen, and what assistance he requires, and how she can provide it, these are the knots for untying; the mysteries to be solved, step by investigative step. She'll begin with the client. Who is he? She takes advantage of a moment when Leonard pauses, raises the veil, lifts his head and lets the snow gather on his lashes. She clicks on his face.

Leonard Cohen. He's a non-fiction kind of guy, practical, with a good business sense, a head for baseball statistics, with scant regard for whimsy, for fancy, for experimentation. He's conscientious. He's decent. He appreciates the familiar. He's a fan of brightly lit surfaces, cares nothing for dark, unplumbed depths, all of which is to say it was entirely out of character for him to sign up, all those years ago, for a self-help weekend workshop at the Russian Community Centre on Fourth Avenue, "Bearing the Names of the Famous: Coming to

Terms with an Unwanted Legacy." The facilitator was Julie Christie, an earnest young woman. It was during those two days of unaccustomed commingling with strangers and enforced soul-searching that Leonard met Edie Fischer, his future wife; Edie, who's now home alone, lying in bed in their Kitsilano duplex on Yew Street, awash in the blue cathode glow of *It's A Wonderful Life*, not thinking much about her husband, certainly not worried about him in any way. She never worries about Leonard. Why would she?

At the time of their meeting, Edie was studying personnel management. On their first proper date, under the pretext of needing a volunteer to help with a homework assignment, Edie asked Leonard if he would complete the Myers–Briggs personality test.

"I guess," he said.

He complied right then and there, in Orestes Taverna on Broadway, undistracted by the heart-quickening thrum of the bouzouki, likewise by the pierced-navel gyrations of the Friday-night belly dancer. He applied himself to the booklet with his accustomed decisiveness, mindful only of Edie's eyes upon him, oblivious to the tintinnabulary enticements of Zorina's come-hither zills.

Later that night, alone at home – they shared a quick kiss at her door, chaste but salty owing to the feta – Edie tabulated his score. She liked that nothing in his revealed character suggested the dangerously idiosyncratic. That was important to Edie. She was on the lookout for someone stable, a father figure. Her own daddy was no Gibraltar, far from it. He was the poisoned wellspring of her angst.

At the seminar that transported Leonard into Edie's gravitational field she spoke at length, with compelling, dreadful candour, of how her father, Frank, had been a fanatical fan of Eddie Fisher, had listened to his recordings – 78s, 45s, LPs – over and over, had paid them maniacal attention, sometimes even imputing Eddie-to-Frank personal messages encoded in the lyrics. Frank Fischer was especially susceptible to Eddie's greatest hit, from 1954, "Oh! My Papa."

Leonard was moved – as were John Lennon, Eva Braun, and Lester B. Pearson – to hear Edie sobbingly recount how her father had prayed for a boy, someone on whom he could confer his hero's moniker. Frank wept when the doctor brought news of her tainted advent, but decided to make the best of it by imposing on his daughter – wide-eyed, defenceless – a gender-adjusted variant. By subjecting the child to repeated playings of "Oh! My Papa" – this was at a time when all the other kids were listening to Burl Ives singing "Big Rock Candy Mountain" – he hoped to inculcate in her tenets of filial piety that would be to Frank's obvious advantage as he grew old. (Which he didn't. Car accident. August 10, 1968. Eddie Fisher's fortieth birthday. Coincidence? Please. We all know better.)

Leonard Cohen heard – so did Julia Child, Sigourney Weaver, and Desmond Tutu – of how Edie's mother, Sylvia, had intended to call her new daughter Debbie, but had caved in to her husband's wishes, which was usual for her; Frank Fischer was impossible to refuse when he'd worked up a head of steam. Sylvia was consoled, a little, by knowing that Eddie Fisher was at least married to a Debbie, to Debbie Reynolds; but when Eddie left Debbie, had the gall to run off with Debbie's best friend, Elizabeth Taylor – the actress, not the English novelist of the same name – Frank and Sylvia became distraught for different, unbreachable reasons. Things spiralled downwards. Unwittingly, they transformed their daughter into a vessel into which they could pour their every carbolic, middle-class resentment.

Joan Crawford, a woman of amplitude and warmth, gathered Edie up off the floor.

"Oh, honey," she said, and clutched Edie to her ample bosom: a worn-out trope, but sometimes that's just what's required, in life as in literature. Edie heaved and sobbed. She sobbed and heaved. Leonard understood that it would fall to him, Leonard Ben-Morley, to be this frail creature's consolation, her comforter, her shield.

Edie required careful management. A man less equanimous than Leonard Cohen might have been worn down by her needs, her passive-aggressive wheedling. Leonard knew her manipulations for what they were. He didn't mind that she was a black hole of neediness, that she devoured the lion's share of the conversation. His only real requirement was that she be willing to coexist in his company, as peaceably as her nature allowed. If she rarely asked him about himself or his work, well, that was okay by him. He didn't have a job that bred much in the way of news. The gowns came in. They rarely went out. They just, you know, hung there. He would have found it a strain, day after day, to spin the straw of this tired quotidian into anecdotal gold.

❄ ❄ ❄

Leonard met Edie six weeks after his father, Morley, died. He was at the bedside as the old man's breathing slowed, as he gathered his strength, spoke his last words.

"Remember, my boy, the three simple rules that will guarantee a happy outcome to anyone who aspires to be a conserver of wedding gowns. Courteous acquisition. Safe storage. Ready retrieval, however rarely it's needed. That's all you'll require to maintain the groundwork I've so carefully laid with the good of the firm, also with your eventual benefit, in mind. Add to that a simple, protective formula of high volume, low overhead, minimal staffing: your ongoing success is ensured. Be good to the business. The business will be good to you. What else can I tell you? Turn out all unnecessary lights. Never buy a German car. One more thing, *boychik*. Your girlfriends so far, none has stuck around. *Nu?* Promise me you're not a *fagela*. It would kill your mother."

While Leonard was wondering whether he should point out that Zita Cohen was already ten years gone, the Angel of Death passed through the room. Morley was dead: to begin with. There is no doubt about that. The undertaker, alerted to this imminence, had been warming up the hearse, was quick to arrive, to ferry Morley off to where the Chevra Kaddisha stood by with their long faces and sponges.

Someone more speculative of mind, more accommodating of the possibility of immortal continuance than Leonard Cohen, might have appreciated an envoi more anodyne than the one Morley delivered; something cuddlier, more replete with platitudes and reassurances. It wasn't that his seven lost years – two in the camps, three as a DP – had hardened Morley against the misty-eyed. He was linear by nature, was hardwired to apply himself to the task at hand, to get on with things, not to fuss and fuss. It wasn't that he believed work would make you free, rather that if you kept yourself busy you wouldn't have the time or energy to agonize about how things could be other than they were. The six numbers on his right forearm were a ready reminder that that was how he survived; not by staring up at the stars, grasping after metaphors, not by constantly noodging and wondering why.

Once a year, typically in May, when wedding season has been amply greased, when caterers and florists are spinning out of control, some journalist will come by the plant, intent on writing a "bright" about Loving You Always. One such story, framed – at Edie's behest, Leonard would never have thought of such a thing – hangs on the wall of the reception area.

> Meet Leonard Cohen. He doesn't live in a tower of song, and he's never visited the Chelsea Hotel, but when it comes to knowing about brides and what they wear, he can always sing "I'm your man." He's the President and CEO of Loving You Always Wedding Gown Storage, a repository for what must certainly be tens of thousands of yards of taffeta and lace, the fairy-tale fabrics worn by would-be princesses on the most important day of their lives.
>
> Loving You Always, a Vancouver Institution since 1961, was founded by Cohen's father, Morley, a Holocaust survivor who had been an apprentice tailor in his native Lithuania.

"He came to Canada and met my mom, Zita, on the ship. She was from Hungary, also via the camps," explains son Leonard, showing the visitor through the temperature-and-humidity-controlled room of this converted meatpacking plant on Alexander Street. "They wound up in Winnipeg, got married there, and when I came along they decided to move west. Mom brought her wedding gown. She wasn't going to wear it, she wasn't going to give it away and our new place was small, there was nowhere to keep it. My dad figured that there must be lots of women in just such a situation, and so –"

Cohen smiles as he gestures at the ranks of gowns, hanging shoulder to shoulder on racks in the same high-ceilinged room where the racks and shoulders were once those of beef and lamb. What a coat of paint can do! Now, we see tulle and organza, satin and velvet. Shrouded in plastic are lustrous charmeuse and slubbed shantung, transparent chiffons and sturdy brocades. Present as well are patterned jacquard and crispy georgette, finely ribbed ottoman and reliable damask. Here is the social history of the last half century. In the varying cuts and styles we can read the cautious optimism of the fifties, the cheeky and revolutionary swing of the sixties, the aesthetically dubious churn of the seventies, the absurdly self-assured swagger of the eighties, the conciliatory, consolidating, somewhat tentative plod of the nineties, and the glass-ceiling shattering verve of the limitless millennial woman.

How often do the owners of these festive frocks come to visit or retrieve them? "Not so very often," says Cohen, "but they always know they'll be here if they want them." And have they ever lost a dress? "No, God forbid," he answers, firmly. And has he ever tried one on? "No," he answers, quickly, then laughs. "What a crazy idea."

❄ ❄ ❄

"You big fat liar," says Zita on Christmas Eve as she watches Leonard Cohen walking home, conspicuously swathed in a wedding gown. She unwraps one of the Perugina chocolates – delicious – then folds the silver foil into a tiny origami crane, a skill she picked up at a workshop given by the Twenty-Six Martyrs of Japan. Nothing she's learned so far suggests how Leonard Cohen has come to be thus attired. To find this out, she'll avail herself of the Time Reversal app, which comes with the option of a live soundtrack. In Heaven, there's an infinite number of choirs, all available at a moment's notice, day or night: a figure of speech since in Heaven there's no divide between the diurnal and nocturnal. Any of these ensembles would deliver a blameless performance, but some are better suited than others to certain situations. The choir that would sing an army into battle is not necessarily the best choir for a neophyte pastry chef making her first baked Alaska. The choir that could most readily sing backup while a coach is giving his team a fiery speech in the locker room before the big game may not be ideally tailored to fit with a man who's about to don, as he does every Christmas Eve, a wedding gown carefully chosen from the many in his keeping. She sends a quick text to Saint Cecilia, the patron saint of music and musicians, explaining the situation and asking her advice about both ensemble and repertoire.

"Since it's you asking," Cecilia replies, "I imagine key will be key."

"Huh?" answers Zita, not always quick on the uptake.

"Never mind. Leave it with me. I'll send someone along."

※ ※ ※

Zita activates Time Reversal. She splits her screen, so that both the immediate past and the evolving present are visible. On the right, in real time, is Leonard Cohen, in the snow; Leonard Cohen, in a wedding gown; Leonard Cohen, walking home. On the left is Leonard Cohen, five years back. The month is May and that journalist has just wrapped up her interview, has left the building. Leonard seems unruffled. He is, Zita discerns, an honest man in the normal run of things, scrupulous, but the lie he read into the public record – "No, what a crazy idea!" – stirred no pang of conscience. What else could he have said? Had he told the truth about his annual metamorphosis – a

Christmas Eve ritual he began the year Morley died, the year he met Edie – what would have happened? A shit storm, that's what. The day after the article appeared he would have come to work to find a lineup stretching around the block, longer than the breadline at the Sisters of Our Lady of Perpetual Help down the way, brides of several generations, none blushing, all red-faced with outrage, all there to rescue their gowns from the potential violation of the custodian who'd taken their money and betrayed their trust. They'd spit at him as he walked by, treat him to vile epithets – "pervert," "asshole," "sissy."

"Your father must be turning over in his grave!" someone would hiss. "A curse be on you and on your children and on your children's children. You are a disgrace to your people!"

That's where "Yes" would have taken him.

Zita advances time as easily as she might move a pawn across a chessboard. Now it's the very recent past, it's Christmas Eve of the present year. Between real-time Leonard on the right, walking home, and Leonard on the left, in the storage facility, is a span of only forty-five minutes. The phone rings. It's Saint Michael at Security. The choir has arrived.

Saint Cecilia is like a sommelier with uncanny intuition. She's the expert; Zita would never have presumed to suggest that a group of sweet-voiced children made up of the unsullied souls of the stillborn might be just the thing, especially if they were to croon some of the hits from the *Charlie Brown Christmas*, a cornerstone of Zita's holiday cheer since 1965. She also wondered if some specialists in Israeli folk songs might not be appropriate since, well, you know. She's surprised, a little, when the group that appears, a blink or two after she'd sent Zita a thumbs-up emoji, was the Hallelujah Holler, an a cappella octet that specializes in the songs of Leonard Cohen. It seems a strangely blunt, reflexive pairing, the steward sending over the same old Sauvignon Blanc because she's too damn busy to go to the cellar and find just the right Pinot Noir to accompany the salmon. Well. Whatever. Christmas is Cecilia's most frantic season.

"What's up?" the director and lead tenor asks Zita. He's wearing a Santa hat and a red-and-white-striped scarf, Phentex, that stretches, quite literally, into eternity. He supposes they've been recruited to accompany something sweet and sentimental, maybe a hayride or a fireside proposal, the engagement ring concealed in a slice of fruitcake or cup of eggnog, perhaps.

"Have a gander," Zita says, and the Hallelujah Holler gathers round to watch.

They see Leonard at a mirror, naked from the chest up. Like Morley, and all his Ashkenazi forebears, dating back to Esau, Leonard is a hairy man; so much so that Zita and the choir at first mistake the wire-brush extrusions from his shoulders, his back, for screen distortion.

"Is that a wedding gown?" asks one of the Hallelujah Holler sopranos as Leonard slowly, reverently strips Shelagh's masterpiece of the protective wrapping that's kept it from the air and light since 1952.

"It's a beauty," says an alto.

"Maybe he's going to try it on for size," says the second tenor, famous for his saucy rejoinders. Everyone chuckles; what chance a man so extravagantly furred would violate the borders of the binary?

"Hush," says Zita. "I need to hear."

Their breathing slows and they watch with a growing sense of awe tempered with unease as Leonard removes his shoes, his socks. He undoes his belt and slides out of his practical khakis. He stands before them in his skivvies.

"I don't feel right about this," says one of the basses, who is hopeless with rhythm, but on whom the Holler relies to settle questions of rectitude.

"Shhhh!" says Zita.

She leans in as Leonard folds his trousers. She hears in his pockets the rattle of change and, yes, she would know it anywhere, the metal-on-metal jingle of keys. House. Car. Warehouse. He places the folded trousers on the countertop. Not even the smart-ass tenor has anything to say when Leonard does next what Leonard does next.

It is a moment of such pure, white, heated holiness that only pure, white, heated silence is a fit accompaniment. Leonard, transformed, stands before the mirror. He is utterly, perfectly, blamelessly still. Zita listens hard. She can hear his heart. She can hear the falling snow. Leonard sighs, and so does everyone gathered around her computer, watching as he turns, as he leaves the room.

"Now?" asks the director?

"Now," says Zita, and they launch into the song for which they're named; they sing "Hallelujah."

There's not much left of Grace Thatcher Rainier. She's wasted away. In 1952, however, the year of her marriage, she was sturdily built, tall and broad-shouldered and not wasplike of waist. Leonard is on the short side, a family trait, and slight of frame, despite being barrel-chested. The gown fits his contours so exactly, it might have been made for him. He looks like a million bucks as he processes up and down the warehouse aisles. A cloud. A ghost. An enigma. He starts out stately, then picks up the pace, skipping down the rows of gowns, prancing, cantering, galloping, clutching his lacy train with one hand, brushing with the well-manicured fingertips of the other – *shoosh, shoosh, shoosh* – all the sadly sidelined bridal wear, all that lacy, gauzy, dreamy stuff upon which so much care had been lavished, so much hope invested; up he dashes, down he dashes, softly, on tiptoe, conferring his blessing, his consolation upon the many, many fine creations of which he was the sole custodian but which he had been compelled to overlook on this one night, this sacred night. This snowy night. Zita nudges him towards the window, so intent on the action that she hardly notices when the choir director says, "One more time," and the Hallelujah Holler gives it another go, sacred chords, please the lord, the fourth, the fifth, the minor lift, and on and on.

"Look out," Zita whispers, and Leonard does. He's surprised to see, illumined by the amber wash of the street lamps, a tumble of flakes so generous he could only imagine how the whole of the sky was hung with enveloping swaths of Lyon lace. No forecast had mentioned this possibility. The unexpected sight of snow on snow on snow on snow fills him with wonder, with a kind of awe.

It's getting late. The dark is deep, concealing. Leonard opens the door a crack. He peers into the alley. Deserted. He steps outside. The door closes behind him. Closes on cash, on credit cards, on street clothes. On keys, Zita's specialty. If only she'd been there earlier, she could have taken some kind of preventive action. But she wasn't. The call came too late. Hence, Leonard in the alley. Leonard in the snow. Zita collapses the screen. She gives herself to the present time, the *hic et nunc*. The past is the past, visitable but unalterable. It is Christmas Eve, it is the evolving now, and Leonard Cohen, keyless and clueless and dressed in Grace Rainier's stunning wedding gown, is walking home.

Zita will do what she can to see he gets there safe and sound. It's not an assignment for which she's uniquely qualified, nor for which she would necessarily have volunteered. Still, she warms to the task, sensing in Leonard, despite the several gulfs between them, the kinship of simplicity. Mortal Zita was a maid, daft and forgetful, as incompetent as she was devout. She was not, by nature, inclined to question, to probe. It would require someone more analytically astute than Zita to understand why Leonard would array himself in the stuff of fairy-tale fantasy on Christmas Eve. She thinks of him, an only child, thinks of him at all those Seders where Morley and Zita – Morley, mostly – told the well-worn story of a people's liberation; told it as only a survivor of unimaginable atrocities could tell it. She thinks of Leonard, so practised at answering the question, "This night, of all nights, what makes it special?" How was it for him, for Leonard, to be the sole heir to the family business, the gift of it, the ball and chain of it; to have always known he would spend his days in the land his father promised him, surrounded by the material remnants of hope, to feel the impossible pressure of so much optimism pressing down upon him, a simple man with unvarnished needs? She can imagine well enough how he might, one Christmas Eve, have wondered what made this night special, how he might have looked around at all these racks hung with limp, white hope, have wondered about their more animate possibilities. It was as though he'd been fed a coin and the idea dropped out, as though from the Accurate Weight and Fortune machine. There was no reason not to. Then, he did. Still, he does.

"And one more time," says the director of the Hallelujah Holler.

"No," says Zita, firmly, because if she has to hear that line about being tied to a kitchen chair and cutting hair again she'll have to leave the room, which she cannot do.

"No?" says the director, nonplussed. He's mystified. Who says "No" to "Hallelujah"? Everyone wants "Hallelujah." All they ever want is "Hallelujah."

"Something else. Anything else."

The Holler – with some reluctance, even resentment, for the singers are as partial to "Hallelujah" as are their fans – begins to sing "Suzanne." Zita, satisfied, turns her attention to the screen. She watches Leonard approach Jackie Chan's little corner store on Jackson and Powell. Business has been slow, Jackie's not making his percentages, no one is smoking as much as they used to, no one is buying the Magnum ice-cream bars in the freezer; he needs something novel to draw customers in. He sees Leonard Cohen pass by, spectral, bright, and then comes an inspiration. Zita smiles as Jackie takes a piece of cardboard, finds a black-felt maker. He makes a sign, he has no idea why, that says, "TEA! ORANGES! ALL THE WAY FROM CHINA!" He puts it in the window. Shoppers cluster.

"Bird on the Wire," the choir sings now – they are adapting to this new aesthetic, they're starting to deepen the groove – and Leonard Cohen passes the intersection of Hastings and Carrall. Zita, her beatified heart nearly breaking, tells Julia Roberts to look up, look up. Julia, who holds a needle to her neck, obeys just in time to see Leonard's long train – in 1952, when Grace Rainier walked down the aisle, it was borne aloft by her little cousin, Fred – lift and flutter in reply to a sudden gust. With her one free hand she reaches for it, a heavenly wing, and apprehends in that moment, in a way both visceral and warming, that sometimes, when you least expect them, when you most need them, angels do appear. She forces the plunger, injects the drug, gives herself over to the numbing, elevating rush; but she will remember this, will ride the wave of it through the dissipating high. That will be something, yes. Something to remember, to watch for again. Something to grab at, when it comes along.

At the corner of Dunsmuir and Seymour, outside the 7-Eleven, Leonard Cohen, walking home, is assailed by a panhandler, a neighbourhood regular whom everyone knows as Scruff but whose proper name is Harrison Ford, a veteran who saw more than he should have seen during his tour in Afghanistan. He shouts to Leonard that he will tell his fortune for a quarter, shrugs philosophically when the offer is declined; a pity because Zita, deciding to put yet more skin in the game, has just given Scruff an hour's worth of unlimited free access to future knowledge; so look out, Lotto 6/49. Look out, Meat Draw at the Legion. "You Want It Darker," sings the choir.

The light turns red at the corner of Georgia and Granville. Joan Didion, returning home on the bus from another sorry assignation with her lover, raises her eyes – no need to ask at whose behest – from her book: *Orlando*, she's giving it a third, no, a fourth chance. Looking down on the creamy apparition that is Leonard Cohen, walking home, she's visited by the rending, necessary insight that her boyfriend has feet of clay. He will never leave his wife; he is, after all, a trifler. Best she should follow her mother's advice, break it off, get on with her life. She has many years still to live. The Hallelujah Holler sings "Hey, That's No Way to Say Goodbye."

At the corner of Helmcken and Burrard, from a high window in St. Paul's Hospital, long-term care patient Sharon Stone looks down to the street, just as the singers take their pitch and begin to harmonize "Lady Midnight." Sharon was a pioneering flight attendant – a "stewardess," as they were called in the industry's infancy. She was compelled by company regulations to abandon her career when she married. She met the first of her three late husbands, Bob Thatcher, way back in 1948, when he was a passenger on her flight to Toronto. Bob! So manly, but she'd never seen a more nervous flyer. He needed special care and attention. She'd taken note of his ring, of course, she knew she should have declined his invitation for drinks, then for dinner, then for what followed, but what can you do? It was a complicated business, messy; when is love not?

"Mother of God," says Sharon at the window, realizing that this is not, as she first believed, a manifestation of macular degeneration, but an actual whiteout, a world transformed. She holds her hand to her heart, a theatrical gesture but unstudied, authentic. She searches her mind – her recall remains acute, even if her eyes are shot – and cannot conjure a single Christmas Eve, not one in all her ninety-six years, that was so picture-perfect, so Norman Rockwell in its presentation. The gift of this perfection, unexpected and unasked for, calms her, settles her mind. She knows now, with surety, that it has gone on long enough, all of it. Never again will there be anything better than this. Another day would be *de trop*; it's time for her to swallow the pills she's been hoarding in the Barney Rubble Pez dispenser the hospital's volunteer Santa left as a gift last year for Sharon's roommate, Grace Rainier. Grace, generous in her dementia, regifted it to Sharon. She was glad to have it, for she had, even then, this eventuality in mind.

Amazingly, Grace, who rarely moves, rises up, takes her walker, joins Sharon at the window. She looks down. She sees what Sharon does not; sees Leonard Cohen, walking home. She doesn't recognize this man, but something about him, about his cladding, seems so very familiar. She has a nanosecond of apprehension before understanding gutters as quickly as the snow obliterates Leonard's trail, fills in the traces left by his boots; boots because her satin slippers – a mercy, really – were too small to fit.

"Oh," says Grace, then "oh," again and she angles her head so it tilts skyward. Sharon supposes she's having some kind of hallucination, has no way of knowing that Grace, deaf as a post, has plugged into the Hallelujah Holler concert. This access is courtesy of Zita who, touched by the old woman's frailty, has provided a backstage pass. "Waiting for the Miracle," the choir sings, and Grace feels the bunching, the gathering of something puffy and white and blameless, something precious, something she has carried with her a long time, all her life, and that she is now ready to release, to consign to the care and keeping of – who? It's the voice of Morley Cohen, known and unknown, remembered and forgotten, that suffuses her being. "We'll take good care of this for you, my dear. Fear not." His calm reassurances echo – *Fear not, fear not, fear not* – as an avalanche of blankness sweeps Grace away. She was there. She is gone.

Zita is surprised by this turn of events; also, troubled. Did she inadvertently overload Grace's circuits, slay her with music? Accidents happen, even to saints. No one would question the benignity of her intentions or doubt that Grace's time was at hand, but none of that will stop Izzy from pressing for a formal inquiry and/or a disciplinary hearing. He's never happier than when he has his nose up someone else's gaffe. For now, she has Leonard to consider. Drivers hoot at him, derisively, as he crosses Davie Street and makes his way towards the Burrard Street Bridge. And Morley, too, strangely enough, has re-entered the picture as a person of interest.

Fear not, fear not, fear not.

His remembered voice had so thoroughly suffused Grace's being that Zita, too, had been privy to it. Simultaneously, she observed on her desktop screen, lower-right corner, the emergence of something dark and formless, like an ominous shadow on an X-ray of a lung. It was made of purpose and intent, not of gristle and bone. And it was, beyond all doubt, following Leonard Cohen.

Fear not, fear not, fear not.

Instinct prompts Zita to call up Morley's records; her security clearance is just sufficient to allow for that. She notes the date of birth, date of passing, the most salient details of what took place between those milestones. Some joy. Much tragedy. Ah. This is what she's looking for, the report from the Bureau of Reassignment.

Morley, having forsaken his flesh, had been surprised to learn that the immortal soul is too precious to be taken out of circulation for more than a few moments. It needs employment, and the agent at the Bureau told him there were a number of options Morley might consider. There was garden-variety reincarnation on Earth, for which most opted, but life on another planet was becoming an increasingly popular choice. Also, there was transmigration.

"Which is what?"

"Taking up residence in another species," the agent explained. "You could return as a butterfly, or a parrot. Ever fancied being a slug or an elephant?"

"Are there any openings for wolves?" Morley inquired; his Hebrew name was Ze'ev, Wolf, so it made as much sense as anything else was making, in that place and in that moment.

"Certainly," said the agent, and proffered a map. "We are unable to guarantee a geographical location, it depends on need, but if you have any requests, we're happy to accommodate them to the best of our ability."

"Here," said Morley, indicating the dense forests near the village in Lithuania where his own boyhood had been interrupted, his family destroyed; the forests where, for two years, he had successfully evaded capture. As a wolf he could do some good, could pass on to others of his eventual kind all he'd learned of the terrain, of being hunted, of hiding, of resistance.

The last notation in the file is the agent's rubber stamp. "REQUEST GRANTED."

The Holler sings "The Partisan," and Zita activates the cameras along the Lithuania–Poland border. She pans the forest, finds what she's looking for, zooms in on the alpha, the pack leader, on Ze'ev. The old wolf – very old, she sees – is asleep, he is dreaming. Of what? Zita activates her Dream Watch app, slips inside his skull, takes a seat, watches the screen of his cataract-encumbered eyes. He is pacing through a city in the snow: a strange place, but familiar in that contradictory/complementary way of the oneiric realm. He has fallen in step with a man gotten up in strange attire, some sort of ceremonial robe, rococo in its elaborations, delicate yet durable, white as the snow, the snow, the endless snow. He is contemptible, this man, and weak, but inexplicably compelling. He is familiar. His smell is known. Ze'ev hears the laboured turning of the stranger's heart, an incipient arrhythmia no physician has yet detected, but he doesn't long to rip the muscle from the man's chest, and devour it on the spot. Look at me, know me: the dream wolf beams out the thought, he has no idea why. No response. The man who walks is an automaton, a somnambulist, a zombie, he's on his own track with its own magnetic field. He's where he needs, where he wants to be. What he's doing is what he's chosen. Why, then, does he seem so indeterminate? Why does he smell so lost?

Oh, Morley. Oh, Leonard.

Zita sees how the ancient beast's four limbs, stiff with age, twitch. He cries aloud. A younger pack member, one of Ze'ev's own spawn, the inheritor of his father's ambitious nature, is awake to hear. He has been asking himself many questions about the present regime. He has been considering challenging this hoary veteran. He has seen others try, fail. Their plans were imperfect. They hadn't taken the time to lay the appropriate groundwork, start rumours, garner support. They were ill-prepared. They were premature in their actions. Now, he senses an emerging chink in the armour. Sniffing the pre-dawn air, he detects a new vulnerability. The buried scent of rot taking root. Soon. Very soon. His time is coming soon.

Oh, fathers. Oh, sons.

Zita wonders, as Leonard never has, what Morley would have said had he learned that Leonard knows better than most men the hug of a Sabrina or Queen Anne neckline, the cinch of an Empire or dropped waist; if he had known that Leonard can distinguish, proprioceptively, Alençon from Calais from Chantilly lace; that Leonard can evince a preference that's far from disinterested in the ballgown over the fishtail skirt, the blusher over the fingertip veil? Would it have mattered to him? Yes. Certainly. To Morley, who permanently soured on Barbra Streisand after *Yentl*, it would have mattered.

Oh, Abraham. Oh, Isaac.

Families. Blood. Ancestry. Devotion. Our necessary, thwarting anchors, our ballast in the hold. Zita thinks of how much we need what weighs us down, how much we resent it, how we cling to it even as we try to shake it off. How accidental is Leonard Cohen's present predicament? What is his endgame? What is he trying to win, out in the world on Christmas Eve, dressed in a wedding gown? What is he trying to lose? So many questions, they make the brain ache. Where is Saint Advil when you need him?

The Hallelujah Holler is still on the case, very much so; they're adding some dance moves, some hand claps, and some fancy finger snaps to a close harmony arrangement of "Closing Time." Gathered round Zita's screen, they watch Leonard Cohen, walking home. He is unwavering in his forward regard. If he thought to pull an Orpheus, to look behind, he would see what Zita sees; what alarms her, and makes her wish she were more inclined to smite the wicked. There's a couple trailing him, they've been following him since he passed the corner of Burrard and Harwood. They are not the shadows of dream, they are fully incarnate, and they have something in mind that is not, Zita feels sure, kindly, this man, this woman, neither of them exactly sober. The woman, Zita can tell, is the alpha. She's calling the shots, and she's taking the shots. Closing time. Closing time. Snap goes the choir and snap goes the woman, snap, snap, snap, with her phone, picture after picture. Why? Zita knows about Instagram, of course. Saint Sebastian is always posting, posting, he can't have so much as a bowl of oatmeal without memorializing it. Is that what this dark agent out in the snow has in mind? Is she an approval addict, trolling for likes, pursuing her own momentary self-aggrandizement through Leonard's enduring debasement? If word of this got out, if his Christmas Eve indulgence were to be revealed, its internet-meme worthiness tested, there'd be no way back. What will happen to Morley's promised land if his son's public and enduring lie – *no, what a crazy idea!* – is exposed? Is this the end of Love You Forever? And what of the cherished millstone of his marriage?

"*Oy gevalt*," says Zita, as Leonard leans into the wind and navigates the slush piles of Cornwall Avenue. He doesn't think much about the imminent fallout of drumming on his own door, of Edie stumbling to let him in, sleep-addled, gummy-eyed, confused. In the persistent susurrations of satin, of snow, Leonard construes a voice, inflected with the agreeable, unfamiliar lilt not of Lithuania, but of Lucca. "Fear not," it says; nor is he afraid. Fear grows from choice, and Leonard knows he's a man in a wedding gown who's run out of narrative options – the truth is all he has to work with. So Leonard Cohen does not fear. Leonard Cohen does what Leonard Cohen can do. Leonard Cohen walks. He walks home.

"Fear not," says Zita, and powers down the main frame. The screen goes dark just as the Holler is about to take on "Famous Blue Raincoat."

"That's it?" says the choir director. He's surprised. From a strictly choral point of view, it had all been going so well.

Zita says, "My work is finished. There's nothing more I can do. There was never much I could do, and that's the truth. Thank you for your service. Merry Christmas."

"How does it all end?" asks the second tenor. "Don't we get to know?"

Zita shakes her head. She feels no need to explain how, ever since she was badly rattled by the shocking conclusion of *The Crying Game*, also *Thelma and Louise*, she makes a habit of checking out before the curtain falls. One hundred fifty-four episodes of *Hazel* are waiting for her at home, and she'll extinguish each before the denouement, even the one where Hazel buys a colour television and the blacks and whites and greys of the series to that point turn vibrantly multi-hued in the closing seconds. Better a happy ending imagined than a sad one revealed.

Neither Saint Zita of Lucca nor the Hallelujah Holler sees Leonard turn up Yew. Home is in view. He's grateful that his passing goes unremarked by his neighbour, Emma Watson, famously fond of a chinwag. Emma is preoccupied. Unable to wait till the morning, she has given in to temptation, has opened the biggest of all the presents under her tree. It was delivered by Purolator earlier in the day – thank goodness her bridge game was cancelled so she was home to sign for it. It came all the way from distant Kamloops, sent by her son, the radiologist, Dr. Watson. It's the leaf blower she was hoping for. Emma Watson, pushing eighty, is out despite the hour, despite the snow – because of the snow, really. She's curious to see how the leaf blower will disperse the drifts, there being presently no leaves upon which to experiment. It makes such a din that Leonard – gingerly mounting his steps, icy, there'll be shovelling to do in the morning – scarcely hears the rumble of what he supposes to be thunder – strange in the snow – but is, in fact, the Sisters of Mercy, high in the heavens, lit by the light that comes through the crack in everything, rolling their dice, feigning surprise with every toss, even though they all know exactly how it will all work out, each and every throw.

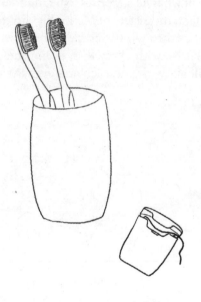

WITH MAN TO DWELL

I looked from our third-floor window. I looked down to the sidewalk. I saw my boyfriend, Gary, half a block away. He was rounding the corner onto Broughton, returning from his twice-yearly carnival of caries detection and plaque routing. Even from that elevation and removal, I could tell he was pleased. No one walks with so self-assured a swagger unless he has secured a promotion, or bagged a moose, or been descaled, X-rayed, and certified blameless by a qualified professional.

I looked from the window. I saw Gary. I listened to my heart, noted with satisfaction that it still accelerated its diphthongs when he hove into view. I was glad. We've been together ten years, long enough to understand that love is a pearl. It must be examined and handled to maintain its lustre. Also, it's easily faked.

"Dazzling," I said, when he came through the door and flashed his Hollywood smile. Gary is proud of his teeth, speaking of pearls. They're well spaced and white, kind of like passengers in a business-class cabin. Or so I gather. My enamel tends to taupe, and I have a smallish mouth, so my molars and incisors and bicuspids are all jammed up in economy. I'm not so anxious about the situation that I'm willing to shell out for adult orthodontics. Forty is behind me. I'm balding. Some things – teeth, hairline, Gary – I have to learn to live with.

Gary showed off the clinic's loot bag.

"Let's see," I said.

It contained a talented new toothbrush, engineered at NASA or some damn place to better sanitize those hard-to-reach places – such as the back of the tongue, or Mars – as well as some bristly, wee toothpicks that looked like silverfish on cocktail picks. Also, there was a sample-size spool of flavoured floss.

"It's bubblegum," said Gary.

"Revolting," I said.

"It was that or mint."

"You had a choice between mint and bubblegum and you chose bubblegum?"

Gary said nothing. Why would he reply? The answer was material and self-evident.

"Bubblegum," I said, sticking my spade one last time in the deepening hole of stupid. I let it go, but it troubled me. If we'd been contestants on one of those "How well do you know your mate?" game shows, and if I'd been asked to predict which flavour of floss Gary was likely to select, I'd never have pegged him for bubblegum. This rent in the fabric of my understanding gave me pause. Was bubblegum floss the gentle, lapping wave on a continuum of behaviour that would culminate in serial killing? Hadn't Gary spoken nostalgically, as recently as last month, of the freezer in his mother's basement, whence was extracted each Sunday's joint of beef or leg of lamb in adequate time to allow for safe and thorough thawing? Was he laying the groundwork for suggesting that we, too, in our accruing maturity, should acquire such an energy-hungry, space-gobbling appliance? If so, why so? I dragged my memory, couldn't retrieve a single instance of Gary complaining, not once in all our time together, that we simply had to do something about the way we didn't have a ready supply of glaciated pork chops or cryogenically advantaged canapés to bung into the oven when unexpected guests dropped in. Which, in fact, they never did. How well do you ever know anyone, after all? I felt a tremor of Christmas nerves. I was preparing his list, the items on which, in the pale pink light of bubblegum floss, seemed needlessly austere. How much was I getting wrong? How much had I always got wrong? How wide had I flung the net of my wrongitude?

"By the way," he said, unsheathing the rebarbative floss from its scabbard, hauling off a length of the stuff, "Cinderella and I have a favour to ask you."

Cinderella is Gary's dentist, Dr. Cinderella Nabokov; no relation to Vlad, apparently. One of the many ways in which Gary and I differ is that I would never, ever encourage or even tolerate a first-name relationship with a medical practitioner to whom I was in professional thrall. Nor would I brook entering into a pact with any plier of the therapeutic trades that would allow for the luring and entrapment of an innocent third party by way of passive-aggressive manipulation, which I felt this was, or might become. I was annoyed. I tamped it down.

"Every good boy deserves favour," I said, as blithely as the deteriorating circumstances allowed.

Gary's answer was a monosyllable that might have been a grudging chuckle, or facsimile of same. It was hard for him to articulate when his mouth was full of floss-festooned finger.

"I don't," had been his indignant reply when I suggested, early on in their relationship, which was early on in our relationship, that he, Gary, might have a crush on Dr. Nabokov.

"It's okay if you do," I said, obligingly, even though my feelings toward him at the time were over-the-top animalistic with territorial imperative.

"Please," he said, with a dismissive snort. We spoke of it no more. Still, it was impossible not to remark how often he managed to insinuate Cinderella's name and her complicated story into any old conversation, whether we were in a group or merely à deux, at dinner or in bed. He would speak admiringly, at length, of how, in her native Leningrad, she was a neurosurgeon. She only turned to dentistry when our stiff-necked health-care regulators wouldn't recognize her qualifications after she landed as a traded-for-grain refugee on these shores almost twenty years ago.

"But surely it would have taken her less time to get relicensed as a neurosurgeon than to become a dentist," I suggested, with the nitpicking Cartesian detachment I so often deploy to spoil a good story.

"She was after a fresh start. New country. New job. New life. A *better* life," Gary added, feelingly, plopping a propagandistic cherry atop a pudding already seasoned with the self-satisfied pieties to which we, as a nation, are lamentably and reflexively heir.

The scenario was compelling but unsettling. Were I a neurosurgeon hankering after a major career change, I'd have turned to, oh I don't know, podiatry, perhaps. Should not Hippocratic prudence have dictated such a measure? I'm no anatomist, but isn't one of the distinguishing marks of the mouth its proximity to the brain? Might Dr. Nabokov not risk being seized by one of the unpredictable episodes of terrible, gnawing nostalgia to which Slavs are famously susceptible? What if, falling prey to some nameless hunger, she were to grab hold of a drill or probe or pick or any of the other sharp objects to which she would have untrammelled access, and pierce a patient's pulpy palate, just for the pleasure of revisiting her old stomping grounds, and scenting anew a fresh cortex?

No eventuality is too strange to imagine, and I should know; my work as a conference organizer routinely lands me in hotels, reliable epicentres of unimagined weirdness. I spared Gary my litany of fears. The fairy in charge of cynicism was uninvited to his christening. He needs heroes; the higher the pedestal the better. I malign his chosen idols, of whom Dr. Nabokov is one, at my peril.

"What might this favour be?" I inquired of my tartar-free spouse equivalent.

He attached the six-months hence appointment-reminder card to the fridge with a red-pepper magnet. On the door of our shiny Inglis such decorative fruits and vegetables vie for space with miniature lavender chips on which are words that enable homosexual gents and their Sapphist sisters in crime to arrange queer-positive messages on magnetic surfaces; if this is what Stonewall has wrought, well, it was worth it. These invert parts of speech were last year's Yuletide token from my best friend, Bonnie. More dutifully than enthusiastically we placed them where they needed to go. No one pays them any mind other than Angelina, our cleaning lady, who always takes time from her more prosaic duties to rearrange them.

CLOSET DYKE SO CUTE

CAMPY BOY HAS BEAUTIFUL BODY

HOT LEATHER DADDY 69 WITH ME

I looked at Angelina with an invigorated regard after she began leaving such snippets in her sparkling wake, along with her routine Post-it note requests that we replenish the Vim.

"4 p.m., May 17, 1996," was the mundane message on the appointment card Gary affixed to the fridge door, adjacent to the free-floating word "suck." It is good to remember May in December, as the darkest day glowers. Light. Blossoms. Fragrant plenitude.

"Does it pertain, perhaps, to a ballroom?" I asked.

I was referencing the favour. I inquired not to make small hay with his dentist's Christian name – Valentina in her homeland, changed to Cinderella on a *nouveau monde* whim; she also secured a maple-leaf tattoo on her ankle – but because I supposed Dr. Nabokov was planning a meeting for some professional association and wanted me to pull some strings. The week doesn't go by that some forgotten school chum or vague associate from days of yore doesn't call up on behalf of a group representing teachers, accountants, social workers, mechanical engineers, you name it, and try to weasel something out of me for next to nothing.

Gary said, "It's a problem of occlusion."

"Sounds like a Graham Greene novel."

Gary motored on.

"Dr. Nabokov says my teeth are showing signs that I grind them at night."

I was touched. Gary, who is not yet thirty-five, is not prone to admissions of vulnerability.

"I've never heard you."

"You wouldn't wake up if I tried to gnaw your arm off."

True enough. Sound sleeping is one of my few gifts.

"So?"

"So, she wonders if you'd mind staying awake some night."

"Awake?"

"To listen. To see whether I do or don't."

"What?"

"Grind. It happens in the REM stage. You'd need to be on the lookout for two hours after I dropped off. Then we'd know."

"About the grinding."

"Yes."

"Does it have to be tonight?"

"Whenever."

"Okay."

"Thanks."

He brushed my lips with his. Faint trace of Dubble Bubble.

▮▮▮

I had minor cavils about Cinderella's tentative diagnosis, which was based on a series of uncertain assumptions: that teeth were being ground at all, that it happened each and every time Gary passed into the land of REM, that it wasn't just some random, now-and-again occurrence, and that therefore I would, of necessity, be able to detect it on the equally random night I sacrificed sleep and kept my adoring vigil. Then again, what the hell did I know? The little I understand of the scientific method I've gleaned from watching arcane films on obscure cable channels with Bonnie. She's a documentary maker, freelance.

Bonnie and I have known each other since the tenth grade. We met when we were plucked from the pool of friendless losers by our biology teacher – name now deleted from all available files – and assigned as lab partners. She could pin down a frog and unseam it from nave to chops, and I would surreptitiously salvage her sewing assignments (aprons, pot holders) in the Home Ec class where I'd been exiled after nearly crucifying myself with a nail gun in wood shop. Our principal, in a post-incident debrief, implied it might have been a self-inflicted wound, that I turned to self-harm as a way to evade that one afternoon a week where the real boys enjoyed the spunky bonhomie particular to adolescent lads set free to roam among implements that can maim. Nope. It was an accident, albeit happy and mutually beneficial. Rasps, hammers, nails, drills: I'd been inept with them all. Our instructor, Husky Pomerantz, the Master of All Tools, held me in ill-concealed disdain. There was no happy future written in our stars; a separation, however regrettable, was inevitable.

Husky died at thirty-nine, or so I was told at the one reunion I was drunk enough to attend. He was, I gather, featured on the yearbook's Memorial page alongside a photo that showed him communing meaningfully with a bandsaw. Husky, Husky. I remember you every time I study my palm, the puckered souvenir, the Braille dot remnant of that long-ago contretemps. A stigma, inexplicably heart-shaped. An interruption in the jagged river of the lifeline.

▐▐▐

"How's it going, Davie Denman?" Bonnie asked, when she called the next morning.

"Okay, I guess."

That I refrained from calling her Nicola Harwood was a tacit signal that Gary was within hearing distance; he was at the table, wrapping gifts, securing them against damage during their upcoming trip to Brandon. Nothing makes him seethe more reliably than hearing Bonnie and I use our soap-opera names, by which we've referred to one another for approximately a hundred years now. He finds it clubby, exclusionary. It makes him doubt his primacy, and much as I wish I could pretend otherwise, I understand why he feels that way. I gave her his news.

"I wouldn't be surprised if that tight-jawed mama's boy is a nocturnal clencher," she said.

"Uh-huh," I said.

Down the line came the raucous shouts of gulls and crows. She was at her mother's apartment, out on the balcony. I heard her lighter click as she ignited what would be her sixth or seventh smoke of the day. It wasn't quite 8:30 a.m. Gloria, her mother, would be propped up in the rented hospital bed from which she now almost never moved. I imagined Bonnie, inhaling deeply, slowly exhaling insubstantial wreaths into the damp December air. She'd never been tempted by cigarettes until the day Gloria was diagnosed with lung cancer, at which point she took up smoking with a vengeance. Bonnie calls it a defiant irony. I see it as a way of venting rage. Gary thinks she's out of her mind.

Between my boyfriend and my best friend, there's no love lost. Each speaks candidly and critically to me about the other, which is inconvenient and embarrassing and a plain old pain in the ass. Bonnie thinks Gary is stuffy, retentive, insufferable. Gary thinks Bonnie is immoral, opportunistic, indiscreet. The one request he made of me when his blood came back from the lab with the chilling descriptor "Positive" attached was that I say nothing to Bonnie. He felt sure she would want to exploit his situation for her own professional gain, that she would pressure me to pressure him to allow her, and her crew, access to his days. The prospect made his bile freeze in its ducts.

I've adhered to his request because it is, after all, his request, and also because I wouldn't want to give him the chance to prove himself right. About Bonnie and about Gary I'm protective, in different ways and for different reasons. I've willingly held my tongue, even though I sometimes feel I'm swelling up with other people's pathologies, which can't be healthy. At times, I think I might explode. At times, I wish I would.

"How's Gloria?"

I held the phone to my ear with my shoulder in exactly the posture the chiropractor warned me against, all the while dicking around with some words on the fridge.

QUEER RIGHTS ARE FABULOUS

OH YOU SEXY LOVER

"Holding. She's looking forward to another round of Christmas hating."

Bonnie's voice broke, no emotive burble, just the muffled burp of call alert. A well-respected virologist was on the line from Dallas, anxious to go over the catering details for the opening-night reception I was organizing for yet another upcoming international AIDS confab. Only in the waning years of this twentieth century could a plague so quickly become an industry.

"Call me tonight," Bonnie said as I prepared to rhapsodize to Dr. Texas about the glories of our local wine and our unimpeachable crab puffs and the fabulous group rate I'd arranged at the posh hotel where, strangely enough, the first person I ever knew who died of what the more forthright obituaries were just then daring to call an "AIDS-related illness" had worked as a concierge.

✤ ✤ ✤

Brandon. That was his name. He told me his parents christened him Brandon because Brandon, Manitoba, was where they went on their honeymoon and Brandon was where he was conceived. I was surprised. With the Wheat City I have a history. Brandon is Gary's hometown. It's there he returns – flying first to Winnipeg, then boarding a Greyhound for the three-hour trip west – each and every

Christmas, to visit his mother. I've never been invited. I'll allow how this troubles me but not so much that I'll ever make a big deal of it. I've done time in Brandon, worked there in a group home one summer as part of a youth exchange. It was nice enough, clean and orderly and with some dynamite agricultural supply emporia. That said, no one would mistake it for, you know, Niagara Falls. But when you are from Deloraine, as were the newlywed Nowickis, and when you've planned your nuptials to accommodate the wear and tear of lambing and sowing and weeding and harvesting, the brightest lights are the ones that burn nearest.

I met the Nowickis, Herb and Joanne, at Brandon's funeral. Married for more than four decades, they wore matching curling sweaters and had otherwise come to resemble each other, as couples of long-standing do. They told me all in a rush that it was their first time outside Manitoba's unguarded borders, and wasn't Vancouver such a great destination, they thought it would rain all the time but no, it's been sunny every day, and aren't those mountains something, and oh, the ocean, well, the bay, whatever it's called, bigger than Pelican or Clear Lake, that's for sure, all those freighters out in the harbour, thirteen there this morning, my goodness, and the tugs hauling the barges, they could certainly see why Brandon loved it here, they understood better now why he hadn't wanted to come back, he was never one for farm life, not even as a little boy, livestock always scared him, even the chickens made him nervous, and oh how they wished that this, their first visit, could have been made under different, under better circumstances, but what was to be done, it was as it was, it was God's will, so they had come to bury their first-born son, and oh how they wished that they could have come to see him when he was well and whole and happy and he could have taken them up Grouse Mountain or to the Sylvia Hotel for tea or to Stanley Park and the Aquarium, and oh how they wished that they could have made the trip during the time of his illness, to comfort him as best they knew how, but how could they have done so, how could they have known when he had kept it from them so carefully, so cruelly, really, when he had told them nothing, truly nothing, had never mentioned the cancer, the lesions, the tortured lungs, the draining sweats, the exhaustion, none of that, not a word, not a hint, and oh how they wished that and oh how they wished that and oh how they wished that and did I think he had suffered, had he suffered at the end?

"No."

Never have I lied more readily or concisely. I listened to them, heard them through, and remembered Brandon's story about his naming, which I had never taken as a literal truth but which I saw now was exactly that. I was filled with wonder and joy at the idea of these two sweet people – I do not say this patronizingly, sweet is what they were, as sweet as anyone I've met – lying together and weeping with the happiness, with the promise, with the rush, of their first night together, never thinking their experimental probings were going to bear such fruit, such pain, such loss. It broke my heart to see their anguish, their confusion.

Brandon found religion in his declining days.

"Is there anything I can do for you?" I asked, thinking I could fetch magazines or assist with phone calls.

"Pray for me."

His voice was so weak I had to make him repeat himself twice before I understood.

"Sure," I said, the only available answer.

Here is a question I sometimes ask myself, and which I might be tempted to spell out on our fridge, had the magnet makers given me words sufficient to the task. What can we do, in these perilous times, to lead honourable lives? Remove the labels from tins and boxes before we put them in the blue box for recycling. Pay the airport improvement fee without complaining. Refrain from smoking pipes and cigars for the comfort of other patrons. Turn off mobile phones and pagers and watch alarms before a concert begins. All these things can we undertake.

Perhaps there is something to be said for honouring our promises, too. Even the dumb ones. Which is why I keep Bonnie in the dark. Which is why I will keep company with Gary in the dark. Which is why, in the gathering dark of that March day, I pulled into the deserted mid-week parking lot of a Catholic holy place. I could have prayed as easily in my own living room, or in the express line at Safeway, come to that, but a church instilled the feeling of going to the source, never mind that the rituals and grammar of Catholicism were not part of my evolved armature. The outright purity of my purpose made me feel less like a clumsy interloper or infidel than I might have done had I gone to gawk at icons or do some digging on Bonnie's behalf for a documentary about priests and altar boys.

I called to mind the antique rituals I'd observed in such helpful movies as *The Trouble with Angels* and *The Nun's Story* and, most particularly, *The Sound of Music*. I took my time going through my prayerful paces. I hummed "Climb Ev'ry Mountain" as I deposited some change from my cache of parking-meter loot into a box, locked and bolted down, on a stand near the door, heard it clunk satisfactorily against the coins of more routinely observant visitors. From a waxy collection of candles I selected a fat, sturdy example that looked like it could bear the weight of the moment. I passed its wick through the flame of one already lit, then added it to the ranks that burned there, unattended, even though they seemed inclined to lean wonkily into one another and would surely incur the wrath of a fire marshal, should one happen to intrude, whether for reasons professional or spiritual. I dared a low whistling of "How Do You Solve a Problem Like Maria?," while walking down the aisle, modest as a bride. I turned churchy words, crossword gleanings, over in my mind. Narthex. Transept. Nave. Monstrance. Sacristy. Host. I moved slowly, with pomp tempered by restraint. I executed a curtsy before the altar; I know genuflection was the required gesture, but what I managed was more in keeping with the end of an undistinguished dance recital than with a nod of respect to the Almighty.

Fearful of committing more grievous procedural gaffes, I settled into a pew. I waited. "Edelweiss," I hummed, surveying the visible statuary. Saints. Angels. Jesus hanging reliably on his cross. Mary, on a less treacherous perch, was the picture of calm, secure in the surety of veneration, turning over the centuries in her marble or possibly alabaster heart. Her eyes were lowered, but her gaze was as steadfast as it was decorous. Hit me up, she seemed to say. Tell me anything. Give me what you've got.

I bowed my head. I began to pray, silently, but moving my lips, much as I will when studying a complicated recipe or deciphering the instructions for DIY furniture. I was surprised at how the untried vocabulary of holy intercession lived within, that it so readily answered when I beckoned it to come.

"Blessed Mary, Mother of God, smile on us sinners. Remember Brandon, and comfort him in his hour of need. Shine thy light upon him ..."

My toe caught, glancingly, on the anachronistic cobble of "thy." I stumbled, opened my eyes, looked up. You would not have to work hard to convince me that what I then beheld was merely a trick of the slanted March light as it traversed the stained-glass depictions of the miracle of the loaves and the fishes, or the mothers of Winston-Salem – that surely can't be right – but the fact is that there, in that moment, what I saw, very clearly, whether or not it was mistaken or hallucinatory, was a trickle of blood, a crimson rivulet issuing from the usually blameless button of the Virgin's nose.

As noted, on the logical dismantling of that detail I am persuadable; what happened next, though, is not so easy to discount or explain away with prismatic theories found in the early chapters of a tenth-grade physics text. For verily, there came a shifting in the room, an atmospheric change so profound that I felt I'd undergone a rapid alteration in altitude. The air coursed hot and electric, the way it will when lightning strikes close by. An unaccustomed current enlivened my spine, as though a universal power source had plugged itself into my central nervous system. Everything that mattered to continuance – time, pulse, respiration, memorized dates for subscription renewals – entered a stage of suspension. I felt – what I'm about to tell you is the strangest of the strange – in the palm of my right hand, emanating from the very place I had pneumatically driven that nail all those years ago, a sensation of – a sensation of – of what? It wasn't heat, exactly, and it wasn't weight, exactly, but it was both those manifestations of energy and matter combined as one and made whole in a manner both infinitely potent and utterly benign. I looked, as who would not, and while I fully expected to see more than I saw – I wish so very much that I could tell you there was an angel there, dancing on the head of a pin – the view was, nonetheless, a long way from unremarkable. On the one hand – predictable phrase – I saw the familiar palmscape, the whorls and lines and the imposed landmark, that heart-shaped scar that had been part of my person for more than twenty years. On the other hand – by which I mean, on the same hand – I saw how that very scar, that very mini-heart, was beating, clearly and vibrantly, dimensionally, clutch and release, clutch and release, the same kind of jellyfish shimmy I'd seen literal hearts perform while watching graphic, surgery-specific documentaries with Bonnie.

I thought then, I think still, that had that supercharged liminality been more attenuated, I might have passed through the tabernacled gates of some eternal portal, gained access to a pure wellspring of knowledge, been able to do more than reliably summon the capital of Moldova or the accurate spelling of "diarrhea." The brass ring of all-knowingness was within my reach, my grasp; then another, more practised parishioner, whose entry into the church I'd not detected, sailed past my pew and executed a flawless genuflection. Mary, well pleased, would have marked her scoresheet ten out of ten. This Janey-come-lately trailed a waft of powerful scent which I recognized as Sergio Soldano's Eau de Toilette for Men. This was 1985, as I don't think I've mentioned, and that happened to be Gary's scent; Gary, whom I had known for scarcely a month at that time, and with whom I was so smitten I hadn't yet mustered the nerve to disclose how repugnant I found the cloying, woodsy waft of Sergio Soldano which, thankfully, he long ago retired. I sneezed. That was that. Mary's nose was Mary's nose. My scar was my scar. From outside the church came the high-pitched *beep beep beep* of a truck, reversing for some reason that could only have been usual. God was dead and so, as it turned out, was Brandon, although I didn't know it until the next day when I called in at St. Paul's with some flowers and a stack of back issues of *Maclean's*.

❦❦❦

On December 21, 1995, midnight draws nigh. A spooky hour. A spooky time of year. I imagine how the atoms of our brass door knocker, made sluggish by the cold, are struggling to rearrange themselves to conform to the features of Marley, of Brandon. Of Husky Pomerantz, God forbid. Having seen what I've seen, I discount no possibility. A quick reconnaissance run would relieve the pressure of wondering, but that would require forsaking this bath, its warmth and fragrant froth. My naked vulnerability and sybaritic posture suggest the luxurious yet saucy repose of an aging odalisque, but I am, rest assured, on my guard; "on tender hooks," as my sister stubbornly insists on saying, no matter how often or how kindly I correct her.

"Tonight's the night," I told Bonnie this morning on the phone.

"For?"

"Watching and waiting."

"Gary?"

"Uh-huh."

"The same old grind?"

Score one for Bonnie, who recommended that, as a preprandial to the "will he or won't he" main event, we watch a short report made by one of her film-school friends. It was slated to run on *The National*, with dishy Peter Mansbridge.

"It's about how statues of Ganesha, all across India, have been drinking offerings of milk."

"The statues themselves?"

"Shiva, too. Same deal."

"I'd have thought Shiva was a blood and tequila gal."

"Scoff all you want. It's been seen by many people in many places. Just watch. Make up your own mind."

Bonnie couldn't know this was a possibility I easily accommodated, given my secret history with graven images. Not to her, not to Gary, not to anyone have I spoken of my close brush with the divine.

We watched. I didn't let on this was a Bonnie recommendation. I summoned up my better angels of hypervigilance, expressed a casual interest in lingering when the milk-drinking statues came up in rotation.

"Jesus, spare me," Gary sneered, when a respected Hindu physicist told the interviewer he had seen this miraculous swilling for himself and took it to be genuine.

"Hooey," said Gary, brandishing the remote with a bravado both secular and effective.

I wondered how Gary would take it if I told him that I myself was nearly fricasseed by the mother of God, way back when things were fundamentally tender between us. Some conversational gambits are best packed away, not necessarily with future use in mind.

"You should get some sleep," I said.

"Can you scratch my back?"

I could.

I did.

⛃⛃⛃

Midnight draws nigh. I am immersed in lavender-scented bubbles in the soaker bath in our glistening ensuite. I can easily hear the low rumble of my boyfriend's snores and the occasional *freep* of a fart. So far, there's been nothing suggesting the deleterious murmur of molar on molar. I wait. I admire my shapely calves, not bad for forty-two, hoist them high in the air, stretch them as far as my hamstrings will allow; they're incredibly tight. I think about Mitzi Gaynor, because someone must. I consider my secret. I turn it this way, then that, study its facets: the marvellous, the deplorable. How different our lives might have been had I merely been able to go all the way, that day in the church, to fully embrace the chance I was given at – what?

Something big was in the offing, had I but stayed the course. Might there not have been, if not absolute omniscience, then the reward of three wishes? How different our present lives would be if I could lift Gloria from her bed of pain or whisper a spell to give Gary the reasonable prospect of believing in the benefits of the retirement savings plans he subscribes to at work. But no. That was not how it played out. And now, the year's darkest day is gasping its last, and over the Burrard Street Bridge, Gloria could be doing likewise. A scant few feet away, the man next to whom it pleases me to typically lie – our joint exhalations, bubblegum and mint, vying for dominance – has a time bomb passed from cell to cell in the secret blood from his sacred heart.

MAKE A WISH

Those were today's words, strangely innocuous, seasonally apt, arranged upon the fridge by Angelina, in a sunny, holiday mood; she is looking forward to her annual return trip to Manila. She goes the day after tomorrow, the same day Gary takes off for his sojourn to Brandon, his ten-day break from ever mentioning my name or otherwise acknowledging my existence. I will be alone, left to my own devices, which are few and unsophisticated and easy enough to either launder or dispose of when their utility has been exhausted.

MAKE A WISH

Suppose those wishes had been granted. Suppose two had been claimed. Suppose I had but one remaining. Whom would I favour? Would I make manifest the circumstances that would culminate in the pronouncement, "And the winner in the Best Documentary Feature category is Bonnie Quigley?" Or would I, not for the first time, do something wasteful and trivial, possibly arrange for the *Girl in a Wetsuit* statue – that Little Mermaid knockoff, the Stanley Park landmark beloved by tourists and locals alike, and a cherished target of incontinent gulls – to wave her flippers the next time Gary and I pass by on one of our seawall walks? No. I think it would be sufficient to put in a bid for wakefulness. That would be enough to ask of a universe already beleaguered by tragedies, requirements. I wish to merely remain alert while the one I work so hard to love makes his solitary REM meander, while his eyeballs do their pinball shuffle under shuttered lids. What will be the result of this short-term, independent inquiry? His incisors will collide or they won't. *Que sera sera.* Were I a better person, I'd be more curious, more concerned than in fact I am. As for Gary, I have no idea what he'll consider good news. Pathology is not without its attractions. It could easily be that, in his heart of hearts, he's looking forward to visiting Cinderella, even before his scheduled appointment, May 17, 1996; maybe just dropping in on spec, affecting a hangdog, why-me look. He doesn't have a best gal pal, someone to fuss over him, to mother him, from whom he'd tolerate the imposition of nicknames. Cinderella could do that – "Look who's come to call, it's Mr. Grindy!" – as well as engineer a mouthguard or some such orthodontic device, all the while spinning exotic tales of dangerous days in her collapsed empire. At the very least it will give him something to jaw over with his mother. Will he tell her about my part – supporting but pivotal, there being no small actors – in confirming or squelching Cinderella's suspicion? I can say with assurance he will not.

This house is bereft of chiming clocks. Midnight, once nigh, has passed but not sounded. Another corner turned. The days grow longer. Morning will come. I'll bring Gary coffee in his favourite mug, the one he won from the CBC for being the eighth to dial in. Is it not amazing, what passes for luck in this world? I'll kiss his stubbly cheek. I'll sit next to him, on the bed.

"Are you ready?"

"Yes," he'll say.

I'll tell him the truth. I'll tell him everything I know. We'll live with it, as best and as long as we can.

And if we can't?

Then I guess we won't.

SINNERS, RECONCILED

Dear Peter,

Best of the season to you! Bonnie Quigley here. You interviewed me on your fine program about eight years ago. We spoke about my documentary on harm reduction. We talked a lot about Amsterdam, I think you were more interested in bicycles and the red-light district than in supervised injection. Who wouldn't be? Maybe you don't remember. It must be hard for you, a pain really, what with people always coming up to you at parties – they must, right? – nattering away like you're best friends, or sending importuning notes that presume an acquaintance just because they made it onto your show once. Funny to have had a job that so many others take personally, kind of like being prime minister but without the official residence. Do you miss it? I bet you do and I bet you don't. Well. Whatever. We miss you. But you know that. Someone at CBC must be forwarding mail to you, so I'll send this off to the old address – M5W 1E6! – and hope for the best.

My purpose in writing this card – isn't it hideous? – is to pass on some sad news, which is that my mother, Gloria Quigley – one of your regular correspondents, and for sure your biggest fan – passed away on October 31. Passed away! She died, Peter. Gloria hated euphemisms. She died. She died on Halloween. I was with her. One last harsh breath. It was done. I sat with her for a few minutes before I went to the nursing station. On the counter was a big bowl filled with mini-packs of Smarties; Gloria favoured the brown and the orange. Did anyone else know that about her? I doubt it. Now you do, Peter. She'd like that. The station was manned – and I do mean manned – by one guy wearing falsies and a Marilyn wig and another who was dressed as Big Bird. It was Big Bird who fetched the gurney and Marilyn who checked her pulse. I think it's nice that menfolk can feel free not only to enter the profession but to be so untethered in their self-expression.

Lung cancer, Peter. She'd had it for years, it's amazing how long you can endure with something like that living inside you, killing you by inches. She went on a year longer than anyone thought she might. In truth – please don't feel bad or implicated when I say this – I think her real decline began with your mutual retirements. For years before she actually left her job she could be depended upon to say, "What I look forward to most about finally getting out of that joint is that I'll be able to listen to Peter every day. No more waiting in the parking lot until an interview is over, no more scheduling a sick day when Alice Munro comes on the show."

Jesus, Peter. My mother and Alice. I swear she had nightmares about being on a ship and seeing that you and Alice had been swept overboard and knowing that she could only save one of you and who would it be?

"Did you happen to hear Peter and Alice last week? She hates doing interviews, that's what I'm told. Who can blame her? Half the time you can tell whoever's asking the questions hasn't read the book. Alice doesn't suffer fools gladly. That's why she'll only talk with Peter. I believe Robertson Davies feels the same way."

Gloria's facial expressions – her range was remarkable – foretold her habitual declarations, of which she had more than a few. A narrowing of the eyes and deepening of the furrow between her brows reliably presaged, "It's fine with me if they choose to spend their grown-up lives sitting on a piece of cardboard outside the 7-Eleven, but I won't be pressured into giving them money." A starboard tilt of the head and a settling of the lips into a subtle moue were a sure sign she was preparing to deliver her homily on the impossibility of procuring a really fine tomato in a supermarket, even in August. And I could always tell when she was aiming to steer the conversation in the direction of "what Peter had to say about it," because her features would assume a wide-eyed longing after peace and transfiguration, most often seen on postulants about to take the veil. Peter, it's a pity

we never got to talk about my last documentary about the slight
resurgence of young women entering convents. There was only one
interview, in fact, on a college station. You would never have asked,
as that young man did, "They're all lesbians, right?" I believe he was
pursuing a degree in engineering.

Bonnie sets down the pen, reaches through a signal plume of
smoke, picks up the smouldering cigarette – Belmont Milds – between
the thumb and index finger of her right hand, takes a long drag,
exhales, stubs the butt out in an ashtray from the Fairmont San
Francisco. It migrated north, to False Creek, in the early eighties,
after Gloria slipped it into her purse in a holiday-crazy spasm of
kleptomania.

Bonnie coughs, sighs, peers through the blue-grey air at the
familiar room: the too-heavy furniture her mother brought from
the house when she downsized, the yesteryear appliances, original
to the building (harvest gold, which is more or less the colour of
everything after all those years of Gloria's smoking), the shelves of
knickknacks and oddments, none that match Bonnie's taste, and all
of which she now owns. And the books, of course, including the three
shelves that are a shrine to Alice and her sister White Goddesses,
Mavis Gallant and Margaret Atwood and Carol Shields. Gloria's
books. Who will want them, permeated as they are by the stink of
the habit that killed her?

∗ ∗ ∗

"I am sitting at the table in the leaky condo of my dead mother."

Bonnie says this out loud, much to her own surprise. Her voice
is hoarse, phlegmy, unused. When did she last have a conversation
with anyone other than Bonnie Quigley? She hasn't even spoken
to her best friend, Philip, and they've talked every day for more
than twenty years. She hasn't charged her mobile, can't say where
it is; Gloria's landline was disconnected weeks ago. If there were an
emergency, she'd have to rely on semaphore, or a note in a bottle. She

has, at least, ample writing supplies. Nor are bottles hard to come by. She reaches for one.

"In the leaky condo of my dead mother I am sitting at the table," Bonnie says, and marvels how much her situation, when reduced to a single sentence, sounds like something from a foreign-phrase book. She can imagine it alongside such unlikely circumlocutions as, "This gin would benefit from a garnish of cucumber," and "I am returning this cutting board because it is warped."

Bonnie, spinning her wheels in a self-flagellatory rut, wonders how she's attained her present age – she is forty-three – without being able to say the word "leaky," or even express the concept, in any language other than English. She sacrifices too many irretrievable moments from her one and only life to the rueful consideration of how superior a race are the polyglot Dutch; to meditating on how much more gilded would be her lily had she been born in The Hague instead of The Dunbar. Depression wouldn't be her steady companion. She'd be taller and blonder and sunnier and waving at the bargemen as she pedalled one of those sturdy bikes – the carrier basket loaded with tulips and a wheel of Gouda – along a canal to her job as an interpreter at the International Court of Justice. "Serves you right, you mean, old warlord," she'd say in flawless German or Swahili or Farsi or whatever the situation required. But no. The Fates had a less glamorous outcome in mind for Bonnie, somewhere far from Babel. She'll never have more than her C+ standing in high-school French and a smattering (*un'infarinatura*) of Italian; she and Philip took an introductory night course years ago, over at the Leonardo da Vinci Centre, back when they were planning a trip to Umbria. That was before Gary the Spoiler came along and everything turned to rat shit. Not that she's bitter.

She tallies the butts that obscure the Fairmont logo. *Uno, due, tre, quattro, cinque, sei.* She extracts *sette* from its nest of foil, lights it, sucks its delicious poisons deep into her body, exhales a toxic ghost, returns to the task at hand. Her final, praise be, Christmas card.

✉ ✉ ✉

My suspicion Peter – naughty me, trying to peek behind the curtain at the great Oz – is that you never saw any of your mail in its raw form. You couldn't have done, there was so much of it, bags and bags, or so I imagine. Well. Before email, anyway. There must have been a minion, one of those people you named in the Friday credits, who did all the opening and reading and selecting and editing and then transcribed everything into some radio-friendly format. Bold type, big fonts, ample spacing, wide margins for doodling or note-taking. The point is that I am writing this card with the VERY PEN my dead mother employed to draft the many missives she dashed off in response to items she heard on your show. (She received prizes in school for her skill with the Palmer Method, Peter, and she never lost the knack. Narrow eyes, hands on hips, a slight widening of the stance was the warning signal for her eruption about "the crying shame of what's happened to penmanship in school these days." Lord, how I miss her.) This pen, Peter, is a good one. She was inclined to view such everyday items as pens (and lighters and gloves and, frequently, her keys) as disposable, but not this weighty Montblanc: a gift from a grateful school board to mark her twenty-five years of service as an itinerant speech pathologist. That was four years before the very same employer declared she was "surplus to her workplace" and offered her a package, which she reluctantly took. She often said, to me, to her friends, to strangers in the elevator, to anyone who would listen, that the one saving grace – and this was where she would assume the look of someone taking a call from the angel Gabriel – was that she would have untrammelled access to your show. And then it ended, your show I mean. It was all downhill from there.

✉ ✉ ✉

Bonnie, absorbed by this riff, forgets her smoke. It's burned down almost to the filter before her concentration is broken by the rude slapping of plastic outside the window. She coaxes another Belmont from the deck – *Questo è numero otto* – and lights it from the radiant corpse of its fallen comrade. She rises, stretches, walks to the window, looks out. Tries to.

Gloria loved this view. It made Bonnie mad, pissed her off, to think how the vista had been obscured during the last few months of her mother's tenancy, before she went to the hospital for good.

Properly, from this window, Bonnie should look down on a landscaped courtyard – a manicured lawn, a fountain, a much-loathed piece of public art that Philip calls "Mouth or Butthole?" – and then beyond, to the creek and the throbbing Granville Island Market, that capitalism theme park crowded with holiday shoppers on the hunt for ready-made soups and free-range fowl and tempting tourtières. They'll be lined up seven deep at the sausage place, everyone with the anxious look of passengers hoping for a berth on the last ship out of Lisbon, clutching their little number tags, desperate to claim some minced pheasant or wild boar or kangaroo, all for prices that require the cooperation of a mortgage broker. But all that's visible is the drapery of blue plastic tarp that's shrouded the whole building since its flawed cladding was removed six months ago. Every day since, the Sabbath excepted, engineers and tradesmen arrive and shake their heads in disbelief at the shoddy work foisted on gullible laymen by their colleagues of yore. They toil slowly, slowly, at the business of setting rot to right. Lacerated stucco, mouldy beam, all the slipshod sins of the booming eighties construction trade now visited upon the carpenters of the century's end. Gloria was a hoarder, but she wasn't much of a saver. After Bonnie has paid out the sixty-thousand-dollar assessment levied by the strata council – a fee that passed by a slim majority of owners at a meeting so rancorous the police had to be called to intervene – there'll be nothing left.

"*Il pleure dans mon cœur comme il pleut sur la ville,*" Bonnie says, her execrable accent a lingering souvenir of her wasted years at Lord Byng Secondary, and then, for good measure, seasons the mood with a smoky and heartfelt, "*Mais où sont les neiges d'antan?*" Her supply of Gallic apophthegms thus depleted – one was Verlaine, one was Villon, she's damned if she can remember which is which – she listens to the percussive scatter of December rain on plastic and watches the cheerful caul of a tarp swell under the influence of one determined gust after another. When did Vancouver become so windy? It's coastal, it's always been breezy, but these last couple of winters gale after gale has blown in, from the north, from the west. Everyone is muttering about that devious brother–sister act, El Niño and La Niña, but Bonnie – and this is consistent with her present mood – is sure something more ominous and lasting has come to live among them, and that this tedious scapegoating of mere ocean currents won't hold water much longer. Which is a pity. There's plenty of water for holding.

It's because of this barometric uncertainty, and also because she is sure there must be a bylaw on the books that prohibits such actions, that Bonnie has chosen to disregard Gloria's wishes that her ashes be dispersed, cast upon the waters of False Creek, somewhere between the Aquatic Centre on one side and the Granville Island Market on the other. Gloria often picked up muffins at the market, then caught the little ferry and went to visit Bonnie in her bright studio apartment on Harwood, over in the West End. When she could no longer manage the steep walk up the Thurlow hill, Gloria relied on cabs. When the Santa Maria went non-smoking, she just stayed home.

"I'd like to be scattered from one of these," she'd once said to Bonnie when they were riding the ferry together.

"Any particular one?"

All the boats are named for persons of no wide fame, friends of whatever family owns the fleet, one supposes.

"I've always liked *Spirit of Mona Elkin.*"

"*Mona Elkin* it is."

Neither brought it up again. Shortly after Gloria's cremains – another cringe-worthy hybrid – were delivered into Bonnie's hands, on a day when she was feeling more than usually resilient, she waited at the ferry stop, urn in hand. She waited for hours, but *Spirit of Mona Elkin* never chugged into view.

"She's in dry dock today," one of the pilots of another vessel told her when finally she asked. "Come aboard, I'll take you where you want to go; we won't sink." But Bonnie had promised her mother "*Mona*," and she wasn't sure how Gloria would warm to "*Spirit of Brigitte Hensel*." She declined with thanks. She went home.

"Next time you try let me know. I'll go with you if you want company," Philip said that night on the phone, when she told him about her failed attempt.

"Okay," said Bonnie, even though she knew Philip would, as always, take over the prow and bellow "Don't Rain on My Parade," like Barbra Streisand, in *Funny Girl*. She needn't have worried. The next time never came. So much mitigated against it: regulations, hungry gulls, unreliable winds. Gloria once recounted a tragicomic letter she'd heard Shelagh Rogers read on Peter's show, all about how a family patriarch died and the extended clan got together in Malibu or Mendocino or one of those mythic California locales for a destination scattering. They gathered cliffside, the six, the eight, the however many of them, the sky a bleached-out blue, the churning surf dashing itself against the rocky shore below, towering redwoods somewhere in the picture. Words were spoken. The urn was upended. The wind blew the cinders back into their faces, they were swatting at themselves as though besieged by a plague of gnats. Bonnie can imagine the warm register of Shelagh's woman-to-woman voice, her ready laugh, can imagine her trying not to crack up as the events turn more and more antic, can imagine Peter's obliging, smoky chuckle at the punchline which, as Gloria told her, was the ashman's widow saying, "Patrick always knew how to get up your nose." God. Hilarious.

Today, however, at last, Bonnie is coming to terms with the urn and its contents. She's devised a plan. The solution to her dilemma was there all along, she'd simply not seen it. It was, quite literally, in the cards.

Alcohol was her project's midwife. Bonnie's original purpose in spending the day at her mother's porous and overstuffed condominium was to make the hard, necessary decisions about which of Gloria's chattels to keep and which to consign. She has no qualms about saying *auf wiedersehen* to the oppressively Schwarzwald walnut sideboard, overwrought and domineering, traits it shared with Heinrich Engels, the transplanted Bavarian who was the monolith's original owner and who had been for a brief – though not brief enough – time, Bonnie's stepfather, Gloria's second husband. Their marriage had not survived a knockdown fight they'd had after Heinrich had struck Bonnie, then seventeen, with the flat of his hand. He was in a rage because she, Bonnie, had loaned to Philip, for a costume party, Heinrich's vintage lederhosen. She had never known Heinrich to wear them, never supposed he harboured for them feelings other than the ironic, couldn't have guessed they were a garment to which he imputed great sentimental value, possibly owing to his time in the Hitler Youth, to which he had once admitted in a schnappsy moment of confidence-sharing, his hand on his stepdaughter's knee.

"And what is this," he said, his accent thickening as he frothed at the chops, pointing to the leather crotch, the white smear.

"Mayonnaise?" was Bonnie's hopeful answer, even though she suspected a DNA sweep might link it more intimately to her friend than to a bowl of dip.

That was when he raised his hand and Gloria showed what she was made of. She made alimony concessions to keep the sideboard, knowing how much he wanted it back.

"Those were the days, my friend," Bonnie crooned, opening its drawers and doors, squinting into its nooks and crannies. That was how she found both the carton of Belmont Milds and a half-dozen dreggy bottles of liqueur. Crème de menthe. Amaretto. Grand Marnier. One thing led to another, and before the cuckoo clock (another souvenir of Heinrich, also marked for redistribution) barked the news of noon, Bonnie was engaged in her present mission.

"*Dieci*? No. *Nove,*" she says, stirred by both her Italianate enumerating skills and her relative temperance. She clicks the lighter, upends another bottle. The treacle trickles and she laments, if only for a moment, all the days of her wasted fertility. Kahlúa would be a lovely name for a daughter. Kahlúa Margarine Quigley. It had a ring, a certain *je ne sais quoi.* She wrote.

✉ ✉ ✉

I miss her, Peter, even though she drove me crazy in many ways. Which I guess is the story most daughters tell about their mothers. She would call me every Sunday morning before eight, and she was forever clipping Cathy cartoons, and "Dear Abby" columns she thought were relevant, and popping them in the mail. But one thing I'll say for Gloria, and for this I will forever bless her name, she never harangued me about giving her grandchildren. She only ever brought it up once – it was at this time last year, now that I think of it – and by then, the grim writing was on the wall, plain for all to read. It was New Year's Eve. She was back in the hospital, she was more often in than out by then. I'd smuggled a half-bottle of Veuve Clicquot onto the ward – I probably didn't need to be so covert, they're incredibly lax about that kind of thing – and it seemed to partner with her meds as a truth serum. Out of the blue, she said, "Lots of women have children and raise them on their own these days. Katrina's done that."

I scarcely know Katrina, have met her once or twice. She's Agnes's daughter. Agnes is another speech pathologist, Gloria's on-again, off-again friend. Agnes can't say enough about her brilliant child and Gloria, a great mimic, would recount the tales of the wunderkind's triumphs, eerily capturing Agnes's slight Hungarian inflection. This time, though, her tone was commendatory.

"Why are you bringing up Katrina?"

"She's raising a child alone. She's doing very nicely."

"Katrina doesn't have to suck up to the Canada Council or go cap in hand to Telefilm. Katrina doesn't need to hold her nose and

swallow when she makes in-house promotional videos for sleazebag corporations. Katrina doesn't live in 450 square feet in a walk-up with a view of the trash and the flasher across the alley. Katrina is a partner in a big Toronto firm, she clears $800,000 a year according to Agnes's last report, more with her bonuses, she has a full-time nanny and a house in Forest Hill. And good for her, she's smart, she works hard, she deserves every good thing that's ever come her way. Katrina manages nicely, for sure. What's your point?"

"I don't want you to be lonely, Bonnie. I know you have Philip, and your other friends, and your work, of course –"

"I have you."

"Bonnie," she said, "oh, Bonnie," with a defeated little shake of her head. Then she had a coughing fit. When she regained her composure, she changed the subject. We never spoke of it again.

Katrina sent a nice note after Gloria died. She'd have heard the news from Agnes, of course; Agnes with her schadenfreude blackbelt. Gloria was the perfect candidate for her gleeful pity, what with her barren, unemployable daughter and her two failed marriages and her slavish dependency on tobacco.

"If only she'd found the strength to quit."

That's what she said to me at the memorial service, standing too close, skewering me with her unblinking Mitteleuropa regard. She had Earl Grey breath and a morsel of brownie on her lower lip that looked satisfyingly like a malignancy. Gloria got caught up in some manufactured administrative squabble towards the end of her career, some outlandish accusation of professional misconduct brought against her by an anonymous accuser. It was absurd, as anyone who knew or worked with her understood, but once that horse was out of the barn, there was no end to its snorting and trampling and rearing and whatever else de-stable-ized horses get up to. She defended herself with dignity and rigour and logic, but facts, however well marshalled, are useless when it comes to expunging such a taint. They wore her down. She took the package. I've always wondered what backstage role Agnes might have played in the drama of that downfall. She wasn't there for

Gloria, that's for sure; wasn't her champion when one was required. It's true what they say about hard times, about how you know who your friends are. What I wouldn't give to be a fly on the wall when she sorts through her mail, Agnes I mean, and finds her card from beyond; her own final package.

"My Christmas Card List."

That's the caption, practical if uninspired, inscribed above a sprig of mistletoe on the plasticized cover of the spiral-bound notebook Bonnie located in an upper drawer of the sideboard, along with an assortment of cocktail napkins, candle stubs, and the tag ends of several boxes of Christmas cards, all purchased, she knew for a fact, at Boxing Day sales over the years. Some of these – there are eighteen, she will use them all – have pipe-smoking snowmen cavorting in wintry fields. Some bristle with holly and pine. Some are Currier and Ives knock-offs: sleigh rides, punch bowls, carollers, stockings hung by the chimney with care. Peter's card, in which Bonnie will enclose the letter that now absorbs her, is the last of the stash. It's a crowded manger scene. The unattributed artist has loaded the frame with Magi and shepherds and villagers and bagpipers and hurdy-gurdy players and the innkeeper and the innkeeper's wife and their children and what might be the stable hand and cherubim in the rafters and every barn animal you could name: Old MacDonald, refracted through the prism of a low-rent Hieronymus Bosch. The Holy Family is front and centre, as you would expect, the baby Jesus in the cradle and Joseph, looking proud, despite his dubious claim to paternity, and Mary, unblemished and whole, no trace of gore anywhere on her divine person, as though the business of pushing the watermelon through the keyhole had been accomplished through osmosis. No one – with the possible exception of Katrina – ever had so easy a birth.

As I mentioned, Peter, you interviewed me once a long time ago. That fifteen-minute conversation was Gloria's finest hour. I imagine her luring Agnes over on some pretext, then binding her to a chair and forcing her to listen. It was such a symbol of arrival. My mother really believed that something fundamental had changed for me, that the world was my forever more oyster. She had seen me reach the pinnacle of achievement. Nothing would eclipse that golden moment. It obviated my many failures. It didn't matter that I still had to temp or waitress to make ends meet because, after all, I had talked to Peter! All of Canada knew my name! What more was there to hope for or expect? I remember how, many years ago, a mayoral candidate whom Gloria backed and who was an underdog was, against all odds, elected. Gloria had a bad head cold, but her elation at this democratic triumph was so heated that all her symptoms simply vanished, just like that. It's true. They were there and they were gone. I saw it. I think it's possible that had my moment of Warholian acclaim come after her diagnosis, she would simply have blasted the evil out of her system, smote the malevolent cells as though they were, say, Pharaoh's men and their horses and chariots, dashed to bits by the Red Sea.

You won't take it amiss, Peter, when I tell you that, beyond stirring maternal pride, the interview had no lasting impact. I was still broke, the phone declined to jangle, and I was grateful for a short-term contract with a publicist who was touting a new restaurant called Confetti. I was assigned to stuff hundreds of envelopes with press releases and – wait for it – confetti. The idea was that unsuspecting reporters would open them up, anticipating another ho-hum, overblown paean to God knows what, and would be thrilled to be showered by the enclosed paper shreds, as though at a wedding. The publicist thought it would be attention-grabbing. I remember thinking at the time that this was a misstep, that were I a busy news professional on the receiving end of such largesse, possibly scarfing down a bowl of soup at my desk, I would be full of feelings and none of them would be charitable. However, as you can tell from the enclosed, it was a ploy that stuck with me. Peter, is it not astonishing, when we look back and trace the influences that

*have shaped us, just how diverse and widespread and unlikely they turn
out to be? This is how culture evolves. This is how art moves forward.*

✉ ✉ ✉

Peter's card, like the others, has been pre-inscribed with a manufactured, all-purpose greeting. Bonnie has crossed out *Merry Christmas
/ Joyeux Noël* and replaced it with her own message, "*And dust to
dust.*" She has done likewise for the seventeen other designated
recipients. To each and every card she has carefully added a line
of her mother's grainy residue: a small funnel she located with the
cocktail supplies has proved useful for the even placement of the
ashes along each card's fold. Bonnie has signed them all with her
mother's name, even though she can't manage even a reasonable
facsimile of Gloria's elegant signature. No one other than Peter, who
is a special case, and whose letter she will soon finish, will receive
any other enclosures, or word of explanation. Will the lucky legatees
even recognize the fulsome trickle for what it is? The artist's eternal
dilemma, as Bonnie knows well, is the risk of being misunderstood
or unappreciated.

"In my mother's house there are many remotes," Bonnie says,
and selects one such gizmo from the coffee table, aims it across
the room at the television, presses "Start," ignites the gas fire. She
mutters a low "damn," lights a cigarette (*Dieci, allora!*), peers about
for the necessary tool.

Bonnie knows the only way she will complete this foray into
performance art, as now she thinks of it, and consign her handiwork
to the mail, will be to make it to the nearest post office before the
effects of the alcohol start to wane. Before she braves the elements,
she needs to reacquaint herself with the world, so inconveniently
obscured by the tarp.

The security camera at her mother's front door pans the street
and broadcasts its findings to channel fifty-nine. Gloria preferred

channel fifty-nine to the news or *Masterpiece Theatre*. She could spend hours watching random passersby, speculating on their needs and motives, commenting on their fashion sense, or lack of same. Channel fifty-nine, in the absence of a working window, will give Bonnie a working pre-exit picture of the weather, the traffic, the possibility of encountering a panhandler. Or cop. Was what she was planning a legal use of the mail? Possibly not. On the other hand, it wasn't as though she was sending anthrax or ricin. There was always next year.

Bonnie broadcasts a beam to douse the fire, sights the device to coax the TV into action, reaches for it, brushes against the pile of cards. The cinders have just enough bulk that the sealed envelopes don't lie flat. They tumble, seventeen cards in seventeen envelopes marked with the seventeen names Bonnie has selected from her mother's Christmas card book. Some fall face up, some face down. Bonnie sighs, takes a long drag on her cigarette – this is it, the last one, no more – and stares down upon the register of the visible elect. Look, there's Agnes, her name leads all the rest, and she's lying next to Hamish MacPherson. They deserve each other. Hamish is the realtor who talked Gloria into buying her apartment in The Regalia; it should have been called The Sieve. There's Anastasia Fournier, Gloria's long-time physician, to whom her mother had remained perversely loyal, and who'd told her it was nothing to worry about, as if her history of a pack and a half a day for fifty years was more or less the same as taking an occasional spoonful of cod liver oil. And Dixie Bruckner, who was the chair of the school board, who oversaw the tribunal that dealt with the complaint against Gloria, then pushed for the cutbacks that led to her redundancy, leaving who knows how many stammerers with no beacon of hope. Bonnie smiles at Martin Collins, gives him a little wave; he's a retired school principal and was her mother's last lover. Bonnie always liked Marty, and he's just sick enough that he'll laugh himself senseless when he wrests the envelope open, perhaps with the engraved silver cutter he was given for thirty years of service. What will Heinrich think? Bonnie wasn't able to make herself write his name. His card is addressed, tartly but not inaccurately, to "Motherfucker." There's also one marked To Whom It May Concern, False Creek Ferry Operation. This she will send on the off-chance they'll recognize the enclosure for what is is, will intuit what needs to be done. Perhaps she could petition them to name one of their boats "*Spirit of Gloria Quigley.*" Yes. Good idea. There must be a way. She will find out.

Bonnie collects the cards, places them all in Gloria's black-canvas Duthie book bag, a real collector's item. She locates channel fifty-nine. The coast looks to be clear. She has only to finish Peter's card. Then she can return to the world, complete the operation.

✉ ✉ ✉

A few days after the "Celebration of Life" – named, I can only suppose, by the same villainous cabal that gave us "cremains" – and before I'd received back the ashes in their thousand-dollar urn, which I now intend to use for spare change – which, if work doesn't come along soon, I'll be collecting on the corner of Davie and Jervis – I went through her files and found one with your name on it, Peter. It contained all the letters she'd written to your show; all the letters as far as I know, there may have been others, who can tell? I was amazed at her prolixity. There were more than fifty, and some of them of novella length. I knew she wrote to you, Peter, she mentioned it from time to time, but I had no idea she was so determined and devoted. So prolific. Such a diversity of narratives, such a testament to a life rich in experience and reflection. There was a story about the time she was canning preserves when she was eight months pregnant and half the jars exploded and she was up all night clearing the pantry of chutney shrapnel and then her water broke: what a hoot! And a truly touching tale about Christmas on the farm and the toboggan her harsh, taciturn, but nonetheless caring father somehow managed to place under the tree, at untold personal sacrifice, a sign of the love he could not otherwise express for his Depression-era progeny. There was one that would have broken your heart about a kitten and a fire and a one-room school. She wrote about being a war bride; that first winter in Cupar, Saskatchewan, my God, it was worse than the Blitz! Memorable, too, was the saucy story about the rude desk clerk who's the reason she keeps going back to her favourite hotel in Paris, L'Auberge de l'Inconnu, hidden away above a fabulous boulangerie on an obscure street in the Marais. It's not in any guides or directories. You have to know someone who knows.

They were good letters, these and all the others, funny, touching, well written, humane, and they didn't contain a single word of truth among them, really, not one. She never canned, not once in her life. She grew up in Montréal, in Westmount. She was fourteen when the war ended. Her father was a little on the withholding side but he was an accountant and a big supporter of the symphony and wouldn't have had to scrimp to buy a Cadillac, let alone a toboggan. Her only experience of Saskatchewan was passing over at thirty-nine thousand feet. I'd be happy to send you her detailed telling of the time she walked with Gandhi. It will amaze you. None of it smells like what it is, and that's unadulterated bullshit.

Gloria never showed me her writing, and I never asked to see it. She would sometimes grouse about how her letters never made the cut – I don't know why I bother, he never picks me! – and I shared her wonderment at this oversight. They're artfully wrought and seem to have been written with your voice, or Shelagh's, in mind. She crafted them with natural pauses to accommodate laughter, bemusement, tears, gasps of astonishment. I'm sure she anticipated a producer adding ambient music played upon the lute or harp, maybe even a lonely harmonica; one story about a summer-long Scrabble marathon in a Muskoka cottage cries out for both the plaintive call of the loon and the aria from the Goldberg *Variations; Glenn Gould, of course. The 1955 version, not the 1981. It took me the longest time to understand she never sent them. It was enough for her to write. She didn't need publication to scratch whatever that itch; she never required the gestalt of mailing. Go figure.*

So, Peter, that's about it. Her name was Gloria Quigley. You made her happy. With you in mind, she probed a vein of inventiveness that

might otherwise have gone unmined. As psychopathologies go, hers
was minor. She never cheated on her taxes. She saved who knows how
many people from the curse of unnecessary sibilance. She loved her
work. They scandalized her name. She got sick. She suffered. She died.
I loved her. What's left of her can be measured in teaspoons. Still, she
holds secrets. Here she is. Here they are. Guess them. All the best for a
happy Christmas and prosperous millennium. Yours, Bonnie Quigley,
Only Child, Orphan, Filmmaker. Soon-to-Be Sober. Ish.

✉ ✉ ✉

Heinrich's cuckoo clock spills the beans. 3 p.m. Bonnie stubs out
her cigarette. She adds Peter's card, sealed with her very own nico-
tine-laced spittle, to the rest in the Duthie sack. She looks under the
kitchen sink, finds a cache of vivid-orange garbage bags. She must
remember they're there. If need be, she can cut arm holes, get a job
as a sign lady on a traffic crew. She selects one, dumps into it the
contents of the ashtray and every bottle from the sideboard, along
with what remains of the carton of Belmont Milds. She finds her coat,
exits the apartment – she leaves the door unlocked, whoever might
break in and haul stuff away would be doing her a favour – then
walks, unsteadily, to the elevator. She waits a long time before she
realizes she hasn't pressed the call button.

The occupants of 806, 503, and 917, all avid fans of channel
fifty-nine, watch Bonnie step onto the sidewalk, book bag in one
hand, garbage bag in the other. Bonnie, alert as only a filmmaker
can be to the presence of a camera, takes care to show her good side.
No one recognizes her as Gloria's daughter. They wonder, casually,
who she is, who she was visiting, where she's going. Angelina, the
cleaning lady for 302, is stretched out on the sofa, having a cup of
tea, petting the cat. She smiles to see that she and Wobble Woman
have the same coat, a popular Bay Day find from a few years back.

Now Bonnie rounds the corner. Now she's out of view. No one
sees her at the dumpster. No one sees what she heaves inside.

BLESS ALL THE DEAR CHILDREN

My father fucked off in the early hours of the morning I turned five. Decamped without notice or warning. Sank without trace. No one pulls off so thorough an evaporation without planning, management. Talent, even. Say there Mr. Houdini, ain't you the cat's ass? My, oh my, my man. Yes, indeed, you surely is.

"How can I tell you what he was wearing?" said my mother. This was to the officer who answered the missing person call. She had a piece of holly pinned to her cap, the cop I mean, and a serious overbite that lent her a look of preternatural, if slightly Paleolithic, concern. She'd been deeded a port-wine birthmark, a ruddy stain that colonized the whole left side of her face. It had a lightning-bolt edge, suggesting a crude zipper inserted from scalp to chin. It fascinated me, as it would any child, distracted me from my brimming stocking, unexplored, and from the pile of presents, wrapped and waiting under the gaudy tree. I longed to touch it, the birthmark, wanted to know if it was scaly, if there was a textural difference between the sullied and unsullied flesh, to find if the jagged borderline was smooth or ridged.

"I was fast asleep when he snuck out. He could be naked as a jailbird for all I know, his coat's still in the hall closet."

"As a jaybird, ma'am."

"What?" my mother barked; then, with a glance in my direction – mindful of setting a good example, even in a time of crisis, and especially in the presence of an authority figure, however antic – corrected herself. "I mean, pardon?"

"It's 'naked as a jaybird.' I'm quite sure that's right. I think if you check it out, you'll find that's so. 'As a jaybird.' Comma. 'Naked as.'"

The policewoman sat with her pen poised over her notebook looking at my mother, who stared in turn at the tree, as though she were expecting from it something revelatory or, at least, diverting; that it would lift up its skirts of tinsel and dance the hoochie coochie. That it would spontaneously combust.

"How do you mean, check it out?"

"I'm sorry, ma'am?"

"Naked as a jailbird. How do you mean, check it out?"

"Jaybird. I mean, look it up. Do you have a copy of, say, *Brewer's Dictionary of Phrase and Fable* handy?"

"We had the *World Book* growing up," said my mother, "but my brother got it, all twenty volumes, God knows why, never had any kids, keeps the damn thing in a box in his garage. In Salmon Arm."

She'd been sitting up straight in her chair at the kitchen table, combative and alert. Something about this disclosure, about the gendered brutishness of primogeniture, about the impediment of the mountain range that stood between her and the proving of her point, took the wind right out of her sails. She wilted, slouched back, collapsed in on herself.

"You could always call the public library," said the cop, brightly, as though this difficult family situation might be mitigated by a more obliging civic service.

"It's Christmas. The library will be closed. I'm sure it will be closed."

I'd been a mute observer. Now, I spoke.

"Everyone knows b-b-b-b-birds have f-f-f-f-"

My mother and the officer stared.

"Why are you stuttering?" said my mother.

"They have f-f-f-f-f-f-f-"

"Something wrong with the boy? Need a glass of water or something? Juice?"

"He's never done that before, always been a good talker, talked before he was a year old, complete sentences, paragraphs, even. His daycare teacher calls him 'the Oscar Wilde of the preschool set.' What's that guy called?"

"T-T-T-T-Tristan."

I pronounced his name with as much reverence as the stammer allowed. I adored Tristan.

"Pansy, of course, name like that he would be, probably changed it from Chuck or Andy or something normal. No criminal record. Sure, I checked. I want my kid to be safe, can't be too careful. Pervs. They're everywhere. It's in the paper all the time."

"F-F-F-F-F-"

"Spit it out."

Her cuff on the ear proved remedial

"F-F-Feathers. Everyone knows they have feathers. Jaybirds. So they're not really n-n-n-naked. Are they?"

"Ha," said my mother, relieved to have found an ally, however pint-sized and tongue-tied and bound to the literal.

The officer was gathering breath, considering her retort, and it might have gone on for a long time, this volley of absurdities, had a seagull not brought a Buñuelesque whiff to the proceedings by smashing, violently, into the apartment window. The force of the impact and the effect of whatever suction comes into play between glass and plumage kept the poor creature in place long enough for us all to study the spread of its wings, the stunned look on its little face, pressed to the pane in awkward profile; to see even the veined webbing between its weirdly balletic toes.

"Jesus," said the officer, less oath than acknowledgment of the apparition's cruciform aspect.

The gull released its hold, or was released by it. It fell seventeen stories to the sidewalk below. A passerby screamed. From the kitchen-counter radio – it had been playing this whole time – Judy Garland pitched the do-mi-so-do opening arpeggio of "Have Yourself a Merry Little Christmas."

What were my presents that year? Were the gifts opened, the stocking unpacked? Was there any pretence of merriment, of muddling through, was the turkey – a Butterball, frozen, left to thaw overnight in the bathtub – stuffed and roasted? I can't remember. My memory ends with the cop, the stuttering, Judy Garland, and later that same morning, my mother on the phone to her sister.

"We'll never see the bastard again, and it's not like the cops give a shit. No, Connie. No, they don't. They sent that girl, right? If there were taking it seriously, you think they'd have sent that girl? What a freak show."

Mother was a MILF, a Monster I'd Like to Forget. Fat fucking chance. Mater was a master monster, and a monster's whole raison d'être is her memorability. At unforgettability, Mother excelled; in the Campground of Recall, where the air is always hazy, she pitched no mere pup tent, but a horizon-obscuring RV.

No one need rear up on a high horse and snarl the news that the vogue for mother-blaming is long out of fashion. I know. It is, what's more, a sentiment with which I'm onside. Nevertheless, I stand by the accuracy of my estimation. I say again, Mother was a monster. If I err, it's only in the baldness of my assertion which would stir the hackles of lydia de'ath. miss de'ath was my high-school English teacher; e.e. cummings was her bright morning star. lydia's insights into what she sincerely, if erroneously, called "creative writing," helped make me all I am today. "*show! don't tell!*" was her cherished, hackneyed maxim. Should she still be alive – unlikely, given her reliance on Dr Pepper as her main fuel, and the burnished nicotine stains on her fingers – and should she ever read this – less likely still – she would hurry to scribble "*show! don't tell! l.d.*" next to my unvarnished maternal "J'accuse"; see above. (miss de'ath, partial to the exclamatory, appended her initials to every annotation, as if to validate their authenticity.) I thought then – and I haven't changed my mind – that telling, sometimes, has its place. Mother was a monster. Monster, monster, monster. I know it now, I knew it then, back when we were the Joan and Christina Crawford of the Pauline

Johnson Mansions. It was from our apartment on the seventeenth floor – via elevator and lobby, one must suppose, given the absence of ripped and knotted bed sheets – that Papa made his midnight flit.

The Mansions look much as they did forty years ago; I passed by on my way here tonight. The building's heraldic crest is still on the door: a lion and unicorn rampant, pawing with their forelegs at the stacked and stylized letters "PJM." I wonder, given the Mohawk (*"Kanien'kehá:ka" is now preferred! l.d.*) ancestry of the building's namesake, that no one has thought to replace it with a more sensitive decal, with flint and feather, perhaps; that it hasn't been renamed the Tekahionwake Longhouse.

However much the PJM could benefit from some selective sprucing and decolonizing touches, I'm glad it hasn't been visibly altered, unlike everything around it. So much of what I knew growing up – the plain, squat apartment buildings, the churches, the corner stores – has been plowed under, rebuilt, changed utterly. This tony trattoria where I've taken shelter from the storm is a case in point. When did it come along with its abundant array of antipasti – who knew so many bocconcini walk abroad in the world? – and its quartz-topped bar where now I perch, two nights before Christmas, scribbling these notes?

Party of four, party of six, one after the other they pile through the door, all in high holiday spirits. These are the very friends of whom doe-eyed Judy G. sang to pensive little Margaret O'Brien in Meet Me in St. Louis, the faithful ones who are dear to us, who gather near to us once more. How young they are, how confident, how au courant. They emanate the scrubbed, prosperous glow of recent graduates from the better universities: architects, surgeons, software engineers. The talk is animated, merry, of course it is, they haven't seen each other in months and months and Instagram, FaceTime, well, they're just not the same. They've been pals since high school – my gosh, has it really been ten years already, how is that possible, feels like prom was yesterday! – and now they're scattered, but they're faithful, just like the song prescribes, so here they are, they've jetted in from

Boston and that pediatrics residency, from Silicon Valley and that promising new start-up, from Basel and that internship at Herzog & de Meuron. They've been looking forward to this reunion, what a relief to get a break from the old folks at home, in Kerrisdale, in West Van, in Deep Cove.

"How's your mom?"

"Really good, considering she's turning, gulp, fifty in the spring."

"No!"

"Uh-huh. She's getting a bit forgetful, maybe, but not too bad."

Jesus Christ. Just you wait, my pretty. Just you wait.

I sit at the swooping bar's far end, my back to the door, wedged in next to the umbrella stand, a popular stop on this pluvial evening. How trusting people are in this sodden city, the way they collapse their dripping brollies and consign them to these ubiquitous tubs – this one is a repurposed waste basket – confident no one will take the thing in error, let alone target it, spirit it away with malice aforethought, whether out of a desperate aversion to the rain or just for the sheer pleasure of larceny. I suspect no one else in this four-star beanery has had the pleasure of discovering their grainy security-camera photo tacked up on the rogue's gallery bulletin board of a Downtown Eastside convenience store beneath the carefully stencilled headline "BEWEAR THESE THEVES!"

Little chance that any of the best and brightest gathered here tonight will have studied and committed to memory that image, which is both far from flattering and far from here. It's highly unlikely that anyone will see me at all, come to that, for I am a middle-aged man, sitting alone, and there is nothing like the double taint of antiquity and isolation to ensure invisibility. Only solitary people pay any mind to solitary people, hence the occasional moments of awkward eye-lock I've had with the unescorted woman at the bar's opposite end. Mostly, her attention is focused on her phone, but once or twice, when I've looked up from my jot-jot-jotting, I've caught her staring. Or so I believe.

⚰ ⚰ ⚰

Dear lady at the other end of the bar,

Who might you be? Curious, you are, and promising, in an ominous way. Let's stay in touch, shall we? As I was saying –

My father fucked off the morning I turned five (*rhetorical repetition! nice! careful not to overuse, though! l.d.*) which also happened to be Christmas Day. Most Christmas-borns – with the notable exception of Jesus, over whom so much fuss is predictably made – sing the same short-shrift song. Blowhard Christmas takes over the room, sucks up all the available air, leaves oxygen insufficient to sustain the candles on the cake inscribed with your own frosted name. To be born on Christmas is to learn, when one's shoots are still tender, what it is to feel slighted, cheated. Ignored. It's hard to sidestep the conclusion – why bother trying, since it's correct? – that your natal day is a kind of seasonal inconvenience, another chore to check off a list, sandwiched between "Buy cranberries" and "Iron table linens." There's no contest. Christmas will always win. You'll never feel like anything other than an interloper, an afterthought at your own party. Boo hoo hoo.

"Get over yourself," I hear my mother say, her reliable retort when I complained about any injustice that might have been visited upon me.

"Do you know how good you've got it? Do you know how many people in this world would crawl over broken grass to eat the food you leave on your plate?"

"G-G-G-Glass."

"Shut your pie hole."

"But L-L-L-L-Lana, you said 'g-g-g-g–'"

"I said shut it."

Daddy got out of Dodge and it took Mother less than twenty-four hours to remove his clothes from the closet, to prise the wedding photo on their dresser from its frame and shred it to ribbons with a box cutter, to disappear the "World's Best Dad" coffee cup from the mug tree. Gone, too, were the seasonal decorations and baubles, all tossed out, sent rattling down the garbage chute to the fiery hell of the furnace room. Fall, angel, fall. No need to wrap the crap in crepe and reconsign it to that special roost on that high shelf; none of it would be required, for with Christmas we were done, and not just with Christmas but with anything connected to that dire day of desertion (*alliteration is the cheap perfume of literary devices! l.d.*), anything that might be "triggering," as I believe we're now meant to say, that might remind Mother of betrayal's terrible sting. (*hackneyed! l.d.*)

"That whole Santa thing is a crock, right? You know that, right?"

This was the news she delivered on Boxing Day morning, when I was one day into my sixth year upon the earth.

"Wipe that stricken look off your face. Think about it. All the children in the whole wide world? Flying reindeer? Fatty, fatty two-by-four coming down the chimney? Look around. You see a chimney? It's a crock. There's no Santa, and you're old enough to know it. Eat your cereal."

I stared into my bowl. I located an *S*, corralled an *A*, searched for a *D*. I found it not. Another *S* paddled by. I could work with that. I put it where it needed to be. Oh what fun, to read "ASS" in milk.

"Things are going to be different around here. No more of this Mummy, Mother, Mama stuff. Makes me crazy."

Alpha-Bits were my go-to breakfast food, not just because they were an excellent source of iron, thiamin, and ten other essential nutrients. With some gentle nudging from Tristan the Beloved at daycare, I had become a reader. I kept this developmental triumph to myself. My father's predictable indifference would have been deflating. Mother would have seen it as more ordnance in my growing arsenal of subversive possibilities; me, a little pitcher with big ears, too smart for my own good, too big for my breeches.

"Call me Lana. That's my name. You're old enough to use it."

I was beginning to feel like a minor carnival attraction, the World's Oldest Five-Year-Old. I gave the milk a stir. "ASS" vanished. Among the bobbing flotsam I found an *L*, an *A*, an *N*, another *A*. I considered the possibilities. I put them in a row.

"Why are you smirking?"

"I'm n-n-n-not."

I scooped up "ANAL" with my spoon. I ate it. (*ugh! l.d.*)

🕯 🕯 🕯

So, Christmas was banished, likewise my birthday. Another change to our family life, notable and surprising, was that Lana began attending church; as, of necessity, did I. Lana was a convert of convenience. A social worker, perhaps at the behest of the Christmas-morning cop, had dropped by, unannounced, a few weeks after the Big Walkout. I had a cold and a snot-encrusted nose, Lana had a hangover and worryingly few cigarettes, and the apartment had the desolate, smoky ambience favoured by the production designers of post-apocalyptic cinema. Jesus would have wept had he opened our fridge. Mrs. Simpson – so her lanyard proclaimed her – was his proxy. Not even he who turned water into wine, who demonstrated the expansive possibilities of a crust of bread and a few fishes could have whipped up something palatable from what mouldered therein. It was an inopportune Saturday morning for a surprise visit from anyone, let alone a card-carrying expert in the art and/or science of child rearing in whom was vested the power to apprehend. Her report was disapproving, more than mildly. Visible, measurable alteration would be required. Or else.

Lana, compliant if not contrite, purchased some air freshener, emptied the ashtrays, and got rid of the bottles, ferrying her bar to the safe harbour of a trunk conveniently located near the front of our basement locker.

"Where's that colander?" she would say most evenings, round about five. "Must be downstairs. Don't let anyone in."

"Did you f-f-f-f-find it?" I would ask, on her eventual return.

"Sure did," she'd say, "and I'm some relieved, I can tell you."

A more public and third-party verifiable demonstration of how we were reclaiming the republic of virtue from the sea of vice (*strained! l.d.*) was our churchgoing. After shopping around for the least offensive possibility, we settled on St. Stephen's United. It had the twin perks of proximity and a minister, Vera Cluster, whose homiletics were exempla of concision and, as I think back on those days, were rather daring in their humanism.

"Women that dykey shouldn't be made to wear collars," Lana would say as we walked home along Cardero Street. "It doesn't do them any favours. She should trim that moustache, too."

"Why c-c-c-c-couldn't we stay for snacks?"

Warm juice and bulk-buy cookies – praise the lard – were served in the church hall, fusty with the smell of liquid floor wax, poster paint, and vomit.

"No need to hang around longer than we need to. You know it's a load of hooey, right? All that Jesus stuff? You get that, right? Hell, I slept for three days once and nobody made a fuss about it when I finally got up. Well. Except my mother."

Sometimes, Reverend Cluster called by the apartment. Her drop-ins were always by appointment, but Lana was persuaded – I'm not sure she was wrong – that she was a spy, checking up on us at the behest of Child and Family Services.

"We'll show those bastards," Lana would say, giving the Glade aerosol can a vigorous shake. Depending on how many of the three elevators were out of service, she had reliably ninety seconds between buzzing the Reverend in and her arrival on the seventeenth floor to transform our apartment into a fragrant, shade-dappled glen.

"We're awfully glad to have you and your son as part of the congregation, Lana," Reverend Cluster would say, smiling professionally, her mottled teeth a testament to just how much tea someone in her profession is compelled to swill. "Would you ever be interested in some committee involvement? The UCW can always use another willing hand."

"Ha!" Lana would say, when these pastoral visits were done and Reverend Cluster was out the door. "If there is a God, and there isn't, that's why he gave us short and curlies, so do-gooders like that could have something to grab onto. What's she want from me anyway? Am I supposed to polish collection plates? Scrub the altar? The UCW. Jesus."

Dear lady at the other end of the bar,

Did you just now, under the pretext of snapping u selfie, take my picture? I feel certain you did. I sensed a slight diminishing, as though some small part of my soul's anatomy broke away and quit my body. Whether you did or whether you didn't, your interest in me is more than passing. Are you perhaps a representative of the MacArthur Foundation, here to determine if I merit a genius grant? Let me help you out with that: the answer is yes. Or are you in the employ of my father, his name so long inscribed on the roll of the missing? Did he make something of himself, build a vast fortune through, say, the brokerage of white sex slaves, the selling of arms, or the mining of uranium? Is he now wanting to make amends, to offer restitution? Will you text him that photo, report your findings? Will he authorize a cheque, something in the high six figures, by way of apology? That would be super-duper, since I have no way of paying for all these drinks. Perhaps I should send you one, just by way of saying hello. Breaking the ice. Well. Later, maybe.

The United Church Women, with its odious prayer and pancake breakfasts, and fundraising teas, and competitive climate around the production of relishes and squares, was not for Lana. Still, certain she was being watched and judged, and the better to demonstrate her adherence to the straight and narrow path required by Mrs. Simpson, and also, mostly, because it was seasonal work of short duration, she signed up for the Christmas Hamper Committee.

"We have a ha-ha-ha-hamster at school," I said.

Harriet slept all day in her cage in the school library, burrowed beneath a piss-scented scattering of wood shavings, colour-coordinated to match her pelt.

"Hamper."

"Oh."

Too bad. I'd hoped this might be an entry into asking if I could bring Harriet home for a holiday furlough. I admired her sloth and envied her camouflage.

"What's a ha-ha-ha–"

"A box of tinned stuff and Kraft Dinner and the like that gets delivered to those less fortunate than we."

Quite who might fall into such a category I couldn't imagine. I knew better than to say so.

"I told them a thing or two," Lana reported when she returned from her first get-together with the hamper-humpers, as she called them. "I told them it was all well and good to load up with baked beans and creamed corn and Spam and such, but what about the fun stuff? Not just toys for kids, they got that covered, but for the grown-ups, too. Treats. Surprises. They tried to shut me up, but I wouldn't let them. So they put me in charge. Meet the Chairwoman of the Luxury Subcommittee."

Lana eschewed Christmas for personal use, but she applied missionary zeal to the task of engineering a bountiful day for disadvantaged strangers, petitioning neighbourhood stores and businesses for donations. She was persuasive. Boxes of Black Magic chocolates, slightly past their sell-by dates, and long overlooked atomizers of Yardley toilet water, and ten-dollar discount gift certificates for Reiki treatments from the massage parlour in the mall where disconsolate Asian women practised on each other while waiting for paying clients, all began to accumulate in the closet where once resided our ornaments.

"You should have seen their faces," my mother reported that first year when she came home from the church on the day of hamper assembly. Over a hundred boxes had been prepared and all had benefited from the sybaritic touch of Lana, Queen of Luxury. They would be delivered by volunteer drivers, not just to homes in the immediate neighbourhood, but all over the vast and marshy reaches of the Lower Mainland. Lana herself had taken charge of the hamper destined for the address that was furthest flung.

Mrs. Winona Rempel lived in a trailer park in the Fraser Valley. It was a two-hour journey by bus; we had no car. Getting there, visiting, and returning would take all day. Thus, Lana could both stake her claim to saintliness and squelch painful, date-associated memories. Winona proved such an effective remedy in this regard that Lana adopted her as our very own enduring Yuletide tradition and destination. Year after year, weighed down with hampers that grew ever more elaborate, we made the long journey, three transfers required, to visit the crumbling double-wide in one of the less salubrious quarters of remote Fort Langley.

Lana was fascinated by Winona, drawn to her in a Diane Arbus kind of way. She was our very own poor and tired and huddled mass, the living proof that, yes, it could be worse. Her hair was long, lank, and greasy, her skin was pale only in the patches that showed through the residue of oil and dust, her nails were a forensic scientist's wet dream, and her eyebrows were as agile as they were feral. She always wore the same voluminous nightgown, its once cheerful floral pattern obliterated by the agent orange of sweat and neglect. She was large, corpulent even, though how she maintained her bulk was a mystery. She ingested, as we gathered, not much more than rusks and black tea and the occasional boiled egg; tinned food from previous hampers was still stacked on the shelves when we returned with a fresh basket of unwanted comestibles. I suspect that whatever got opened was enjoyed not by Winona but by her many animal companions.

Mrs. Rempel had "the touch." Whoever found an injured squirrel, or a fledgling crow fallen too early from the nest, or a muskrat that had gnawed off its own leg to escape a trap, would take it to Winona, who would nurse it back to health. There was no release program in effect, nor were the salvaged creatures restrained. They simply elected, so it seemed, to stay put once their healing was done. The trailer was a malodorous but harmonious Assisi of cheeping and whirring and underfoot scuttling.

"You brought the boy," she'd say every year when we arrived with our burgeoning box. "Will you sing for me, sonny?"

"Go on," Lana would say, "sing."

The air was fetid enough to be dimensional. Steeling myself against the unpleasant necessity of inhalation, I let the carols flow.

🕯 🕯 🕯

Dear lady at the other end of the bar,

Just look at you, beavering away at your smartphone. Texting. Emailing. Note-taking. And me with my well-chewed Bic, scratching like a medieval monk in my wee black cahier, another lydia de'ath artifact. I was her special case for cultivation, for enrichment. She would pass on to me books from which she thought I might benefit, might even – imagine it! – enjoy. One such text was On the Black Hill, *Bruce Chatwin's evocation of the rigours of Welsh agrarianism and the complexities of fraternal affection. It made me rejoice at being a citified only child, otherwise it was a slog. What thrilled me was the author's flyleaf photo: his pallid complexion and Weltschmerz eyes, his baby face and bad-boy mien. "How are you enjoying Chatwin?" l.d. inquired, after a lunchtime meeting of the Creative Writing Club, for which she was the "faculty supervisor." The one other boy who attended was Glen Glenn – or was it "Glenn Glen"? – the eventual author of pamphlets for both the Canadian Wildlife Service and the St. John Ambulance Association. He recently won a commendation*

*from the Port Moody Society of Technical Writers for his concise yet
vivid description of how best to treat a wolverine bite when one is deep
in the woods and no professional assistance is near to hand. I found
it profoundly moving, especially the way it reinforced the necessity of
never leaving home without a supply of cheesecloth and a roll of duct
tape. The other de'athian acolytes were pale young women who wrote
desperate, confessional poetry and knew by heart long passages from
The Outsiders and The Bell Jar. "I'm enjoying Chatwin very much,"
I said, omitting the details of my nocturnal inventions, fictions that
hinged on miscreant behaviour on my part, misdeeds that required
corporal punishment administered by the sternly disapproving Mr. C.
"I want you to have this, too," said lydia, "It's a Moleskine, the same
notebook Chatwin uses. If you want to be a writer, you should follow
his example." From that day to this, dear lady, I have always had a
Moleskine, although I have never actually, you know, like, purchased
one. They are as pleasing to write in as they are tempting to lift as they
are easy to conceal: perhaps not an endorsement the manufacturer will
hurry to post on their website adjacent to Chatwin's loving appraisal.
It is to my trusted Moleskine I confide this now. All I remember. All I
observe. I observe you, dear lady at the other end of the bar. I observe
you observing me for your own reasons, whether for good or for ill.
You are a distraction on which I hadn't counted. Where was I? Oh, yes.*

☙ ☙ ☙

My father fucked off when I turned five (*starting to lose impact! l.d.*)
and thus commenced my career as a stammerer.

"I don't know, Connie. I don't know why he started all of a sudden," said Lana to her sister on the phone. "Probably a phase, like
bed-wetting. Thank God that's stopped. Mostly."

The stutter was stubborn, though; the stutter settled in. Predictably,
I was bullied. Shunned. I took to hiding in the girl's washroom – I
thought, correctly for a while, that no one would ever think to look

for me there – to avoid recess. Eventually, my cover was blown. Difference was detected, if not full-blown deviance. Phone calls ensued.

"It will only get worse," the teacher told Lana, who was fully aware of the problem, but content to wait for me to grow out of it. "I'd like you to meet Mrs. Quigley, our itinerant speech pathologist. She travels around to different schools in the district."

"I know what 'itinerant' means," said Lana, indignant.

"She'll be here tomorrow," the teacher continued, "and I've arranged a get-together for you all."

"Snippy little thing," Lana told Connie that night on the phone. "Setting up a meeting without so much as a by-your-leave. It's not as if I don't have things to do, places to be."

"Wh-Wh-Wh-Where have you g-g-g-got to b-b-b-be?" I asked when she hung up, knowing her days to be steppe-like with vacancy.

"None of your b-b-b-beeswax," she replied, the tenderest of empaths.

🕯 🕯 🕯

We gathered the next day – Lana must have rejigged her hectic schedule – in the office of Miss Sargent, the vice-principal. Her window offered an unobstructed view of the playing fields, not quite of Eton, where I'd been on the receiving end of so many inventive humiliations. Prominent on the wall were a framed Cecil Beaton photograph of young Elizabeth II, and a thick leather strap for the persuasion of difficult cases: Sergeant Sargent and Corporal Punishment, as we delighted in saying. (*perhaps creeping beyond the margin of credibility! l.d.*) I liked Mrs. Quigley, liked her right away. Cigarette smoke hung heavy around her, adhered to her well-tailored suit, her breath. I longed to sit in her lap and cuddle close and take comfort from the venial reek of her person.

"I hear you have some trouble talking, darling. You get a little stumbly. Is that true?"

Silence. In tantalizing view on the desk was a bag of Oreos. Were they Miss Sargent's, for her elevenses? Or were they Mrs. Quigley's, the sugary carrot to her stick?

"I'm going to tell you a secret. I know this and as soon I've whispered in your ear, you'll know it, too. Are you ready?"

I nodded, agreeably. I knew I was being patronized, but if I could stretch it out another seven minutes, I'd be able to not only miss the horrors of the 10:15 recess but, perhaps, snag an Oreo, too.

"It's this," she said, leaning in, her warm exhalations layered with the taint of tobacco and the cloying whiff of breath mints. "Sometimes people who have trouble saying words can sing them."

I gaped in wide-eyed amazement, which I gauged to be the naive reaction the revelation required.

"It's strange, but true. Would you like to try? Can you sing for me?"

Twelve minutes past ten. To draw her out, I shrugged and composed my features into a look I intended to convey a willing spirit incarcerated in feeble flesh. Three minutes of urging might be required!

"Is it because you can't think of a song? Nothing at all?"

Head shake no, and the modest, downcast gaze of Bess, the landlord's daughter, disavowing all knowledge of the highwayman who's galloping towards the old inn door. (*glad to see you paid attention in english 9! l.d.*)

"'My Bonnie Lies over the Ocean' is my favourite. Do you know why? It's because my daughter is called Bonnie. She's a little older than you, not so very much. You must know that one. If I help you out?"

She began.

"My Bonnie lies over the –"

Then came the rude braying of the bell that announced recess. Typically, this stirred in me a Pavlovian response of sweating and shaking and the urge to vomit; on this occasion I felt only relief and triumph.

"– ocean, My Bonnie lies over –"

I watched the other children run from the school, making animal noises, eager to begin their play.

"– *the sea, My Bonnie* –"

I was so grateful to Mrs. Gloria Quigley, itinerant speech pathologist, for providing the diversion that saved me from having to join in those reindeer games, in the roughing and the tumbling that always ended with me held hard against a wall and forced to grapple with "Peter Piper picked a peck" while everyone stood around and laughed, that I offered up the reward of compliance. I opened my mouth. I joined in.

"– *lies over the ocean, Oh* –"

Mrs. Quigley smiled encouragement, stepped away from the footlights, ceded me the stage. It was a perilous moment to embark upon a solo career, owing to the text's impending alliterative minefield. So many *B*'s in the offing! They were my particular stuttering bugaboo, worse, even, than *P*'s; I could always be counted on to mangle *B*'s terribly. Determined to succeed, I sharpened my focus. I imagined myself – not for the first time, nor the last – as the young Elizabeth Taylor, astride her beloved Velvet, approaching some lofty show jumping obstacle, a twisted pile of *B*'s upon which a hoof might easily snag and bring both horse and rider down. But no. Triumph was in the cards. Never have I seen anyone beam as broadly as did Mrs. Q. when I vaulted over the dangerous consonants, as easily as a thoroughbred jumping egg cartons.

"– *bring back my Bonnie to me.*"

"Wonderful! Keep it up, darling!"

"*Bring back* –"

Now on a roll, I essayed the same artful *r* roll I'd heard from Kathleen Ferrier on *Gilmour's Albums*.

"– *bring back, Oh* –"

I sang with deepening assurance, volume, purity.

"– *bring back my Bonnie to* –"

I sang with a strength and quality of voice foreign to one so young and so hobbled.

"– *me, to me, Bring back, bring back, Oh –*"

I sang and never doubted my own rarity. I'd always understood, intuitively, that I was inhabited by a freakish, uninvited guest. Now, for the first time, under the placid, approving gaze of the Queen, and while my tormentors thundered about the pitted pitch, kicking up divots in their pursuit of soccer balls, I met what I'd always harboured, the alien who would prove to be my saviour, my redeemer. I saw in Lana, and in Mrs. Quigley, too, the widening of eyes and the slackening of jaws I'd grow accustomed to witnessing over the years, whenever The Voice revealed itself to first-time listeners.

"– *bring back my Bonnie to me.*"

As the last note faded – I held it strong to the end of my breath, even introduced a measured vibrato – I threw back my head, as though in ecstasy or triumph, and extended my arms upwards, an heroic gesture I'd seen Bernadette Peters employ to telling effect on *The Carol Burnet* (*Burnett! l.d.*) *Show* and which drove the audience into a frenzy of applause and stamping and cheering.

Lana said, "Sweet Jesus Christ."

Gloria said, "You can say that again."

"C-C-C-Can I have a c-c-c-cookie?"

I worked hard with Mrs. Quigley for the rest of that year, and throughout the summer, too.

"I'm not paying her," Lana explained to Connie on the phone, "she just seems to like the kid. Brings along her dictaphone, makes recordings, takes notes. Whatever she's doing, it's working."

Under Mrs. Quigley's patient tutelage, I learned to hold the stammer at bay. Its irrevocable banishment, she said, was unlikely.

"Darling, there's nothing so stubborn or sneaky as a stutter. It never quite goes away, it's always waiting to creep up and surprise you when you least expect it. Just remember," she would tell me, like

Julie Andrews prescribing a musical cure for the fear of lightning to the junior von Trapps, or Deborah Kerr advocating the merits of whistling a happy tune to the children of the King of Siam (*clunky: one example would suffice! l.d.*): "If you ever get stuck, just take a deep breath and sing. Sing! It works every time. For you, especially."

Mrs. Quigley consulted her musical colleagues in the itinerant specialist pool. They sent out feelers, commissioned informants, learned that she had not exaggerated. I was soon bumped up from the cramped back row of Special Needs to the spacious front cabin of Gifted. (*overreaching, again! l.d.*) Being the Boy Who Sings was a great deal more pleasant than being the Boy Who Stutters. Everyone stared in wonder when my diamantine tones sliced through the pale glass of "The More We Get Together" or "Row, Row, Row Your Boat." Word spread. Seas parted. I did the hokey-pokey and I turned it all about. Life, at last, was good.

I began to understand and to appreciate the responsibilities and privileges accorded those on whom the angels beam. I parlayed my lark-like soprano, and my willingness to employ the reliable ping of its stratospheric reaches in the service of the school's greater good at assemblies and festivals and so on, into the winning of such concessions as exemptions from the twice-weekly torture of physical education. One well-placed expression of concern about the deleterious effect on my cords of an errant football was all it took.

The Voice was nimble, muscular, never tired or worn. It grew the more burnished with time and use, showed no inclination to break or change. Twelve, thirteen, fourteen all came and went. Some of my coevals – boys, in the main – sprouted whiskers. Not I. I'd rise with the sun and pop off the high Fs in the Queen of the Night's aria without benefit of clearing my throat. Ah, but then there came the day when – oh!

Dear lady at the other end of the bar,

How can I have been so blinkered, so obtuse? You turned just now to signal the bartender – he with his eyes of hazel and his marmoreal ass by Bernini and his ill-considered man bun, Bjorn he's called – and I saw you in a certain angle of profile and in a certain slant of light and I had my very own road-to-Damascus moment. Did you hear the tinkle of scales dropping from my peepers? How could I not have seen it at once? You look just like her, a younger version – though not by much – of the photo that appeared with her obit, minus the Dorothy Hamill wedge cut. My condolences, by the way. I was sorry to read of her passing. Despite what happened, despite all the evidence to the contrary, I was fond of Gloria, once. Dear Gloria. Was it you who took that picture? I suspect so, just as I imagine it was you who wrote the warm appraisal that accompanied it. You handled the delicate bits very, well, delicately. Failing to mention them at all was exactly what I would have done. Good work. And now you've tracked me down. But how? To what end? I feel like Moriarty caught in the Holmesian high beams. This calls for a drink, n'est-ce pas? Where's Bjorn? And where was I? Oh, yes.

🕯 🕯 🕯

My father fucked off the day I turned five (*stop! l.d.*) and after that my birthday, along with Christmas, became a non-event. (*you've made this point clearly already! l.d.*) Time passed without the untidy rupture of celebration. Not even the mythic prospect of sweet six-teen – driving! cigarettes! shaving kits! – engaged my attention. I was just two days shy of that milestone, with no plan to mark it, when Lana came home from work with what had been delivered to her as a request and then passed on to me as a command, a *fait accompli*.

"Jennifer's sister is in a jam," she said.

Jennifer was the supervisor at the No Frills Market where Lana, at the earnest urging of Mrs. Simpson, had secured employment as a

"Checkout Associate." She was celebrated among her colleagues for her speedy accuracy, and feared by customers for her uncompromising refusal to allow more than ten items through the Express Line, and universally admired for her gift for remembering the four-digit codes assigned to over a hundred different bulk-food items. Dried papaya, trail mix, pitted prunes, rye flour, whatever: she was unstumpable. With Lana on the case there was no need to search out the elusive pencil stubs or to scratch out the relevant digits on the too-narrow twist ties; indeed, she was offended if any shopper bothered.

"Rachel's at her wit's end."

Rachel was Jennifer's sister.

"I told Jennifer you'd be happy to help out."

Jennifer was Hitler to Lana's Chamberlain; her appeasement was paramount, especially at Christmastime. Lana, citing her employer's requirement that she be available to serve Sabbath-shopping infidels, severed her connection with St. Stephen's United. Reliable sources, parishioners who stationed their trolleys in her line, confided that things were not the same in Hamperland since Lana's retirement. She persisted, though, in acting as Mrs. Rempel's Yuletide handmaid, continued to lavish more attention than the evidence suggested was warranted on the assembly of her box of goodies. It was astonishing, the quantity and quality of foodstuffs and luxury items that No Frills would make available for this charitable purpose, gratis, depending on Jennifer's mood of the moment.

"You know she's the recreation director over at that loony bin in Coquitlam, right?"

She meant Rachel, about whom Jennifer shared an unseemly amount of intelligence to which I became privy at each workday's end when Lana returned to the Pauline Johnson Mansions, worn-out but replete with gossip. I knew about how Rachel had nearly been ousted from her role as treasurer of the Occupational Therapists' Association after some kerfuffle involving the logging of membership dues that turned out to be a bank mix-up, and about the skin cancer scare that proved to be only a rashy reaction to a new moisturizer, and the feared prolapsing of her uterus that was no more than a nasty bout of gas which was put right by a regime of probiotics prescribed by a Chinese herbalist. Rachel was forever teetering on disaster's precipice. Typically, she stepped back, but this time she looked poised to slip over the edge.

"She had this string quartet booked to play the Christmas Eve show and they've all come down with mumps or mono or measles or I don't know what the hell else. They're high-school kids, probably they all got the clap. The point is, Rachel needs someone to go out there tomorrow night and entertain or there'll be hell to pay. Seems the director is gunning for the poor girl, apparently he's a real piece of work, and I told Jennifer you'd make yourself available. You haven't got anything planned, have you?"

"No," I said, "but Bless-the-Day has gone to Seoul for the holidays."

Bless-the-Day Park, a mathematics and piano prodigy, the daughter of immigrant Korean evangelists, had become my reliable accompanist; "keyboard collaborator," as she preferred to say. Bless-the-Day was possessed of an across-the-board brilliance that should have ensured her exemption from the long tedium that was high school. Her teachers, whom she alarmed to the point of paralysis, all advocated for early university entrance, but her parents, concerned for her social well-being – she had already skipped three grades – held her back. Having memorized all of Scarlatti's and Mozart's piano sonatas and the entire book of Leviticus, she applied her energies, which were abundant, to the organizing and running of a teenage prostitution ring that kept a dozen girls in vodka and cigarettes. The entire second clarinet section of the senior band, three of whom were named Tiffany, were in her employ; the embouchure jokes were as legion as they were predictable. The enthusiastic participation of so many Lolitas in her stable – her "whores de combat," as she wittily called them – allowed Bless-the-Day to make the cash purchase of the BMW convertible in which she fled when, inevitably, the cops turned up, cutting a big blue swath and demanding access to her locker. I happened to come down the hall just as the janitor, under the direction of the authorities, took a crowbar and brought brute force to bear.

"Nothing but *Fowler's Dictionary of Modern English Usage* and the score for Bach's *The Well-Tempered Clavier*," proclaimed the officer in charge who was, I was thrilled to see, the same affable dame who had come to our apartment all those years before and who had been promoted – at least, one would suppose it to be an elevation – from General Duty to Vice. I could have told her – and might have done, if asked – that Bless-the-Day would never have kept a Moleskine or any kind of written or even computerized record of her employees' or clients' details. She understood the need for discretion. Everything – dates, addresses, numbers – was safely and securely filed in the deep furrows of her pliant brain. They could have waterboarded her from here to Sunday and she would never have broken or caved.

Despite the issuing of warrants and the slavering of the media and the intemperate splashing about by the authorities of her photograph, Bless-the-Day managed to elude all dragnets, traverse a mountain range, penetrate the border undetected and then to die, a mere few hours later, in a – wait for it – fiery crash near Spokane. Of all places. A police chase, an errant three-point stag, a frosty road, and a sturdy elm were all complicit in her demise. She was fourteen. I often think of how much richer, perhaps even safer, a place the world would be, if Bless-the-Day Park still walked upon the earth.

Lana was undeterred by the absence of my regular sidekick.

"Rachel can play for you, so don't get your panties in a twist. Jennifer says she's rounded up a whole shitload of sheet music, so anything you want to sing she's pretty much sure to have."

Rachel, I knew, had attained the hoary heights of Grade 8 Piano, Toronto Conservatory. She'd have gone further, perhaps even taken a teaching diploma, but for a suspected rheumatoid arthritis in her hands that proved to be nothing more than a transient stiffness of fingers attributable to the overworking of bread dough. Even so, it rattled her confidence. It was proof that the mechanism was unreliable, there was just no telling when it would give way, it was all just too,

too tremble-making. Timorous Rachel would never have been my first or fourth choice as a musical partner, but I could only trust in Lana's assurances that she would rise to the occasion, and that my radiance would obscure her inadequacies.

"Anyway, they'll be drugged out of their minds, most of them won't even know you're there. Here's her number."

Rachel and I agreed on a set list that included a generous selection of four encores, and a few more that would be suitable for singing along, in the unlikely event that lithium and electroshock allowed anyone to be up for such an indulgence. On Christmas Eve afternoon, as the sun angled low in the western sky, and the flocks of crows began to decamp from their daytime downtown roosts for their mysterious end-of-day flight to their dormitories in Burnaby – why then? why there? – I mounted a bus at the corner of Georgia and Denman and followed their scattershot trail. I made my tuneful way to the fairyland of Coquitlam.

🕯 🕯 🕯

Dear lady at the other end of the bar,
Dear Bonnie Quigley,

I have so many questions! Principal among them is how you found me. I was assured my cloak of anonymity would resist all tattering. I had imagined the file containing the events I described would have been stored in some desanctified salt mine, under twenty-four-hour guard, surrounded by barrels of plutonium and radioactive bats. You must have tracked down some good old friend of your good old ma, someone with a key, a combination, with nothing to lose. A rogue operative. You'll have questions, too. You'll want to know why. Such a simple query, but trickier to parse than you might expect. I can't tell you, for example, precisely what it was that moved me to visit the public library on a day that was bright with more alluring possibilities. In the periodicals division I spent an irretrievable afternoon leafing through back copies – grudgingly retrieved from the closed stacks by a frayed looking clerk – of The Forum of Speech P-P-P-Pathology, *lol. Imagine my surprise, my delight, when my random gaze fell upon her byline. Gloria Quigley, M.A. Your ma was an M.A.! A peer-approved paper in a prestigious publication, what a Peter Piper picked a pickled feather in her cap. "A Case of Post-Traumatic Stuttering," was the title of her study; intriguing, even if it didn't suggest an eventual starring role for Tom Hanks. I began to read, was quickly taken by a frisson of déjà vu. Her account was eerily familiar, and it didn't take me long to grasp the how of it, or the why. "The subject, whom I shall call Craig, was by every account in the normal range of development and demonstrated no trace of pathological inconsistency in his speech patterns until the morning his father abandoned the family. The effect, as remarked by his mother, was immediate. That it was both Christmas morning and Craig's fifth birthday made the desertion the more traumatic, a compounding of tragic circumstances."*

🕯 🕯 🕯

My father fucked off the morning I turned five, which also happened to be Christmas morning, (*i could scream! i will scream! i am screaming! l.d.*) and he was summarily stricken from the record of family life, never again mentioned, which is not to say his molecular traces were utterly purged. They lingered, free-floating particles that would sometimes gather, like late-spring swarms of midges, and assemble, Busby Berkeley–style, into a pattern that was a misty simulacrum of his face, an opaque balloon bobbing above the bread box or the percolator. I wondered after his whereabouts, searched for him in crowds, even anticipated the wonderments of Photoshop by enhancing his image for age or circumstance using nothing but the power of my very own brain. Daddy with a handlebar moustache. Daddy with a salt-and-pepper beard. Daddy with a brand new and more satisfactory family. Or perhaps he'd been tragically derailed, committed, confined to a locked ward in the fabled Xanadu of Coquitlam, whither I repaired to meet Rachel on that fateful Christmas Eve, the night before my sixteenth birthday.

I stood on the stage where so many elementary-school choirs and prepubescent highland dancers and amateur ventriloquists had gone before. I surveyed our audience – involuntary would be my best guess – while Rachel adjusted her stool. It was not an upholstered bench with convenient handles on each side, but a wooden contrivance that was raised or lowered through revolving. It was in serious need of greasing; it squeaked and moaned while Rachel spun, clockwise, counterclockwise, like a demented, indecisive figurine in a music box, much to the amusement of the one patient who was brave enough to take a seat in the front row. His maniacal applause was what every singer craves – albeit after a performance, rather than before. Or also during, as turned out to be the case.

I had ample time to look for Daddy, who was neither among the patients nor the staff. The attendants leaned against the walls, yawning, checking their watches, examining their nails; perhaps they'd have been more demonstrative and attentive had we been the promised string quartet. A slight cough from nearby stage right indicated that Rachel had located her sweet spot and was in a position to begin. I answered with a subtle nod to indicate that I, too, was primed to let the good times roll. Bless-the-Day Park would have telegraphed a conspiratorial wink and mouthed the words "Let's give these motherfuckers what for," but Rachel only hunched over the chipped ivories and pounded out the introductory chords to "Hark! The Herald Angels Sing." Her instrument, a vintage upright, battered and scarred, could have benefited from revarnishing and was even more badly in need of tuning; the middle register burred with the twang of a cigar-box banjo.

Hark! The herald-angels sing,
"Glory to the newborn king..."

A seasoned performer, I knew I could rise above any imposed adversity.

> *"Peace on earth and mercy mild,*
> *God and sinners reconciled."*
> *Joyful all ye nations rise ...*

I would give it my all, unfazed even by that solitary occupant of the front row, One Man Clapping, sending out his SOS in a demonic code of his own devising.

> *Join the triumph of the skies*
> *With the angelic host proclaim ...*

I would bring him to my side, convert him using only the cudgel of musical excellence.

> *"Christ is born in Bethlehem."*

My sails were a long way from unfurled. I took the last lines up an entire octave – easily done! – and threw in a trill or two for good measure.

> *Hark! The herald-angels sing*
> *"Glory to the newborn king!"*

Rachel, catching my spark, burned off sufficient torpor to fracture the chords of the four-bar bridge between verses, roll them out with clamouring merriment like the wakened Golem thudding through the streets of Prague. (*??????! l.d.*) For the second verse, with its daft abstract of the doctrine of immaculate conception, I ornamented the treble line to a warbling fare-thee-well, like an amphetamine-fuelled Kiri Te Kanawa.

Christ, by highest heaven adored,
Christ, the everlasting Lord,
Late in time behold Him come,
Offspring of a Virgin's womb ...

It was then, as though obedient to the stage direction "late in time," that the door to the hall swung wide and a tardy concertgoer entered. Ignoring the centre aisle, she described an eccentric corkscrew arc through the room, weaving in and out among the mostly vacant seats.

She arrived at the front row and, as there was nowhere further to go, dropped down heavily, immediately adjacent to One Man Clapping, who was no more moved by her arrival than he had been by my expert, tasteless exertions.

That I was able to continue, to make it through the balance of the verse without stumbling, I attribute to nerve, discipline, and the vocal equivalent of automatic pilot; muscle memory got me through. It was all I could do not to stop outright and gape, for the new arrival was none other than Winona Rempel. The pocked moon of her face, its wan beam, her crater eyes: there was no mistaking her. I thought of Lana, home by now from the No Frills, putting the finishing touches on the hamper, the translation of which from the PJM to Fort Langley was to be the diverting centrepiece of the looming morrow. I thought of how she would be gobsmacked, Lana I mean, when I passed on the news.

"Winona?"

"Winona."

"No!"

"Yes."

"It can't be."

"I saw her, with my own eyes."

"You're sure?"

"Pinky swear."

I imagined her incredulity, her fatuous demanding of details I would be unable to provide. What had happened to bring Winona to so unfortunate a pass and place? True, the timing was extraordinary, but the happenstance was not unexpected. If Winona were destined to fall, she didn't have far to tumble; this, or some similar destination, should long ago have been her landing pad.

"Hark! The Herald Angels Sing" was rewarded with a subtle round of applause, mostly from the attendants. Rachel was once again suffering from loose stool (*beneath you, but i guess you had to get it out of your system! l.d.*) and during the time of her dizzying adjustments I looked steadily at Mrs. Rempel who returned my gaze smilingly, unblinkingly. If she recognized me, she gave no sign; she'd come to roost in a place where such unconsidered collisions were a long way from remarkable. I found her presence, however surprising, oddly reassuring. She was, after all, the centrepiece of my Christmas and birthday, both. She was all I had of tradition, Winona and her menagerie of damaged creatures. What had become of them, the flightless crows, the lame skunks, the blind foxes? I would worry about them later. I had a job to do.

I sang all the sturdy carols that night, all the tireless warhorses, "Angels We Have Heard on High," and "Away in a Manger," and "Good King Wenceslas," a personal favourite with its three distinct voices that allow the performer to show off his Stanislavskian breadth. I worked hard, purposefully, with fierce focus. By rights, I should have been flagging, but I had slipped the surly bonds of Earth (*cite your source! l.d.*), was more exhilarated than exhausted. Never had I felt so in command of my gift, so authoritative, so fully myself. Finally, we came to "Silent Night," the Serene Queen of All Carols, a balm for troubled minds that I would spin out with my most lilting, gossamer pianissimo.

All is calm, all is bright

I imagined myself a healing oracle, direct from Delphi, up from whose floodlit depths and into the room spilled wave after wholesome wave of song, washing first and foremost over Mrs. Rempel, our darling

Winona, whose flesh slackened, seemed almost to melt, extruding lavishly from the inadequate confines of her stacking chair.

Round yon virgin mother and child.

I invested this text with the nuanced particularity of one whose maternal connection was, even when on its firmest footing, prone to teetering.

Holy infant, so tender –

Winona, beneath her thin blue robe, which had come unfastened, wore her accustomed tent of a nightgown: impossible to say where the faded floral print ended and the stains began.

– and mild,
Sleep in heavenly –

I now observed a vigorous kineticism in the region of her sternum, the heave in heavenly. The nightgown was stirring, pulsing, as though Winona had come by a stripper's talent for isolating movement in her breasts: righty tighty, lefty loosey.

– peace,
Sleep –

I sent Rachel a sideways glance to see if she was taking this in, but she was impervious, her eyes steady on the score. I looked back to Mrs. Rempel who, speedy and deft, hoisted her nightie to reveal two junior suckling raccoons, clinging to her breasts and feeding, as it appeared.

– in heavenly –

Whatever dam restrained the shouldering tides of adolescence gave way. It broke, as did my voice, my treasure, my precious. It was washed away with the flood.

– peace.

It was a baritone rasp that might as well have been a belch. My hitherto unimagined fallibility registered in my knees, cartilaginous liquefaction. Thinking I might faint, I clutched at the piano, its sticky casing the tacky aftermath of so many carelessly placed soft drinks. Rachel's probiotics packed it in; from her gut came the rumble of a passing train. She hit the closing chord hard to compensate for her borborygmus broadcast, misjudged her hand placement: a dissonant clatter. It was an inglorious finale, one for the record books, alongside curtain fires and stage daggers that proved to be the genuine items, and magician's doves that fly into the rafters, there to rain down pigeon shit on the ladies in the stalls. Done. We were done. No further verses were offered, no encores. There were stiff bows, then the attendants corralling the patients, directing them to the exits, shuffle, shuffle, everyone not quite marching to the not-quite-steady, percussive beat of One Man Clapping. I wondered if Winona might linger, but no. She joined the herd. I watched her recede, hoped desperately she'd turn, wave, offer some kind of acknowledgment. She did not.

I packed my music in my leather satchel, upon which were embossed my once-glorious initials, and which also contained the Moleskine devoted to detailed accounts of previous triumphs: dates, places, repertoire, duration of ovation. I kept it with the care and maintenance of future biographers in mind. Rachel buttoned her coat of heather-coloured tweed. Neither of us spoke. We proceeded down halls of scarred linoleum. Photographs of past Presidents of the Board lined the walls. Near the door was a Dantesque vision of the Inferno, a mural in progress someone had been crayoning before being interrupted. In other circumstances, I might have studied it more closely, it had promise. Lingering departures were not in order.

It was raining. We made our mute and squelching way to the glamorous Lougheed Highway. Rachel rumbled and cried all the way to the bus stop. She cried and rumbled all the way home. I peered through the ghostly reflection of my own face in the Plexiglas window. I watched the past tatter and shred. Gone for good was my accustomed means of whoring. What now? A question more thrilling than daunting. It had long been my habit to create a life soundtrack by humming whatever tune matched the moment. I essayed a few measures of "Sixteen Going on Seventeen" from *The Sound of Music*. I sounded like a stalled backhoe. Rain pelted. I imagined myself dashing for cover, taking shelter from the storm in an elegant gazebo, dancing the night away with an attractive Nazi who looked just like Bruce Chatwin. Sprouting hair tickled my armpits.

"Goodbye, Rachel," I said as the bus approached my stop. Those were the first words I'd spoken as a man. My shattered voice was already beginning to reassemble itself, timbre of smoke and walnut; gone for good its lapidary shimmer. Rachel looked aghast, as though I'd popped the buttons on my lambskin and stood before her revealed as a wolf. She reached into her bag. I thought she might be searching out a pearl-handled Derringer, loaded with a silver bullet.

"For you," she said.

She placed into my hands the thank-you gift she had thoughtfully acquired and carefully wrapped, a family-size bottle of imitation maple syrup.

"I thought it might be something you could have with your Christmas-morning p-p-p-p-p-pancakes."

I knew from the look on her face that this was the first time she had ever stammered. I could tell from the lightness that invaded my being that we were now partners, donor and recipient, in a living transplant experiment that surely would have been fodder for many scholarly articles by Gloria Quigley and her ilk.

"Good luck, Rachel," I said.

I descended the bus.

Lana was in bed by the time I got home, resting up for the morning's incredible journey. I wouldn't be available to tell her, at the break of giftless dawn, about Winona's change in circumstances and locale. She would have to discover it for herself, the hard and interesting way. I added Rachel's imitation maple syrup to the hamper. It was nothing I required, not for what I had in mind. I was sweet, and I was sixteen, and I was gone. I never sang, never saw Winona, and never took public transportation again.

🕯 🕯 🕯

Dear Lady Bonnie, not lying over the ocean but sitting at the other end of the bar,

I did, you may or may not care to know, continue to see Lana; caught up with her after a prolonged hiatus. She was the same old monster and it was the same old hell between us, but I came to appreciate, at least a little, some of the underpinnings of her perfidy; to understand some of the slings and arrows that underwrote her paid-in-full membership in the Society of Bad Mommies. She was given more of the shitty end of the stick than anyone deserves, that's the truth of it, and that was her lifelong situation, start to finish, right to the end. I know this, lady Bonnie, for I was there at the end, there with Lana for three excruciating months of deepening monsterhood and mortal uncoiling and she didn't die easy when her time came. All that brutality was fresh in my mind when I made my trip to the public library. I was feeling tender towards her, Lana I mean, and took umbrage on her behalf when I read sainted Gloria's accurate but pitiless assessment of her maternal and domestic inadequacies. She might as well have hiked up her skirts and squatted on her grave. She was my mother, after all, and I bristled to see her laid bare, cut open, all her harridan organs revealed, for the delectation of readers of The Forum of Speech Pathology. *Rosemary. That's what Gloria named her. Rosemary and her baby, poor little C-C-C-Craig! I might have been kinder had dear*

Gloria saddled me with a handle more to my taste. Peregrine, maybe, or Neville. My mother was a monster and yours was a twat. I wanted her punished. The letter I wrote and circulated – to whom it may concern – was masterful, restrained, reasoned, full of damning specifics, incidents, and dates, a memorable synthesis of show and tell. Had it gone only to the school board perhaps nothing would have come of it, they would have circled the wagons, protected one of their own, but copying that crusading reporter was inspired. God bless the fourth estate, especially on a slow news day in August. Once they started sniffing around, there was no stopping it; the wheels of abuse go round and round, all day long. But I think you've probably deduced most of this, Lady Bonnie, you with your phone at the ready. And look, here's Bjorn of the preternaturally shapely ass, a terrible beauty is Bjorn, coming this way, regarding me with what I think I can reasonably interpret as intent, not of the friendly variety, nor is he alone, he's got the manager with him, pigtails are always a mistake in a woman past forty, don't you agree? I suppose she wasn't counting on being seen, she's been in the office, applying herself to holiday schedules, payroll, bonuses, oh, she's a hard-looking woman, she's seen it all, she's not one over whose eyes the wool is easily pulled, there's something about me that's just not right, perhaps it's the velocity of my scribbling, perhaps that last bottle of wine was a mistake, perhaps I've knocked over just one too many glasses, I imagine she's bent on verifying my creditworthiness before she makes a none-too-subtle suggestion about the night and the outside and my place in it and doesn't she have a surprise in store, have yourself a merry little Christmas, Lady Bonnie, and get your camera ready, you'll want to have this on record. See? Here. I take this vessel. I catch your eye. I see you see. I raise a toast. To you and your ma and to my ma, too! There's so much more to say, but it won't be me who's saying it. For now, for forever more, my tongue is t-t-t-tied, my lips are sealed.

☙ ☙ ☙

"Jesus, Nicola Harwood. Holy, holy Jesus."

"Mary and Joseph and the little donkey, too."

It's late. Bonnie's plastered and not done drinking. It's not even two hours since she arrived and Philip has already sacrificed two of the three bottles of Malbec he'd been keeping for Christmas dinner; now he's opened the Estonian liqueur Gloria gave him twenty years ago, a regifting of the duty-free token her neighbours brought back from Tallinn to thank her for cat-sitting.

"I remember this," Bonnie said when Philip dug it out from his cache of earthquake supplies. "She told me, 'I thanked them, of course, I said I was sure it was going to be swell, even though I suspect swill will prove *le mot juste*.' You want to see it again?"

She means the video.

Philip says, "Twice is more than plenty. Did that really happen?"

"Just like you saw. Two hours ago. At Tabula. Who knew a butch number like Bjorn would have so nelly a scream? Jesus."

"Jesus."

"What else is there to say, right? Jesus."

"Jesus. I wonder if dude's okay."

"How could dude be okay? Was dude ever okay? Dude is a major fuck-up."

"I can't believe you tracked him down."

Philip knew nothing about Bonnie's Harriet the Spying. He had no idea she'd scented a trail and followed, no idea she'd spent the evening at Tabula. Philip loves Tabula. He could have been there with her, shared in the adventure. Once, his involvement would have been automatic, a given. Why this exclusion?

"How'd you find him? How'd you get his name?"

"I can't say. It was sordid."

"When did you become someone who shuns admissions of sordidity?"

"That's not even a word."

"Is, bitch."

"Isn't, faggot."

"Is. Anyway, you know what I mean."

The fact is, they've grown apart, not chasm-wide, but still, the distance is discernible. Philip is sad. For so many years they were joined at the hip. Why this dividing? When did it begin? When the Santa Maria came down? When Bonnie left the West End, moved across the creek, took over Gloria's apartment? It's not just Bonnie who's to blame. Philip's grown withholding in his own way, guarded and opaque. He observes his unaccustomed reticence. It unnerves him. Is this what happens to men as the prostate starts to atrophy, the ass to sag, the veins to varicose? Is this part of the same range of symptoms that includes the way he now rises early, goes into Alexander Park and loiters near the heritage bandstand where, next to the sign that forbids feeding pigeons, he feeds the pigeons? He's taken to folding his tea towels into precise squares, to ironing them. He counts his chews. He's named his kettle. He gets lost online doing comparison shopping for bathtub bars. He finds he does, in fact, have a favourite member of the Royal Family, and it's Prince Edward. He hasn't yet walked the labyrinth at the Anglican church, but he thinks he might. He knows the hours. These are not his habits, they belong to a stranger who's slowly but surely moving in, taking over, prescribing the agenda. None of this has he shared with Bonnie; how can he blame her for her maddening discretion?

"I can't say how I found out, Philip. I got his name. I got his address, East Hastings. I started hanging around, asking the locals, trading cigarettes for information. Someone pointed him out as he was coming out of the hotel. What a dump."

Philip exhales Bette Davis ghost smoke. "What a dump."

The old lines are the good lines. Some things never change. A relief.

"That was weeks back. I figured if I just knew what the bastard looked like, I could move on. I thought I had. But I saw him go into Tabula. I followed."

"Then?"

"I sat. I watched, grabbed a few shots. He had this notebook, he was writing like he was taking dictation from the other side. Crazy. Exorcist stuff."

"Automatic writing?"

"Exactly. He was becoming more and more erratic. People were starting to notice. Someone complained. Bjorn got Marcella. That was when –"

Words fail. She activates the video. Philip, over her shoulder, watches pigtailed Marcella approach the bar. The quarry reaches for, as anyone would suppose, his wine glass. In fact, he lays hands on the ample globe in which burns a candle, red for Christmas. For hours it's been weeping, the flame wavering, struggling against the molten tides that wash around it. He looks across the bar, addresses the camera, offers a toast, you can just hear him over the noise, the clatter of the restaurant.

"*Gloria in excelsis!*"

He drinks the lava down. He –

"Enough," says Philip, "turn it off."

He doesn't need to see or hear what happens next. Not again.

"How did you manage to film it?"

"Filming is what I do, remember?"

"But it's as if you were ready. As if you knew."

"Instinct. How did so many people film the towers?"

"What now?"

"Don't know."

"Liar, liar, pants on fire."

"I could post it."

"YouTube?"

"Serve him right."

"Would it? Anyway, they'll take it down."

"It would get enough hits. I'd make my point."

"Which is what, exactly?"

Bonnie shrugs, hoists the Estonian hooch.

"*Gloria in excelsis.* That couch looks good."

"You want to stay?"

"Can I?"

"Since when do you need to ask?"

"Love you madly, Davie Denman."

"Love you right back, Nicola Harwood."

Philip goes to find a blanket, a pillow, pauses to look out at the world. He's seventeen floors up. A gull smashed into his window earlier that day, not the first time this has happened. It didn't end well, it never does – a terrible whack, and then the appalling evidence, the bits of feather and goo that adhere to the pane, still there now despite the steady rain. His building must be on some kind of path, a gull trade route. They're monogamous, yes? Is there some gull spouse wondering what could have happened, nursing a horrible doubt, the grievous wound of unexplained abandonment at Christmastime? Maybe these kamikaze seabirds will find another rendezvous with death when the hulking mass of Three Ships rises up past the seventeenth-storey mark. Philip can't imagine that gulls of the future will fly around it to seek out his window. Who knows? Philip is more conversant with pigeons, whose requirements end with crusts, millet. Time will tell. Soon, the sun will rise on 2020. Should a year of perfect vision not be in store? You'd think. But by June, his view of English Bay, what's left of it, will be utterly gone. It was always going to happen. There was never anything to be done. For years now, it's been getting harder and harder to see what's out there. For years now, it's been getting harder and harder to know what to do.

IN FLESH REVEALING

*"Jim, darling," she cried, "don't look at me that way. I had
my hair cut off and sold because I couldn't have lived
through Christmas without giving you a present."*

—O. HENRY, "THE GIFT OF THE MAGI"

Frances is no joiner. She was on the rolls of the Sierra Club one year.
Her daughter, Marcia, gave her a membership for Christmas. That
was yonks ago. Now, come mid-December, Marcia always sends a
document certifying that a goat has been gifted, in Frances's name, to
an Ethiopian villager; someone who will benefit more from and rise
more readily to the challenges of goat husbandry than will Frances.
As near as Frances knows it's a different villager and a different goat,
every year, she's never read the literature or followed up on the
details. It's enough to imagine that, hundreds of miles in whatever
direction from Addis Ababa, in a dusty outpost, as she supposes,
someone poised to slit a goat throat, someone with kebabs in their
immediate future, pauses long enough to say, "Thank you, Frances.
I wish you could join us."

But Frances is no joiner. Once, to help out a second cousin who
was chasing a riding nomination and needed the signatures of party
members, Frances allied herself with the NDP. She paid a nominal
fee, filled out a form, and that was the extent of her involvement.
Did they provide an ID card, a decoding ring, a cyanide capsule to
take in case of capture by Conservatives? She can't recall. A couple
of times a month, always around 6 p.m., typically when her omelette
is at some pivotal moment in its evolution, someone more loyal to

175

the cause than Frances will phone her up to discuss the socialist agenda, will insinuate that she, Frances, isn't doing as much as she might to ensure the coast remain unblemished by bitumen spills. She still receives in the mail brochures, importunate circulars, or so she imagines; she recycles them, unopened.

Not much else arrives via post anymore. The letter carrier – Frances sometimes catches herself saying "mailman" – passes over her box, as though it's marked by the blood of a lamb. A goat. Whatever. Every second week, from far-off Kingston, come Marcia's hand-written letters, breezy accounts of her busy life detailing all the activities she enjoys with people Frances has never met. She wishes they could simply Skype or FaceTime. Text, even.

"U OK?"

"👍"

"TTYL!"

For most of her friends with adult children – everyone busy, busy, busy – this is sufficient contact, maybe with the booster shot of an annual family getaway at an all-inclusive in Waikīkī.

Marcia stopped emailing after she was seduced by the Slow Food movement and its tenets expanded their influence. Acoustic, unplugged, analog: Frances notes these frequent, cherished bywords cropping up in Marcia's correspondence. "Crop" is germane. Marcia makes her own paper, coarse and grainy, devoutly vegan. Sometimes a word or phrase is smudged or lost when the nib of her fountain pen collides with a blender-resistant fragment of bark or carrot or lentil or whatever other vegetative matter makes the stationery.

"Mom, I hope you're considering complementary therapies. Reiki? Acupuncture? There must be meditation groups you could –"

Indecipherable. Ambush by sinkhole.

Marcia works at Queen's, in the library. She's an assistant bibliographer. Always a joiner – she belongs to a feminist choir, a women's writing collective, a community crumhorn consort – Marcia is also part of a group that safeguards the interests of LGBTQ+ library workers. She's chair of the conference planning committee. She wrote about it, at length, in a letter to Frances.

Frances answers by email, an innovation Marcia can't escape at work.

"Are there actual impediments?" she asks, not confrontational, just in the spirit of inquiry. "In the NHL I could imagine it, but libraries?"

Frances's surmise is that libraries are staffed, also largely patronized, by persons who are tolerant of any expression of human longing, or who simply don't give a cold crap as long as the latest John Grisham is available for borrowing, free of bedbugs, in a reasonable period of time.

"Readiness is all," Marcia answers, by hand, in her next letter. "We must cultivate our allies."

"She has a point, Trix," Frances says. "Are you ready for whatever comes next? Are you still my ally?"

Trix is a Pomeranian. People they meet on their plodding walks ask after Trix's age, then try to calculate what twenty-one is in dog years. Frances keeps her seven-times table well lubricated. Trix is held together by stubbornness and cysts. To pet her is to read a page of Braille. She's blind, she's deaf, she's apparently mute.

"Helen Keller, but on four legs," is how Bonnie recently summed her up. "More flatulent, too."

"Oh, you're terrible," said Frances, thrilled at the irreverence. "Philip, who is this girl you keep bringing around? Why is she so terrible?"

✂ ✂ ✂

When Philip began hanging out with Bonnie, back in high school, Frances never considered it might be a boyfriend/girlfriend thing. She foresaw Philip's charted course long before he took a paper route with the express intention of saving enough money to buy Diaghilev-themed wallpaper. He was seventeen when he called a family meeting to come out. Frances listened calmly and attentively;

she was only surprised when Marcia, three years his junior, burst into tears.

"But so am I," she sobbed. "So am I!"

Frances was quick to offer assurances that it made no difference to her, that hers was a love that would not alter when it alteration found, and et cetera. Nonetheless, Marcia was disconsolate, irrational, pouty, even. Frances guessed she was out of sorts because her claim to an anticipated primacy of specialness had been subverted. Marcia had always been a hoarder; her toilet training was a nightmare. Was same-sex identification a distinction she wanted to cling to uniquely, to claim for herself alone and to manipulate to her particular advantage? Had Philip, not for the first time, stolen her thunder?

"I only want for both of you to be happy," said Frances. "Also, if you can, stay out of prison."

Marcia was impatient with her mother's jokey equanimity, her reflexive default to the dismissive, the flip. She urged Frances to seek counselling, find a parents' support group, march in the Pride Parade. Frances, not a joiner, declined. She's never care for therapy, its guilt-based prescriptions. Against guilt she is, by nature, Kevlar-vested.

"You're in denial," Marcia would say.

"I'm in the kitchen. I'm trying to do the crossword."

When Marcia moved to Kingston, Frances identified her primary response as relief. She felt no guilt. At the oncologist's office, she completed a *Cosmopolitan* questionnaire. Without hesitation, in red ink, she circled "Yes" to the question about preferring one child over the other. Again, no pang; nor did shame or anything like it figure when it was to Bonnie, rather than Philip or Marcia, that she first confided her sad tidings.

"Fuck," said Bonnie, which pretty much summed things up.

"All this time I thought stage IV was an attractive venue at the Folk Festival," said Frances, determined to make light.

✂ ✂ ✂

Frances's first appointment at the clinic was scheduled for Monday morning. She cooked family dinner on Sunday night. Family meant Philip and Bonnie. Dinner meant roast and two vegetables: "hashtag meat-two," Frances had taken to calling it.

"Have I ever told you how I adore the smell of searing flesh?" Frances asked, taking the roast from the oven, patting it, sniffing to test its doneness.

"You're going to love radiation," said Bonnie, because she knew she could. Frances roared. After dessert, she told them she'd made an appointment to have her head shaved.

"Pre-emptive strike."

"When?" asked Bonnie.

"Tomorrow, right after the clinic."

"The dog needs a walk," said Philip.

"She doesn't," said Frances.

"She does."

He woke Trix. They took the elevator to the lobby, stepped outside, didn't stray beyond the porte-cochère. The dog had no need to pee. Philip did. He took advantage of a convenient and concealing gap in the hedge at the building's edge. He'd seen occasional raccoons emerge from it, wondered if they might take this as a territorial challenge. Down came the rain, the November rain. Philip remembered how, as a little boy, his mother would let him brush her hair. He loved the static sparks, loose strands in the bristles, the smell of her shampoo, conditioner, talcum; smell of her scalp, smell of her person. Frances the Unsinkable. Frances the Immutable. Photos from twenty or thirty years ago attested to how age could not wither her, nor custom stale. Her hair was striking, the hair of a woman half her age, thick and long and coal-coloured, shot through sparingly with white. Godiva hair. Rapunzel hair.

Monday, the rain still fell. The wind was strong but indecisive, it seemed to blow from all directions: climate change, the brain-scrambled Gulf Stream, arguing with itself. Frances stood in the lobby, trying to call a cab, the concierge doing the same. Redial, busy. Redial, busy. She watched the water pool on the streets, the sidewalks, water with nowhere left to run, the drains clogged with fallen foliage. She watched the last of the leaves come down. Naked branches. Stripped trees. The day that stretched ahead. The incapacitating surprise of a sob. She breathed in, out. None of that, my lady. None of that. She would break her habit of taking into account the future. She allowed herself to run her hands through her hair, which she had not troubled to pin up. She pulled it till it hurt. Done. Over. She would not go there again.

"No luck," said the concierge.

"Fuck it," said Frances.

She walked.

>< >< ><

Bonnie had arranged to pick her up, to take her from the clinic to the salon.

"Are you up to this?"

"I'm fine. I expect the puking will kick in later."

"Good to have something to look forward to."

Frances knew she ought to keep the volley going. She couldn't. Bonnie turned on the radio. More news of homelessness. Fentanyl. Oil spills. Another recession, Frances couldn't even count how many she'd lived through, it truly was a dismal science. Bonnie turned off the radio.

"I've been thinking."

"About?"

"Your hair."

They were at a red. Bonnie reached, took a strand between her fingers.

"It's beautiful. You can't just let it go."

A honk from behind. Bonnie drove. They were on Broadway. The sun was breaking through the clouds, smashing to smithereens the bathetic pleasures of pathetic fallacy.

"What do you have in mind, lovey?"

"I've got this friend, Patti, she's in the industry."

"As?"

"A wigmaker."

"Oh."

"I talked to her last night. I asked her if she could help you out."

"Help me?"

"Come on, Frances, you know what I mean. You're not going to want to go around all bald and vulnerable, and there's nothing worse than a nasty wig."

Frances knew there was nothing to be gained from reciting a long litany of worse.

"So why put up with synthetic crap when you can have your own gorgeous hair, your own colour? It's not cheap, but I'd like to do it for you. A gift."

Bonnie was parallel parking, making a mess of it.

"What else?"

Frances loved Bonnie and knew that Bonnie loved her back, and she didn't think Bonnie's love was tainted, just because it was conditional.

"I'd like to film it. The shaving. The wig. The fitting. Make a documentary."

"But the shaving is now."

"That's why I'm asking."

"What about equipment? A camera, microphones? A crew? A grip?"

Frances had no idea what a grip was or did, but she knew one was required. She always sat through the credits.

"Welcome to the new century, baby," said Bonnie, palming her phone.

Frances waited in the car while Bonnie dealt with the meter. She thought about how her image would be digitized, edited, dispersed. She thought about how her scalp, which she was about to meet for the first time, would be revealed in razor-wide increments to who knew how many strangers, tens of thousands, maybe more, people who might be drinking tea or knitting or fucking or making sandwiches. She thought about her hair, which she had imagined might be turned over to a bird sanctuary for the building of nests, or composted, or summarily tossed out. But this? To preserve it? To follow it along?

"I know it's a big ask, Frances. I know."

Bonnie, Bonnie. Was she already fantasizing the plaudits? *Tender, yet hard-edged. Honest. Revealing. Unforgettable. Pure joy to watch.* Was she forecasting nominations, ceremonies, acceptance speeches? Would she acknowledge Frances, the woman without whom? Would it be a posthumous nod? Would she press Philip to show it at the funeral? No. Celebration of Life. An urn, an organ, a giant flat screen. Thank God she wouldn't be there.

"If you say no, Frances, I'll totally get it. I won't mention it again."

Maybe it was the first blush of chemo brain; Frances couldn't say. From nowhere, spurred on by who knows what synaptic firing, rose an image of her father, thirty years dead, running across the beach at Dunkirk, staggering through the sand, men dying all around him, the blood, the screaming, the confusion, the stupidity: bullets, bullets, bullets everywhere in the air, everywhere except where he was. He was in her mind. He was gone. Where he'd been was a deep, strange, inexplicable calm, dark as a shell hole.

"Go ahead, Bonnie. Just go ahead."

✂   ✂   ✂

When Gary left, moved back to Brandon to look after his mother, when he declared that it wasn't for the short term, that he wouldn't be returning, Philip decided to make some changes. He'd been miserable in his work as a convention organizer, didn't want to spend the rest of his days ricocheting from minor crisis to minor crisis, sucking back the smell of chicken or salmon, listening to after-dinner speeches of dubious quality on unsound sound systems. Frances helped him out with a loan, the generosity of which was duly noted by Marcia, who filed it away for future reference. He took a lease on a storefront in Gastown, on a street that was already well gentrified.

A Killing Curiosity is a seemingly random but carefully curated jumble of antiques, gilded dross, latter-day kitsch: a magpie mess of Dickensiana. The shop, open now for three years, has been a big success, especially at Christmastime. Philip has an assistant, Edie Fischer. Edie is odd, but Philip likes her, so does Frances who, as the season ramps up, when the volume is too much for two to handle, lends a hand.

"Are you sure you're up to it this year?" Philip asks her when she appears, unbidden, ready to do what she can do.

"Why would I stay at home when I have all these lovely scarves to show off?"

She and Bonnie had gone hog-wild at Holt Renfrew. Bonnie, a shameless vicarious shopper, had urged Frances on; she's a Hermès poster girl now.

"You'll take it easy."

"I'll be fine," Frances says. "I'll be fine."

She putters. She dusts. She chats. She helps Edie put clown noses on the snouts of two mounted stag heads that stare balefully from either end of the store. She gives directions to tourists, advises them on what not to miss, on where to eat. Woman after woman takes her measure – the scarf, the pallor – then lets it be known that she, too, has pulled her term, done her time, come through it. Survival is not impossible, far from it; what are good outcomes but a hybrid of luck and determination and maintenance? Survival belongs to those who keep their appointments at the clinic, and who also manage to be somewhere other than in the path of the bullets when they come zinging through. It's that simple and that unlikely.

                          ✂   ✂   ✂

On that first day back on the job, Frances arrives just before noon.
Edie goes for lunch. Frances spells her off. Edie returns. There's a
lull. Frances, never one for idleness, goes to check out the storeroom
where there's always something that needs tending to.

"What on earth?"

A catastrophe of boxes.

"That pawnshop on Main went belly-up," says Philip, who's
followed her in; he watches her every move, it's driving Frances
crazy; she feels like a Samoan under the surveillance of Margaret
Mead. "I got it as a case lot, on spec. Lord knows what's in them."

"Potluck."

"Exactly."

"One way to find out."

Frances locates a blade. She sets to. Someone has labelled the
cartons with a blue-felt marker, neatly but with no regard for accuracy.
In the box marked "Jewellery," she finds a collection of paperbacks,
guitar picks, also strings, possibly for a banjo, as well as a mouthpiece
for something brassy, a trumpet or French horn. A euphonium? Her
first serious boyfriend played the euphonium in the school band. He
was given to talking way, way, way more than was necessary about
how a euphonium was no more a baritone than a trumpet was a
cornet. He was a bore, but a terrific kisser.

In "Misc. Bike Parts," Frances discovers a silver-plated Buddha
incense holder she knows will move quickly. Alongside, wrapped in a
page from the *Vancouver Sun*, 1955, she finds a bronze door knocker
in the shape of a hand, a piece of real weight and substance. The
day doesn't go by during the ramp-up to Christmas that someone
doesn't come in looking for a door knocker, typically having seen
or read *A Christmas Carol*.

Frances gasps, says, "Jesus save us," when one box, upon which is a
crude sketch of a warning skull, proves to contain several photograph
albums. On every page is a snap of a man with a bearish pelt of chest

hair, grinning maniacally while demonstrating the several stages of self-abuse. Someone she knows knew such an exhibitionist once. Who? No matter. They're gag-making, bound for the incinerator.

In "Etc., Etc." – Frances senses the interest of the packer beginning to wane – she finds clocks and watches, most in states of disassembly, a few intact, none in working order. There's a variety of tools plainly intended for fine, patient tinkering; Frances supposes they have some horological significance. Inside the box is a tidy regiment of purpose-built containers into which have been sorted the cogs, the flywheels, the springs a watchmaker could probably name. One has cracked. Its slight freight is strewn about the box bottom. So minuscule, so light. Like taking seeds from a packet to pick them up.

"Oh," says Frances, when she makes contact with something more substantial, a silver watch chain for which the delicate guts were a kind of camouflage. "What have we here?"

Frances is no connoisseur, but she knows quality when she sees it. Substance. Consistency. No reliance on the showy, the gaudy. No weak links. She holds it up. She lets the diffuse pewter light from the storeroom's one window fall upon it. It draws her in, exerts a mesmeric tug. Perhaps it had once belonged to a hypnotist. Watch the watch. You are getting sleepy, sleepy. Frances winds the chain around her left wrist; she's lost weight, it takes three turns for her to complete the circling. She feels a mini-rush of vertigo, a slight numbing of her extremities. Nothing unusual, now. Perhaps she should sit. A short rest. One more, then she'll call it quits. Because the handwriting is different from the script on every other box, and for every other reason that's easy to discern, "Wigs" snags her attention.

The box disgorges a puff of dust, mould, sweat. Something else, particular in its sourness. Disappointment? Despair? The wigs sigh as a group, rise up slightly, as might a genie, long compressed, contemplating an exit from the bottle. All those inanimate curls, red, raven, auburn, blond, undulatory, responsive to the currents from the overhead fan, put Frances in mind of the specimen case where her uncle, an entomologist, displayed his tropical exotics.

Frances hasn't disclosed to Bonnie, nor could she ever reveal to Patti, that she, Frances, is wig-averse. Not paralyzingly so. They give her the creeps, that's all. Spiders, snakes, clowns, heights – to such run-of-the-mill triggers she's indifferent. Wigs, however, stir up the murk. She's steeled herself against the eventual delivery of her own reconstituted hair. She'll try it on, exclaim happily "Frabjous day," smile for the camera, serve some tea, some biscuits, endure whatever social exigencies the occasion requires, bid everyone a fond farewell, remove the horrible hank, store it, never wear it again. She can put up with hairlessness. It's temporary. After three months of drug-enforced baldness, the drought will end. The crop will sprout. Regeneration will occur. It will be glorious.

Now, in this moment, alone in the storeroom – the afternoon sun angles through the high, barred window, charmingly illuminating a wide wedge of dust motes – she feels no curiosity about trying on one of the pieces that threaten to spill from the box, odoriferous, surely in need of a disinfecting spray: this platinum fall from grace, or this ash-blond sticky bun, or this big-banged Bond girl number. Her phone alerts her to an incoming text. Philip.

"U good?"

"🐱," she replies, not the emoji she intended. It reminds her of how her first-born, her only son, had a cat pyjama bag he loved more than anything. That was when he was five, when her marriage seemed solid, when they had the big house in MacKenzie Heights. One day, in a fit of pique stirred up by Frances can't recall what imagined slight – something to do with baby Marcia, probably – Philip ran away from home. He packed a few of his most cherished belongings, mostly stuffed toys, into that cat bag – its lining was quilted, she now recalls, and pink. He demonstrated a practical streak in his choice of a can opener, which he'd added to his stash anticipating that hunger would track him down before the police did. He'd taken no tins of food. Perhaps he trusted in the lord to provide. From her purse, Philip helped himself to twenty-two dollars. There was more to take. When Frances eventually inquired why he'd swiped so specific an amount, he allowed that twenty-two was the upper limit of his ability to count. To take more seemed folly. He wanted to be able to keep track. Once the trip was funded, Philip selected a going-away outfit. To judge by the state of her closet, he'd tried on pretty much everything before settling on his Winnie-the-Pooh pyjamas and the fox stole (head intact, grim rictus of a snarl) that had been her mother's. This he accessorized with a pair of chunky bracelets, along with many colourful strands of costume jewellery beads: Cleopatra at the five and dime. He teetered out of the house in a pair of pumps with three-inch heels. The crowning touch was a hat, also her mother's, black, with a veil, only ever worn for funerals. Who knows how far he might have travelled, thus arrayed, had he not been distracted by a yard sale two doors down? He forgot all about whatever it was that had so annoyed him.

"He spent a real long time browsing," said the neighbour, who brought him home. "This was what he chose."

It was a plaster bust from the 1940s, a woman with finely chiselled features, incarnadine lips, bald: Veronica Lake with alopecia. It was intended for the display of wigs in windows.

"I'm so sorry," said Frances, mortified, trying desperately not to guffaw. "Did he steal it?"

This was before she knew about his cash grab.

"Oh, no," said the neighbour, a friendly fellow called Conrad. "He insisted on paying more than we were asking. He gave me twenty-two dollars. I brought it back, of course. He's a strange little boy, isn't he?"

"Who," said Frances, "Philip? No. I don't think so."

They laughed and laughed, Philip too, though he didn't understand why or at what. Conrad thought the whole business was hilarious. He always brought it up whenever they'd meet at the market. It's a story Frances loved to tell, Philip likewise.

Conrad insisted Philip keep his purchase: a gift. He has it still – the ur-bust, the mother of them all. Many others have been acquired in the intervening decades: busts, dress dummies, mannequins entire and members of mannequins. Much can be accomplished with a foot, a hand, an arm. A shapely rubber leg, Philip knows, can solve problems of decor that haven't yet been articulated. Much of the collection had been relegated to a rented locker; now, it's migrated to the store. The dummies earn their keep modelling vintage jackets, skirts, jewellery. Those not presently in service linger in the storeroom, attending eventual deployment; Philip, a kinder, gentler Bluebeard, has locked them away. They peer down from every corner, all those bald, unblinking ladies. Frances imagines them wondering what she's discovered in the box she grasps before her, what she stares at, transfixed. As if in reply to their collective curiosity, the better for them to see, she turns it over, gives it a shake. Out tumble the wigs, more fledglings than so small a nest could reasonably have accommodated.

A barometric shuffle. Frances feels it more than she hears it, a whoosh of air as if from a collective gasp of wonder, expectation. Wigs! Wigs! So many wigs! There must be enough for every bald lady in this room, wouldn't you say? Frances feels her dials adjusted. Static resolves into a plangent chorus.

"Now or never, lady."

"You know you want to."

"Just do it."

She does. She bends, a gleaner in a Flemish painting, gathers up the scattered pieces, begins disbursing them, a relief worker, a bald lady benefactor, placing, patting, fussing, shaping, getting them all just so. A triumph. Everyone taken care of.

"Gorgeous," says Frances, "all of you gorgeous."

Some instinct prompts her to look down. On the floor, half-wrapped around the base of an old bird cage, curled like a cobra, is a winding, black plait. Frances bends again, examines, strokes it with her finger. It doesn't stir. She picks it up. Oh! A cut above. Here was difference. Weight. Thickness. Lustre. This was not some petroleum-based facsimile. This, for sure, was the real thing.

"Now or never, lady."

"You know you want to."

"Just do it."

Not even Frances, with her disdain for wigs; not even Frances, who's no joiner, can withstand this persuasive gathering into community. She does as bidden. There's a Venetian mirror hanging next to a dartboard. Frances looks at Frances. Frances is gone.

✂   ✂   ✂

When Philip was eighteen, just out of high school, he went through a drag phase. It was short-lived. Frances was glad. She didn't want to be the one to tell him that no matter how partial he was to show tunes, he would always have a fullback's shoulders. Some of the friends Philip made during that brief rhinestone immersion went on to become the city's busiest female impersonators. They often pop by A Killing Curiosity to sift through the new arrivals, to see what might be adapted to stagecraft purpose. Philip has learned to be careful about what he discloses on social media. Only once did he make the mistake of digitally crowing about the spectacular bin of showgirl castoffs, just arrived, now on offer. There was a stampede of takers. No one could remember the last time Princess Wanda Getyerocksoff and the Countess of Monte Crisco had been seen in the same room. Casual shoppers, lay people, received an education they might not necessarily have chosen on just how mean-spirited rival drag queens can be when what's in contention is a peach-coloured boa with Vegas bona fides.

On this particular afternoon, when Frances is in the storeroom, transfixed by her own reflection, it's Allen Feldman, a.k.a. Amber Flashing, who stops in for a look-see. In the past, as a friend and regular, he's been allowed to investigate the nether reaches of the storeroom without adult supervision. Both Philip and Edie are busy with customers when he arrives. Rather than interrupt or, heaven forbid, wait; unable to imagine being denied access, and without announcing himself or asking permission, he enters.

"What the hell?" says Edie, when a scream ricochets through the store.

Philip assumes – why would he not, given the high soprano – his mother is in distress.

"The storeroom," he yells, which is where they both dash. Allen is teetering on a chair, as might a maiden of old, startled by a mouse, clutching in his hand a plaited wig. Frances is dazed, confused, in need of a tall glass of water, which Edie fetches.

"Oh, Jesus," says Allen, by far the most upset of the two, "I'm so sorry, I had no idea anyone was in here. Your back was to the door, you were so still, I supposed you were one of the mannequins, I just thought, 'Yes, perfect, that's the one, that's the wig I need,' so I helped myself."

"I don't believe we've properly met," says Frances, gathering herself, extending her hand, noticing how the silver watch chain is blood warm, how it grips her like a tendril vine or snake. She takes it from her wrist, but doesn't return it to the box. She puts it in her pocket.

✂   ✂   ✂

Later on, after supper, Philip calls Frances. He talks to her every night on the phone; she's tried Skype, can't abide it, can't stand the fuss of looking put together just to shoot the breeze. Philip gives her the lowdown on how what happened happened. Allen is adding Cher to his formidable cast of divas. He'd come to the store for accessories, sequined halter tops, platform shoes, the oddities Philip often had in stock. That was what he was after when he discovered Frances in the subfusc demi-gloom. He saw the wig. Perfection! He pulled. He screamed.

"Tell me he bought it at least," says Frances.

"You can see it for yourself tonight at the club."

"Perhaps not."

"I support that decision."

"How did he look? In the wig, I mean."

"Like a million bucks. I only wish he'd paid that much."

"And how did he seem?"

"Seem?"

"In the wig. Did he seem, you know, all right? Himself?"

"I think so."

"Good."

"Mom. You okay?"

"Smiley-face emoji."

"Sure?"

"Yes. Dozy. Meds. Are you coming for dinner tomorrow?"

"Is it Sunday?"

"Yes."

"Then I'm coming for dinner."

"There may be meat."

"That'll be novel. I'm asking one last time. You're okay?"

"I'm fine, Philip. I'm going, now. Trix needs her walk. I'm fine."

✂   ✂   ✂

Frances told Philip she was fine. Frances was fine. Fine is how Frances will be, for a time. Frances will know fine, then the winnowing of fine for another Christmas, maybe two. She will outlive Trix. No one, not about the dog, nor about Frances, when her time comes, will be able to say, "Too young, too soon."

Early in the new year, Frances will take delivery of the wig. She will follow her plan, meticulously laid out, carefully rehearsed; will coo her compliments, suppress the impulse to push it away. The niceties still come when she whistles, so she will make the ingratiating noises decency dictates she must. What else could she do with Patti so pleased and proud and with Bonnie filming, filming, stopping to adjust lights, asking for retakes, telling them to just go about their business as if she weren't there? Frances will be a good little actress. It's all she can do. She could have said no at the outset. She didn't. Weak moments are not inconsequential. She gave in to

Bonnie, acceded to her request, let her film the shaving. The very next day, the chemo poisons asserting themselves, Frances sat in her dining room with Patti – Bonnie filming, filming – and leafed through many binders replete with photos, samples. It was like going to the tile store to choose a kitchen backsplash. Bonnie had gathered up Frances's long hair, removed it from the salon in a green plastic garbage bag. This she upended on the table; it was like wool gathered up from the shearing room floor, raw, uncarded. Frances, woozy from the anti-nausea meds, tried to concentrate while Patti explained what would happen next, how it would be gathered, treated, sculpted, styled. All those fallen tresses – cold and dead, coiled and feral – piled in an ungodly centrepiece, Martha Stewart channelling Jack the Ripper. Bonnie came in for closeups whenever one or the other would pick up a strand, examine it as they considered a range of stylistic options. Frances couldn't shake the feeling that she was assisting at her own autopsy.

Come Wig Day, Frances will summon all her positivity, as Marcia likes to say. She offered no resistance when Patti suggested the shape of cut on which they'd settled, a kind of suits-all-occasions do. What drugs was she on? Were "sapping of common sense" or "aesthetic neutering" listed side effects? Why would she have given her consent to something that, no matter the skill of the artisan, could only ever resemble a failed meringue? How will it be possible for the thing to seem so foreign in sight, smell, feel; how possible for something, the raw materials of which originated with her own body, to hit so discordant, so jarring a sensory note? For Patti's sake, for Bonnie's too, she will be convincing on camera, won't spoil the moment of revelation, the tear-jerking climax of the documentary, by looking askance or laughing out loud. By setting a match to the thing. She won't want to get in the way of Bonnie's chances for success, nor will she be ashamed if she herself, Frances, is invited to attend the occasional film festival. It's possible, after all. People love to gawk at the dying. She imagines audiences, having seen her on stage at post-screen Q and As, leaving the theatre, saying, "You'd never guess she only has months to live."

"I know! She looks fine, just fine."

Frances is fine. She will go on being fine long enough to understand that she never had cause for worry, alarm, or hope. This project, like so many Bonnie undertakes, will never be completed. Bonnie will get distracted by some more lucrative, shorter-term, less quixotic assignment. Someone else's venture. Something Bonnie doesn't have to manage. Frances will be just as glad. She loves Bonnie for her hopelessness as much as for anything else. When her own hair grows back she'll start wearing it in a sensible cut not unlike the one Patti designed for her.

Sometimes, when Frances wakes from one of the afternoon naps that will become ever more routine, a cooling cup of Darjeeling on her bedside table, perhaps Marcia's latest testament spread out on the duvet, the paper smelling ever so slightly like her crisper drawer, she will see Patti's wig; see it on her vanity table, warming the skull of the mannequin head Philip will give her for just this purpose of display, will give to her at Christmas, the same bust he purchased for twenty-two dollars almost fifty years ago. Was that the only time he stole from her? As near as she knows. She could ask, but never will. She might feel compelled to confess her own minor larceny, not a theft so much as a long-term borrowing. The silver chain is in the drawer of her bedside table, along with the vibrator Bonnie gave her years ago when she was researching a documentary (never made) on women's sex toys and which Frances used only once to try, unsuccessfully, to coax egg whites to hold a stiff peak. The Femme Fun Ultra Bullet, with twenty vibration modes, startled her awake one night when, obedient to some occult impulse, it took its own purpose to heart and "turned itself on." Frances found it bouncing and rattling around the narrow confines of the drawer like an animate, freedom-striving sausage in a half-remembered story from the Brothers Grimm. She removed the batteries and lay awake all the rest of the night, wondering what was wrong with her life that she couldn't think of one single person she could decently call, never mind the hour; no one with whom she could share this inexplicable turn of events, perhaps the funniest thing that had ever befallen her. It's a story she'll take to her grave, soon enough. Soon enough, her things will be inconveniences to be gone through, argued over. She wonders who will find the vibrator, Philip or Marcia? What will they make of it, and of the lovely chain? She has considered attaching a note to the latter requesting it go to Allen Feldman. Would he understand that he was to wear it in tandem with the wig? Would it complete the circuit for him as it had for her? Perhaps he'd enjoy the Bullet too; let him have it if so.

It will happen that, when suspended halfway between waking and dreaming, Frances will catch a glimpse, fleeting, of the eye that opened for her that afternoon in the gloom of the storeroom, the eye that invited her in, offered her a chance at belonging, at absorption; a chance to which, she had felt in the moment, she might possibly accede. Frances will conjure that wide, infinite eye in whose returned regard she had been able to see every woman from every age who, for whatever reason, whether for good or ill, whether out of whim or necessity, whether willingly or under duress, had sacrificed or surrendered or been stripped of her hair. She saw them all, all the members of that strange communion – the victim, the survivor, the outraged; heard the murmur of their voices, their unique stories, felt the warmth of their individual exhalations, the welcoming, spacious expanse of their millions of opening arms. Felt the intricacy of their braiding. She saw in that moment that they were no less than the total sum of history, all of it, from the first grunts of recorded time on: not the history of record, but the history of the lost, which is the history that will embrace her, too. Soon. She understood. It gave her great comfort, this joining she might willingly, even joyfully, undertake. She looked the eye in the eye. She saw her end, in all its enormity, all its insignificance. She understood it all, even though she would keep nothing of it but the tiniest grain to hold, to ponder in her heart.

"I'm fine," Frances tells Philip on the phone, testing the elasticity of truth. Come the morning, after a decent night's sleep, fine is indeed how she'll feel. She'll rise early. She'll get to the shop by opening time. She'll put in a full, busy day. Now, in bed, she imagines Allen Feldman, backstage at the club, at Celebrities, immersed in the Ovidian business of turning himself into Amber Flashing. He'll be shaving his chest stubble, tucking up his genitals, taping them to his well-waxed inner thigh, squeezing himself into a bustier, attaching his new extension, strutting about fearlessly in six-inch spikes. What will he sing? Something new? Will Amber cover Cher covering Abba? Or something classic? "Gypsies, Tramps & Thieves"? She bears him no grudge, regrets only that the spell was broken, that she was pulled back from a place she would gladly have stayed forever. She feels like a foreigner now in the element to which she's confined, transported there unwillingly, a mermaid hauled to the deck in a net of herring.

Frances thinks of that place.

She wants it again.

She wants it now.

In the oncologist's waiting room, in *Redbook* or *Marie Claire*, Frances had more than enough time to read a long article about how dreams can be controlled through post-hypnotic suggestion. What was the term? "Lucid dreaming." That's right. She floods her mind with the assurance that that place, so accidentally achieved, is not lost to her, that she can have it, that it will come to her, that she will have the leisure to linger, that she'll find a way to take it all in, to keep it, live in it, yet not combust or explode.

Frances will sleep. Frances will wake. Frances will feel fine, just fine, but disappointed, too. Let down. All her retentive resolutions will have been for naught. She'll have no memory of the dream in which she, Frances, is a rib, drawn from the side of Cher; a rib that's passed, unassailed, through a torrent of bullets, into the hands of God, who is a goat, around whose waist is tied an impressive silver

chain, no watch attached. For Frances, the atheist, God, the goat –
indiscriminately ravenous, timeless, capricious – had something
particular and unexpected in mind. The what of it, the why of it, the
when and the how and the all of it she'll have seen and known, but
none of it will glimmer in memory. No matter. The planet will spin
without undue wobbling and Frances will make another journey,
maybe two, around the sun, and for most of what remains of her
time on Earth, she will be fine, just fine. For Frances, as for all God's
children, whether bonded or estranged, fine, just fine, is more than
enough. It is, as it turns out, plenty.

SIN ERROR PINING

We know this world is good enough
Because it has to be.

—JOHN K. SAMSON, "WINTER WHEAT"

Every Sunday afternoon, during the years of his Western Exile –
as now he thinks of them, not with as much irony as you might
expect – Gary's mother, a waste-not, want-not daughter of the Great
Depression, indulged in the extravagance of long-distance. Jean would
lift the heavy Bakelite receiver of the phone that a well-mannered
fellow from the Manitoba Telephone System had attached to her
kitchen wall, in Brandon, in 1956. She listened with satisfaction to
the dependable tone, then rotary-dialled the eleven digits inscribed
in her "Wheat City Co-op Phone and Address Book" under G, for
Gary. Jean checked each number, including the obligatory 1, before
she committed herself to it. You could never be too careful. Errors
were costly, costlier even than operator-assisted person-to-person,
from which obligation Jean had weaned herself, in the name of
economy, after taking a free continuing-education night course in
modern telephonics at the local community centre.

"Whoever could it be?" Philip would crow when the phone
brayed in their Broughton Street apartment, always on the dot, at
1:07 (Pacific Time), 3:07 (Central Time). The timing allowed for
the possibility that Gary had attended church, attended the IHOP,
listened to the CBC Radio news: a Godly Canadian Sunday, as Jean
had demonstrated to Gary, by way of unfailing example, all the years
of his growing up.

Anyone meeting Jean now would quickly name her as a conscript in the army of the addled. Back then, during the epoch of the unholy interregnum, when her son had fallen under the spell of the Magus of the Pacific Northwest, she was nobody's fool. She knew very well that her weekly call was as dreaded as it was expected, knew that it would be Gary's friend – she preferred "roommate" – Philip who would pick up. Eventually. In his own good time. Philip the Spoiler. Philip the Instigator. Philip the Weasel. Jean imagined him rolling his eyes. It hurt her to think of her son smiling conspiratorially. Let them have their fun. It was to be expected. Gary wasn't young, exactly, but nor was he yet so long in the tooth that he would have extinguished the burner upon which simmered the possibility of filial insurgence.

Jean listened while the phone in far-off Vancouver rang and rang. She tried not to imagine the room in which they sat, her boy with his corruptor. The mustard-coloured walls that mimicked something they'd seen in a design magazine. The abstract geometries of the paintings, primitive, a child could do them. Flowers, flowers, flowers everywhere, fussily arranged. Dolls' heads displayed on shelves, on the mantel, the most trivial kind of whimsy. All those mannequins. Grotesque. Horrible. Affected. She had never visited but she had seen it in the photographs they used for their Christmas cards, the two of them cuddling on a love seat that looked as uncomfortable as it was impractical – prone to staining, hard to clean. Ring, ring, ring. Jean used her time constructively, checking her calendar for the week to come, noting dental and hair appointments, making grocery lists. She was annoyed, but not overly concerned, by a delay she knew to be an artless contrivance. She had worked diligently on the mixing and pouring of her child's foundation, improvising on the formulas prescribed by Dr. Spock. She was certain the masonry would hold, withstand any shifting of the ground. There was never any doubt, certainly not in her mind, about who would triumph in a tussle for Gary's loyalties; about whether, when it counted at the ballot box, he would ink his X for Blood or Water. All she had to do was withstand, to endure the notion, implanted by Philip – carelessly, imperfectly – that she, Jean – pursed, prudish, recalcitrant – merited punishment, censure, resistance. Bring it on. She knew how to take it. She was in it for the long term. Philip was a trifler, good for short spurts, not built to last the distance.

"One ringy-dingy. Two ringy-dingy."

Philip did a top-drawer impersonation, really killing, of Lily Tomlin as the switchboard operator Ernestine. He would count out a whole octave of ringy-dingies before picking up, cooing, "Good afternoon, thank you for calling the Friendly Giant Sauna for Gentlemen of Adequate Style and Ample Dimensions. To which of our esteemed clientele may I direct your call?"

"This is Jean Bruce speaking."

Philip switched to his civilian voice.

"Hi, Jean, how are you? This is Philip, we've spoken before. Often. As recently as last week, in fact."

"I'm calling long-distance from Brandon, Manitoba. I'm holding on the line for Gary Bruce."

"I'm fine, too, Jean, thanks for asking. Just a moment. I'll see if he's available ... Ga-a-a-a-r-r-y! It's for you, darling!"

This went on for years. Not once did Jean rise to his bait. Not once did she acknowledge Philip by name, accord him the status of anything other than inconvenient intermediary. Few people under the age of fifty can accommodate how such mutual, willful torment, such passive-aggressive grandstanding, was not only practised but was usual. This was not so long ago, not in the overarching scheme of things. It remains, for many who continue to walk upright, more or less, the stuff of pixilated, living memory.

☎   ☎   ☎

Weldon Bedford joined the church choir when he was thirty. He was anxious about the future, unexpectedly full of dynastic longings. Weldon was of a mind to marry. He had been told, by people whose judgment he didn't discount, that he had a pleasant tenor voice. Also, he'd heard from a friend at work, who had a friend who had a friend for whom this strategy had paid off, that a church choir was a first-rate place to find a wife. Church choirs, he was given to understand, were magnets for women who were sprinting towards spinsterhood and were possessed, as was Weldon, of procreative urges, but had no peg upon which to hang them.

That was nearly sixty years ago. Now, Weldon verges on ninety. He's still single. The closest he came to the erasure of bachelorhood was an episode involving a choir party, some spiked punch, and a willing alto. Willing, so he wants to believe. These days, with so much in the news about women and men, about power and consent, he wonders if he might have been the unfeeling agent of trauma. Did he press his advantage? His memory is foggy. He'd thought the punch was fruit juice and soda, nothing more; he'd spent a long time at the trough. Well. They both had, that was the truth. Something hasty and secretive and grabby happened between them. It left Weldon feeling queasy. He couldn't look at Ginny after that, nor could he bring himself to enter the closet that contained the Sunday School craft supplies, as well as the stacks of decommissioned hymnals they managed to topple. It beggared belief, really, how much clutter they kicked up in that narrow space, in not quite five minutes.

Ginny was a nurse. She moved to Victoria more than forty years ago. Had she fled west because she couldn't bear the constant reminder of what had taken place? Perhaps. Afterwards, Weldon himself had felt pretty, well, roughed up. She was younger by ten years, at least; that she was still alive seemed likely. Someone would have heard if she'd passed, there would have been an obit in the paper, some mention made in the choir column of the church newsletter. He wonders if he should write to her, explain himself as best he might. Apologize, if an apology is in order. Is it? His grandmother, who raised him, would have said, "If you think you should maybe say sorry, there's really no maybe about it." His grandmother, had she known any of the details of what had happened with Ginny, would have told Weldon he had no choice, only an obligation.

"You marry that girl," she would have said. "You make things right."

Weldon's troubling session with Ginny scotched his marriage aspirations. It didn't change his feelings for the choir, though. That attachment deepened. In the sixty years he's been a mainstay of the tenor section, Weldon has never once missed a rehearsal or a performance – a fact much marvelled at by other choir members, by all the church congregants, really. His reliability has been occasionally reported, on a slow news day, in the community press; once, even, in *The Brandon Sun*.

☎ ☎ ☎

Gary is an only child, his mother a single parent. Jean had been married, of course, happily so. All things being equal she'd be married still, married to her beloved Callum. Equal, though, is not how all things were. Callum died in childbirth.

Jean is persuaded she saw it happen but has never been able to bring herself to speak of it. How could she? Her recollections, vividly detailed, make no sense; Jean has always valued sense above all. Well. That was true until a few years back when she set sense down, somewhere along the way, then wandered off, forgot all about it, left it yipping helplessly like a puppy in a hot car.

What Jean remembers – remembered reliably, prior to the perforating of her powers of recall, but these days, can only summon up in fragments – was that her time had come; the baby was on the way. They'd driven to the hospital in their powder-blue Studebaker, Callum steady, calm at the wheel, Jean in the passenger seat beside him, nauseated but elated. They were separated the moment she was admitted. She was stripped, shaved, gowned. She was battened down, taken into a room that was too cold, too bright. They gave her something to allay the waves of pain, something to make her sleep. Jean didn't want to sleep. Everything in her nature told her she needed to be alert, she needed to be able to fight, needed every available animal resource. But the doctors knew what the doctors knew, the nurses likewise. This was their business. There was no need for her to suffer, it wasn't the modern way: lie back, lie back, no point struggling, give in, give in.

What she remembers – until recently she would have been the first to acknowledge this was a fabrication, how could it have been otherwise? – is that she became unmoored, slipped outside her own flesh, that the essential part of herself – she does not want to risk impiety by calling it her soul, though that is what she believes it to have been – hovered, no gauzy cloud but an invisible gas, above the table. She saw the doctor waiting with his forceps, like some kind of barbecue accessory. One of the nurses lit a cigarette, blew smoke rings into the air. Jean, abstemious, tobacco-averse, was offended; even so, she felt herself more at one with those acrid exhalations than with anything made of sinew, blood, bone. It seemed impossible to her, to conscious Jean, released from the constraints of gravity, that unconscious Jean, laid out like a specimen for anatomizing, would be able to do what Jean would need to do to make what had to happen happen, to expel her burden, to transfer her passenger from the aqueous to the terrestrial. But she was powerless just when power was most required. The mere understanding of her needlessness was enough to give her a hallway pass. As though in reply to an urgent call, she passed through the walls of the operating theatre, its dry-mouth plaster, its tickling circuitry, out into the waiting room where she collided, as though in a midway bumper car, for an incalculably brief, heated moment with the soul – that was surely the word – of her husband, Callum, as it departed the world. He was there and gone, as real, as rapid as a speeding car's headlight passing through the window at night. Jean looked down, observed the clay of her mate, saw Callum akimbo on the floor, noted the six celebratory cigars scattered round about. Cigars! Of all things! Why six? The expense! And for whom were they intended? The one other expectant father, who had been dozing, startled awake. He bellowed for help, help. Needless shouting. Callum had passed beyond aid. An aneurysm. A soft spot in the brain. Cerebral hemorrhage. Snuffed in a heartbeat. Catastrophic failure. Gone for good.

Back in the delivery room, despite the drugs, despite the straps, Jean arched, screamed. The gore-caked baby emerged with the violent insistence of a rodeo bull goaded into an arena.

"Son of a biscuit eater," said the smoking nurse, grinding out her butt on the terrazzo floor, rushing for sponges, for sutures, for scissors to cut the cord.

Just a few metres away from this busy scene, a young resident checked Callum for a pulse. He shook his head, already sensing how this tragic turn of events, so gothic, so unforeseen, contained a moral that was quintessential to his chosen work. He began to compose the lines he would speak to the poor fellow's wife. Something candid yet consoling would be required. He was concerned that so dire, so shocking a turn of events might precipitate the enervated mother's own decline, even allowed himself to dally in a daydream in which he, nobly, despite his youth and inexperience, claimed the orphaned infant, raised him as his own son, doing no harm. It was with this eventuality in mind that he took the six cigars, went to the bank, rented a safe deposit box, placed them there with the idea that one day he would show them to his ward, explain their significance, pass them on to him ceremonially. They're still there. One day, soon, his only child, a daughter, a school principal, her father's executor, will discover the box noted in his papers, will enter the vault, will turn the key. Will wonder.

New mother Jean, the baby at her breast, took the news of Callum's death calmly, with preternatural, almost off-putting, equanimity, which tends to be how one receives news one already knows.

☎   ☎   ☎

Had Weldon Bedford ever come clean about his main reason for joining the church choir, some Cupid could have brokered a meeting with the widow Bruce. It would have been a good match. Jean was no singer – she was tone-deaf, a liability she passed on to Gary – but was fondly allied with that same United Church. She was an active member of the UCW, also of the Finance Committee where she was famous for her arid stringencies, which many attributed, fondly yet wryly, to her Hibernian heritage: Jean Bruce, née MacDonald, fluid when it came to the choosing of a tartan for formal occasions. But their paths, however proximate, remained resolutely parallel. Weldon was too reticent to let it be overtly known he was scouting for a companion. He thought such clarity, such specificity might scare off potential candidates. And wouldn't the right girl just make herself known, somehow? Would it not just transpire of a Sabbath morning – Weldon liked to imagine it in January, with its twin pillars of hope and sterility – that this elusive, ineffable she would allow her mind to wander during a laboured bit of sermonizing, of which there were always more than a few; that she would look across the crowded sanctuary, would see Weldon elevated in the choir loft: his magenta robe, with its wizard sleeves and expansive taupe lapels and crisp white piping; the robe he took home every Sunday after the service to launder – singing was sweaty work – and to iron on Saturday night while he watched the hockey, then *Juliette*. His beloved-to-be would see Weldon, whom she would know by name at least and certainly by musical reputation, as though for the first time, radiant with the winter light that angled through the stained-glass representations of the raising of Lazarus, or Jesus the Exorcist, evicting demons from human hosts, compelling them to take up residence in swine. She would understand that here was a project she could reasonably undertake; know in her heart that she was uniquely equipped, among all the women in the world, to stoke the fire of his needs, to bring him to salvation. Was that not how it was meant to work? Was that now how it happened, spontaneously, borne on the back of a vision? Wouldn't she simply come along?

Nope.

Many supposed, Jean among them, that Weldon, an obvious catch, inexplicably single, was quietly, regrettably homosexual; she had heard it said that a condition of inversion afflicted many in the tenor voice range. She supposed, on the one occasion she gave it any thought, that he'd done as decency, even the law, dictated he must, that he had balled up his needs, stored them away, out of sight, out of mind. It was best not to pry. It was probably not a good idea to leave him unsupervised around children.

As for Jean, her chance collision with the essence of Callum, as it lifted into orbit, affected her so profoundly, so lastingly, that she never again felt the need to cleave to husband. Callum had been, not just figuratively, her soulmate; she knew for a fact they would meet again in Heaven. What would happen then, what would happen there, the nature of their reunion, its possible erotic dimensions, remained to be seen and were best not imagined. But here, on Earth, her carnal needs had been adequately, productively met. She could do no better than Callum. Pointless to try. For the rest of Jean's days she would cultivate the companionship of only one other man, the one she had brought forth fully formed into the world, who had startled her by knocking on the hot side of her oven door, whom she had decorated with eyes and nose, with mouth and buttons. She always knew he would follow the maxim of run, run, as fast as you can. She had missed him. Now, Gary is back.

☎   ☎   ☎

Gary belongs to the last generation of men called Gary. For the past fifty years, at least, no one has thought to name a baby Gary. It seems unlikely that anyone, anywhere, ever will again. Gary is a name like Dorcas, popular once upon a time but not susceptible to revival. Gary is now a name bestowed, with irony, upon Dalmatians, say, who accompany their owners, typically software engineers or video-game designers, to dog-tolerant workplaces where breaks are routinely taken for the playing of foosball. To anyone born within spitting distance of the present millennium the name Gary is aromatic of the quaint, the anachronistic. For Gary, a midstream boomer, Weldon, the moniker, also the man, is redolent of exactly the same whiff.

Gary knows Weldon by face, by name, but about his person, his reasons, he is enduringly incurious. Then again, there is much about which he never scruples to wonder. Gary favours the hammered down; Callum was the same. Callum was, as Gary is, not the type to let his gaze settle for long on the wavering middle distance, to look for the emergence of alternatives to the established or known. It has never occurred to Gary to imagine how Jean and Weldon could so easily, so logically, have been intertwined, how his own life might have taken on so different a cast. This trait of personality, his partiality to the hardtack, his impatience with the inchoate, perhaps explains how it is that Gary has never wondered why he feels himself so strangely bound to the older man; feels so once-a-year, in any case; feels as though they are roped together, scaling a steep rock face, in the dark and the cold.

This is how.

This why.

Gary was born on December 15. Many congregants at his mother's church, at Weldon's church, having scarcely recomposed themselves after the kilter-shattering circumstances attending the lad's nativity, were wonderstruck when, on Christmas Eve of that same year, Jean Bruce had the strength of body and spirit, to say nothing of the bloodiness of mind, to attend the service. (Inexplicably, given that it began promptly at eight, given that it was rigorously Protestant in its aesthetic, its rituals, it was called "Midnight Mass.") Jean drove herself in the Studebaker, the baby in a bassinet on the back seat. Some were admiring; most thought it in dubious taste. Jean knew, surely, that her presence would require all kinds of concessions, of complicated, awkward expressions of congratulation tempered by remorse that would distract from the candles, the carols, the cakes; from the main event, in other words.

Jean was reared to impute more value to the needs of others than to her own. But her drug-induced, *in extremis* reconnaissance flight, what she observed from her astral vantage point, her violent re-entry into her own body, had landed her in a place somewhere on the other side of caring. She was a new woman, herself reborn, with a unique perspective, a fresh purpose. She was a mother on her own whose first order of business was the defence of her child, the insuring of his continuance, his moral buttressing. A warning growl had taken up residence in the upper reaches of her thorax. She would do whatever she must to simply get on with things.

As it happens, it was on this selfsame Christmas Eve that Weldon Bedford, newly appointed to the tenor section of the church choir, was chosen to sing his first solo, the famously challenging "O, Holy Night." As it happens, Gary was not quite ten days old when he heard, however passively, for the very first time, Weldon Bedford sing "O, Holy Night." As it happens, on every Christmas Eve of Gary's already long tenure upon the earth – he has now lived more than twice as many years as were accorded his father – he has heard Weldon Bedford sing "O, Holy Night."

Gary, born without a musical bone in his body, nevertheless intuited, early on, that "O, Holy Night" is a daunting undertaking. Weldon's performance, so focused in its execution, so transfigurative in its effect, stirred in him the same nervous currents he felt when he watched, with Jean, figure skating on television. This was among their favourite shared pastimes, they clutched at one another when gripped by the commingling of hope, of dread that would flood into the blink-of-an-eye space between a jump's launch, its landing. Glory or shame. Each stood by, ready to claim the moment. Gary would listen to Weldon's clarion call of "Fall on your knees! O hear the angel voices! O night divine, O night when Christ was born," would inch forward in the pew, would white-knuckle the little shelf that held the hymnals – all the texts revised, now, with gender inclusivity, with the squashing of serpent-headed patriarchy in mind – would clutch at his mother's hand, would hold, literally, his breath, as Weldon ramped up to the awe-inspiring climax, the ringing, stratospheric reprise of "O, night divine," which was full of danger, ripe with the risk that

that note, teetering at the extremity of the voice's range, would crack, crumble, that every good thing that had been poured into the carol until then would drain out.

Gary can't say at what very young age this moment became portentous, can't pinpoint the year that he entered into a game of magical association with Weldon's singing. He would be hard-pressed to explain how it's come to resonate so tellingly within the low-ceilinged chapel of his own brain. That fact is that, over the years, Gary's own prospects for happiness have come to rely on Weldon's successful execution of that heroic, arduous note. Over the years Gary has told himself, "If he nails it, I will get an A on my essay, I will ace the spelling bee, I will win first prize in the science fair, I will get into McGill, I will get the job, I will get the transfer, someone will love me, Philip will love me, my blood counts will hold, a wonder drug will be found."

Every year, as it happens, Gary's granted wish has dovetailed with Weldon's stentorian success. Every year. It has been a remarkable partnership, even if one half of the firm lives in ignorance of it.

☎   ☎   ☎

On Christmas Eve –

Mid-afternoon. Light already on the wane. Jean fussing in her room when she should be napping. Gary at the kitchen table, thinking about making a phone call. He looks out at the backyard. Not much snow this year, not so far. That's usual, now, different from how it was, half a century back. All his childhood photos from this time of year – looking through those albums is one way of spending time with Jean, a productive goad to memory – show him suited up against the cold, standing atop mountainous drifts.

"King of the castle!"

"Lord of all he surveys!"

"Is this Kilimanjaro or Everest?"

These are a few of the cartoony captions Jean took it upon herself to compose: a summer project, once upon a while back. Gary tries to imagine himself in a situation where it would strike him as a fine idea, a useful pastime, to go to the attic, to risk inhaling rogue asbestos tailings from the old insulation, to find the box where the albums were stored, to take them downstairs, to arrange them, spread them out, on this very table, grey Formica, then to go painstakingly through, page after page, to inscribe – with a fine-point silver sharpie especially acquired for just this purpose – a cute little descriptor, none the same, under each and every photo. Hundreds of them.

In some of the pictures, Gary is astride a sleigh of which he has no recollection; worrying, given what runs in the family. He spends more time than nine out of ten physicians would recommend staring from his conning tower, trepidatious, on the lookout for incoming torpedoes. They strike when you least expect them, come silently, swiftly, often by night. Kablooey. All gone. So much already jettisoned, apparently. A sleigh. He searches hard, sifts the cinders. Nowhere can he find it, neither in flotsam nor guttering flames. Rosebud.

Maybe it's not so sinister. Other childhood conveyances he remembers well enough. His roller skates. His several bicycles. The little red wagon he used as a pram to haul around the sprinkler he pretended was a doll. Maybe the absent sleigh was a more straight-forward, tragicomic instance of repression, a self-protective measure. He never cared for the cold. Why wouldn't he scrub clean his hard drive, delete all frosty references? He hated it when his mother would zip him into his snowsuit, banish him from the house, compel him to get some fresh, sub-zero air. His favourite winter sport as a child was to assume the foetal position in front of the hot-air register, to lick his fingers, to pretend he was a cat, curled before the fire. He loved more than anything the enveloping warmth, the smell of the paste wax Jean applied every second Saturday morning to the oak floor, which she would buff to a high gloss.

There's an oak in the big backyard – the house is on a double lot – that every fall hails acorns. There's a sheltering cottonwood, similarly messy, a couple of lilacs, the obligatory caragana hedge, standard prairie issue. Most of the trees, though, are ash, a hardy strain. They take strength from frigidity. Gary has read that in a relatively few years – within his lifetime, potentially – the Canadian prairies will have surrendered so much of their claim on cold that the climate will more resemble present day north Texas; what that means for north Texas is the stuff of dystopic speculation.

"Nothing's assured but death and Texas," Gary says to himself, considering the yard, the ash trees having too easy a time of it. It's chilly now, as properly it should be on Christmas Eve, but just last week a sweater was all he needed when he walked to the corner store. Why wasn't there more widespread panic? Why were people locked away in their basements playing *Fortnite* instead of spearheading movements to fend off the devouring ash borer that was being tempted north, then west, by the seductive warmth; that would, within a few years, turn his backyard – for by then, in all likelihood, his it will be – into an arid, unshaded wasteland? Winter kept us warm. Isn't that what Eliot wrote? Or was it Larkin? Shantih, shantih. Whatever. Tra-la.

Eight. That's the tally of ash trees. Buried beneath one of them – this much Gary remembers – is the kitten he found in a culvert the summer he turned seven. He'd been looking for pop bottles he could cash in to buy a Barbie. Quite how he'd manage the necessary subterfuge such a purchase would require, to say nothing of the doll's concealment, he had yet to work out. The kitten was alone, no sign of litter mates. How had it come to be there? Gary couldn't say, couldn't have cared less. It was scarcely breathing, was too limp to offer any resistance when he slipped it into his shirt, rode home as fast as his little legs could pedal.

"It won't survive," said Jean.

"It will," he said.

"It's too weak, darling. It's been too long away from its mother."

"It will live. I will love it to life."

She'd been so touched by his belief in his own powers that she put her experience on hold. She didn't take it to the vet, didn't simply finish it off in a bucket. She let him try, let it die, let him cry. She offered comfort, never said "I told you so" when it was refused.

God, how he'd wept. That he remembers, for sure. He has never, not for anyone, not for any reason, not in all the intervening years, sobbed so violently. The shoebox coffin, the kitten's tiny ribs, its fragile skull – all gone, by now. Long gone. Even so, if circumstances dictated he must, Gary could take a shovel, show you exactly where.

Now he thinks of the kitten, thinks of every other thing that proved resistant to his love, that died in spite of him. He picks up the phone, dials. He counts.

One ringy-dingy.

Perhaps when the ash trees come down, as surely they will, the arborist, out of curiosity if for no other reason, might number their rings. Gary could calculate, were he of a mind to do so, the exact age, to the day, of the tree nearest to hand, the frosty-boughed artificial pine he assembled yesterday, not without difficulty. He'd spent a happy evening with Jean clipping on the strings of lights, hanging it with the ornaments he's known since childhood; draping the tinsel that she removes, year after year, strand by strand, then irons between two tea towels before storing it in its original box; tinsel that must be at least thirty years old. She's past doing that now. Will Gary? Probably. The receipt from the tree's purchase, at Canadian Tire, is still taped to the inside lid of the carton. Boxing Day, 1980. The year of his exodus, his flight to the coast. Never did he imagine a permanent return.

Two ringy-dingy.

During the years of Gary's growing up, such fir fakery would have been mock-worthy. They always had the real thing, he and Jean, a pine or spruce, fragrant, sticky, oozing with resin. The trees were harvested by the Boy Scouts affiliated with their United church, chopped down in woods nearby, sold as a fundraiser. The cash collected was used to underwrite troop travel to far-flung jamborees.

Three ringy-dingy.

Gary's first crush, age five, had been on Bert McKeever, age thirteen, a Baden-Powell acolyte. His many badges attested to his expertise at starting fires with flint and moss, crafting splints from poplar boughs, tapping out messages with Morse code. Bert lived down the street; it was he who delivered the tree. Mindful that the widow Bruce was, necessarily, by dint of both gender and social station, fragile, Bert stayed to trim the tree to fit the room, to make sure it was steady in its stand. Jean was impressed by his competence, already manly, also by his courtesy. Gary was touched by his swagger, his unlaundered smell of cheese rind, of meat. Of something tartly ammoniac. Bert would stay for hot chocolate, topped with a marshmallow.

"Hey kid, wanna see how I look with a moustache?"

Yes, Gary would nod, too shy to speak.

Bert took a sloppy sip of the hot drink, grinned when Gary laughed at the sticky coating, white and brown.

"Oh, Bert," said Jean, who would never have tolerated mucky shenanigans from her own son.

Later, in bed, Gary imagined slowly licking Bert's lips clean. He was a mother cat. Bert was his kitten.

Four ringy-dingy.

Jean suggested Gary join the Cub Scouts, the feeder organization for the more paramilitary operation of which Bert was an adherent. Compelling though he found the notion that this might propel the circumstances that would land him in a tent, alone, with Bert McKeever, Gary declined. It was a miscalculation on his part to confess he'd rather the Brownies, the sturdy cut of whose tunics and tams he adored, along with their uniforms' practical accessories: the pouch, the kerchief, the little pencil on its silver fob that attached to the belt, dangled there, stubby and jaunty, primed for easy deployment whenever a pencil was required.

Five ringy-dingy.

Jean shut that down, quickly, no negotiation. She became watchful, censorious, forbade Gary to enter her room where he had loved to try on her shoes, to fondle the treasures in her jewellery box; loved, even more than what the box contained, the little figure skater that sprang to pirouette position when the lid was lifted; who twirled around on the mirrored surface that was her rink, to the "Air des bijoux" from Gounod's *Faust*. Never did he fear she would fall.

Six ringy-dingy.

Jean kept that jewellery box in perfect working order. For a long time, Gary was driven to distraction by the obsessive, disciplined care his mother took with the house, with everything in it – a behavioural branch attached to the same trunk that supported her parsimony. Now, he's glad of her vigilance. The house is as the house was, has always been. It's what he prizes most about this place, its immutability; materials conservation of museum quality.

Seven ringy-dingy.

His own room is exactly as he left it, exactly as he has found it on all those Christmases when he came back from the coast for a week or ten days. The desk, the bed, the Hopalong Cassidy spread upon it: one of the masculinizing ploys with which Jean sometimes surprised him and eventually abandoned. The kitchen is the same, never updated, other than the fridge and stove; they had given out after decades of service, were replaced, once only, with models identical to the originals. Jean searched high and low to find them, made herself a nuisance at Sears until they tracked down what she wanted in a warehouse somewhere in Burnaby. Not to forget the phone. This great, hulking, rotary dial phone.

Eight ringy-dingy.

"Gary?"

"Hi, Philip. Merry Christmas."

On Christmas Eve –

Jean enters the kitchen in her cream-coloured blouse, grey cardigan, wool skirt of Bruce tartan, its reds and greens so amenable to the season. She has applied her lipstick evenly – not always a given – has worked a little into her cheeks, not so much that she looks like a demented clown.

"I'm ready any time, Callum."

She often calls Gary by his father's name. He's stopped correcting her.

"Ready for?"

"Why, church. What else?"

"It's not even three o'clock, love."

"Oh. What does that mean, exactly?"

This is the question she most often asks. It's a good one, really, Socratic in scope, precision.

"It means we have miles to go before we sleep."

"Oh. What does that mean, exactly?"

By 5:30, supper done, Gary has exhausted his repertoire of diversionary tactics. Jean wears the muskrat coat that was her own mother's, has found her galoshes, applied them to the wrong feet. She's standing at the door.

"I'll walk," she says.

"Unwise," says Gary.

They're not experiencing the killing cold of his childhood, but it's plenty brisk. He's heard too many stories about back-in-a-minute, unsupervised walks around the block that end in hypothermia miles from home.

Gary warms up the 1994 Subaru that replaced the Studebaker Jean sold, in mint condition, for a song, to a collector who now drives it all over southwestern Manitoba to all the classic car rallies, of which there's an unaccountable number, every summer, in every poky town.

Young mother Jean would load baby Gary in the car, would drive up the street, down the street, drive around the block, until the motion, the purr of the motor, put him to sleep. She was a good driver; even Callum, always critical of women behind the wheel, thought so. She cried when she surrendered her licence, not at her doctor's or Gary's or anyone's urging. It was her own decision. She knew what was coming. She could scent the prevailing wind.

Gary drives now, of course. They take a lot of little road trips – not with sleep in mind, just time. With the available hours. With their disposal. Now, on Christmas Eve, Jean squirms as he buckles her in. He rolls down the windows, despite the cold; her fur has spent the year in a trunk and the pungent flex of mothballs almost knocks him out. They head downtown to look at the lights, cruise past the mall that stands where Jean's high school had been.

"That was where we met, Callum, remember?"

At Jean's request, they route themselves past the house where she'd grown up.

"I don't care for those shutters, do you? Periwinkle is not a suitable outdoors colour. I do think blinking lights are in bad taste, too showy. My mother would never have allowed such a thing. Shouldn't we be at the church by now? You're not lost again, are you Callum?"

"No, love."

At 6:45, Gary parks in one of the four available disabled parking spaces. The lot is empty, save for the van that occupies the stall designated for the "Director of Musical Praise." Even "Clergy" is vacant.

"I don't care for that sign, do you?" says Jean, pointing to the placard adjacent to the entrance. "So cheap-looking."

It's one of those portable billboard contrivances, backlit with neon, the kind so ubiquitous at strip malls. Its application here is for the display of inspirational messages.

"*GOD NEVER GAVE YOU A BURDEN TOO HEAVY TO CARRY.*"

"*YOU CAN BANK ON GOD WITH PLENTY OF INTEREST.*"

"*SHOW YOU CARE WITH A PRAYER TO SPARE.*"

Gary wonders if they're the original work of the church secretary or if they come from a source book, maybe a Reddit group. He assumes that the cold, such as it is, must test the adhesiveness of the stick-on letters. The message on this Christmas Eve reads, "SERVICE BEGINS AT 8! EVERYONE WE COME!"

"Everyone we come? What does that even mean?" Jean asks.

"It's what happens when 'L' freezes over," says Gary.

Jean looks at him blankly.

"Gary?"

"Yes, ma'am."

"I thought it was you."

"And you were right."

"Shall we go in?"

☎   ☎   ☎

On Christmas Eve –

The Midnight Mass is now a Family-Friendly Holiday Celebration. It still begins at eight.

Jean studies her left wrist. She's forgotten her watch, a Timex she's never overwound or immersed in soapy dishwater, and that works as well now as it did when she bought it, in 1969.

"They're late starting this year."

"They certainly are," says Gary, for whom reflexive agreeability has become a habit.

He checks his phone. It's 7:35. Worshippers are just starting to arrive. Cheerful voices, seasons greetings. Stomp of boots. Rorschach of melt marks on the worn linoleum. Rush of cold air as the doors open, close.

Jean and Gary have taken seats near the front. She likes to be close to the sacramental action, not in the first pew, though, which would seem overeager, indecorous. One bench back suits her.

"Did you know," said Jean, lowering her voice, not quite enough, "that the new minister here is coloured?"

Gary's reply is a stiff smile and silencing nod.

"And a woman," says Jean, her tone expressive of both wonder and dismay at the world, at what it's become: its ready accommodation; the sloppy leniency of the new order; how perimeters, once clearly demarcated with solid lines, have become frangible, permeable.

This church, their church, is, in fact, now in the pastoral care and keeping of a married team, an interracial couple. Elspeth and Malcolm are young, relatively; they were fresh out of the seminary when they arrived, five years ago. They've worked hard to spark a spirit of renewal, to encourage families of all stripes to attend (Single Parents! Lesbian Moms!), to support refugees, to undertake meaningful acts of truth and reconciliation, to foster interfaith dialogue: what Gary would consider God's work, if Gary could consider God. He can't. Never really could.

"I just don't understand what they believe," said Jean, who was steeped in a tradition of Presbyterianism shot through with lead-coloured bolts of Calvinism. "I'm not sure they know themselves, and that's a fact."

"What do you mean?" Gary asked.

He was still in Vancouver, then, and this was during one of their Sunday afternoon phone chats. Jean could be relied upon to make at least one benighted pronouncement about race or gender or some such hot-button topic. Gary would roll his eyes and later report it to Philip who would howl with outrage and delight.

"No! She didn't say that? Did she? *Did she?*"

"I believe I've mentioned," said Jean on this occasion, "that they're always inviting someone from some other faith to come and preach. A Catholic priest. A Jewish rabbi. Today, it was a Muslim islam."

"You mean an imam?"

"That is what I said, yes. He talked about Mohammed and the Koran and made us all say 'Peace be with you' in whatever his language. I didn't, of course."

"Why not?"

"I'm no fool, Gary. 'Peace be with you'? It was just gibberish to me. How could I be sure that was really what it meant? It might have been 'I am a donkey's bottom' for all I know. What if he was toying with us? What if he was trying to convert us? That's how it works, you know; a few words, and it's done. You're a Muslim, whether you like it or not. They don't even have confirmation classes. Can you imagine? I suppose it won't be long before we'll all be expected to fly off to Mecca, on a Raj."

"'On a Raj'!" he heard Philip say on the phone that night, talking to Bonnie. "Yes! I kid you not. That's what she said. 'On a Raj'!"

Ho.

Ho.

Ho.

Gary thinks of Philip now, two time zones west, locking up the store, the cash register spooling out its ticker tape testament, Bonnie wresting the foil from the bottle of bubbly one or the other of them will surely have thought to bring with toasting in mind.

"To you, Davie Denman."

"To you, Nicola Harwood."

"To us."

Gary thinks of Philip and he grows flush with feeling, with something akin to sorrow, and something close to regret, and something that's not quite loathing but getting close, and something he can name reliably as shame; shame at the way he used Jean's intolerance, her foolishness as a currency to purchase what little Philip was willing to sell him of favour.

Feckless. Hateful. Treacherous. These should be the names of his Three Kings. How Gary despises himself, here on Christmas Eve, here in the house of the Lord, remembering how easily he betrayed her, his own mother, Jean, a fading echo of her once-resonant self.

"I do believe," says Jean, touching his arm, calling him back, "there's a bun in that oven."

She refers to Elspeth, who has just emerged from the wings – or whatever the proper term for the backstage area of a

United Church – and is lighting candles on the altar. Gary nods agreement. Even in her voluminous robe, it's clear that Elspeth is great with child.

"Do you suppose it will come out coffee or cream?" asks Jean, and Gary fakes a coughing fit, anything to kick up enough dust to mask her traces.

He thinks how brave it is, how possibly ill-advised, to bring a child into a world that has sloughed off its carapace of civility. No place is safe now, and no place is sacred. Churches in Charleston and Colombo, synagogues in Paris and Pittsburgh, mosques in Québec City and Christchurch. It keeps on happening. There is no good reason to imagine it will end. It could happen here, in this church, here, in Brandon, Manitoba, here, on Christmas Eve, just as readily as any place, anywhere else, at any other time. All it takes is the hardware, which is easy enough to come by, and an impulse, which is really nothing at all. Gary thinks of this all the time. He has a knack for contingencies. He always knows where the exits are. He always has a plan.

"'On a Raj'!"

It became one of Philip's favourite stories, one he could dine out on. Indeed, dining out with Bonnie is what they were doing on what proved a decisive Saturday evening, two years ago.

"'We'll all be expected to fly off to Mecca,'" said Philip, the tears streaming down his cheeks, "'on a Raj'!"

"Stop," said Gary. "You've worn that out. You make her sound worse than she is. She's harmless."

"She's not," said Bonnie, sniffing a weakness, quick to seize the advantage, to bring down her prey. "She's no more harmless than Dylann Roof or Alexandre Bissonnette. She just doesn't have the internet. She doesn't have a gun."

"Ergo," said Gary, tight-lipped, "harmless. Unable to do harm."

"No," said Bonnie. "It's a continuum. Not harmless. Not at all."

Gary couldn't swallow. He excused himself. He walked the three miles home. He walked ten times around the block. Philip was in bed by the time he felt rational enough to enter the apartment.

Gary said, "I'm leaving."

Philip said, "I know."

They didn't speak in the morning. Philip went out, didn't say where he was going. Gary was alone when Jean made her ritual call.

"How was church today?"

"I didn't go," said Jean. "I've decided not to attend any longer."

"Why?"

"I just don't care for it. It's not to my taste, too much like an old-time revival meeting, what with everyone raising their hands and saying 'Hallelujah,' and so on. Tasteless. You can hardly walk into the place any more without getting hugged, and there's always someone passing around a petition to save the whales or stop a pipeline. Such idiocy. Don't they drive? Don't they know where their gas comes from? What does any of that have to do with Jesus? It's all so different, Callum."

"Gary."

"Pardon?"

"Gary. You called me Callum."

"Nonsense. I never did. I was telling you about church. She's even taken down the picture of the Queen from the hall. It's nowhere to be found."

"Who did that?"

"That minister. Reverend Harrison. I don't know why she doesn't take her husband's name."

"Because it's Pickle?"

"Don't be smart."

For more than sixty years, Jean had been a regular Sunday presence. Her absence, even after a week, did not go unremarked or unquestioned. It was Malcolm Pickle (M.Div., McMaster) who made a home visit to inquire after the reasons. It was he who contacted Gary.

Gary came.

Gary saw.

Gary stayed.

"Black as the Ace of Spades," says Jean, now, on Christmas Eve; it's been a year since they were last here. She shakes her head. She opens her purse. It's one Gary hasn't seen before. She must have found it in the nether reaches of her closet. God knows what it contains. Jean is determined to find out. She peers into its interior, begins the slow business of extraction, starting with the tissues.

"Aren't the flowers on the altar lovely," says Gary, by way of diversionary tactic. "What are they called?"

"Poinsettias, of course," says Jean, without looking up. There's much that she can summon at will.

"Poinsettias. You know that, Callum."

But there's just as much that she cannot.

☎   ☎   ☎

On Christmas Eve –

Gary's phone buzzes in his left breast pocket. A text. He steals a surreptitious glance.

"thinking of u!!!!!! 😜 "

He can't reply, not here, not now, not at 8:17, not as the congregation is enjoined to rise for "While Shepherds Watched Their Flocks"; not with his mother beside him, not Jean, a woman whose incremental diminishment is a daily reminder of her once expansive capacities, her intelligence, even, yes, her humour. Never, however, not even when she was at her considerable peak, did she command the spaciousness of mind or liberality that would allow her to credit how any man, let alone her son, might have a hard-on in church. He feels a flush of something unnameable, a hybrid of shame and delight, when he thinks of how, for the last several months, several nights a week, when Jean is in bed, her hearing aids dormant on the table beside her, he has opened the door of her house to – yes, really – Randy; Randy, in the steady employ of the phone company, as it turns out; Randy, willing to turn up after hours to make a service call; Randy, age twenty-six, who contacted Gary via a website that hooks up mature men – old men, at least – with their younger admirers; Randy, who goes by the handle "The Son Also Rises"; Gary, who answers to "The Silver Standard."

"Thanks," said Randy, on the occasion of their first meeting. They had satisfactorily, efficiently dealt with the one item on their agenda. He was headed for the door.

"Stay for a drink if you'd like," said Gary, taken aback at his own nerve. His effrontery. This was not how these transactions usually proceeded, with something that might lead to conversation.

"I don't touch spirits," said Randy. His primness made Gary's ventricles flutter with avuncular affection.

"Hot chocolate?"

Randy wavered.

"I have marshmallows."

"Okay."

They sat at the kitchen table. They didn't say much. Randy stared in wonder at the Bakelite extravagance of the phone.

"That's a museum piece. Does it work?"

Gary wondered if he'd had similar thoughts twenty minutes earlier when they were getting down to the business that had brought them together.

"It does."

Randy lifted the receiver, listened to the dial tone, grinned.

"Mind if I take a picture?" Randy asked, not for the first time that evening.

☎   ☎   ☎

On Christmas Eve –

Jean neither stands nor sings. She pays no mind to the reading of the lessons. She sits in her pew, clutches at her son's or husband's arm with her left hand. With her right, she mines her purse. Beneath the wads of tissue that now spill onto the church floor – some crusty with use, some smeared with lipstick – lie fortune cookies, individually wrapped, crisply resonant in cellophane.

Gary remembers Jean telling him, in one of their weekly phone conversations, how her bridge club – all now dead or confined – voted to switch their time of play to afternoon, the better to avoid unnecessary driving at night. ("I never thought she'd be the type to enjoy a rubber before dark," is what Philip had said on that far-off Sunday afternoon when he heard this bit of news from home.) If they finished up early enough they'd "go for Chinese," as Jean liked to say. Sweet and Sour Pork. Chow Mein. Egg Foo Young. This purse, Gary surmises, was the one in everyday use however many years ago. Now comes a pair of chopsticks. Now a little packet of soy, a few after-dinner mints. Lint. Now more fortune cookies. How many can there be? Ten have been excavated, lined up on the ledge, an activity readily observed from the pulpit. Gary has been exchanging "Yes, I know, but what can I do?" looks with Elspeth Harrison.

"Do not be afraid," the Reverend says, reporting the words of the herald angel, "I bring you good news that will cause great joy for all people."

Jean is attentive enough to snort at this earnest, clunky rendering of Luke. "Fear not: for, behold, I bring you good tidings of great joy, which shall be to all people" had been good enough for King James and good enough for her, too. All this modernizing; it was enough to drive anyone into the arms of Rome.

Oh, God. It's horrible. It's hilarious. It needs sharing. Gary aches with the narrative equivalent of blue balls. Who has he got to tell, with whom can he share this anecdotal accumulation; this, well, mother lode? Once, not so long ago, Philip would have been his ready remedy.

"How's your mom?" Gary asked him earlier in the day, Philip on his mobile at the store in Vancouver, Gary anchored to the vintage Bakelite in the kitchen in Brandon.

"Frances is amazing. She swears this is her last Christmas. She's probably right. She said the same thing last year, though. Jesus, Gary. You should see her. There's hardly anything left. She's a husk, but a busy husk. She was here earlier today, toting barges, lifting bales. Can't last though. Can't."

"That's hard."

"It's going to get harder. As the actress said to the bishop. Anyway, it's not as though you don't know first-hand how it is. How's Miss Brodie?"

This was Philip's not necessarily fond nickname for Gary's mother; he was famous in their circle for his Maggie Smith as Jean Brodie impersonation.

"Jean is – herself."

Philip didn't press for details. Why would he? After so much time, after so long an aversion, after he and Jean had for so many years made each other's lives miserable by remote control, he's not going to offer a pretence of concern. Also, he had plenty on his plate. There were customers coming in, anxious to spend just about anything just to get it over with. Just to have done. Over the din of the last-minute shoppers, Gary hears a shout.

"Davie Denman! Take the till, I'm desperate for a slash."

His nemesis. Decency requires he send her best wishes, season's greetings. He doesn't have that much decency.

"You should go. It sounds crazy there."

"The glorious symphony of fools and their money, parting ways. What about you, Gary? You're well?"

"I'm fine, Philip. Just fine."

"Let's talk soon."

"Sure. Let's."

Click.

"Or not."

On Christmas Eve –

The texts keep coming, insistent waves of pornographic palpations from Randy by name, randy by nature. Gary didn't buy him a Christmas present; that would have been weird. He did, however, take the precaution of placing an Amazon order for some high-end, fair-trade cocoa, just to have something reciprocal at the ready in case Randy surprised him with a special little something. Gary had spoken admiringly of the young man's cock ring, thought he saw him take note. Who knows? He might just come to the door with a little something for under the tree. As it were. He has decided that tonight, assuming Randy can get away – he has family obligations, but they're plainly not keeping him from his phone – he'll lead his young man upstairs, up to his room, up to his nun-like twin bed with the Hopalong Cassidy spread. It pleases him to think of playing in the place he used to ache. So far, their conjoinings have taken place on an old mattress in the basement, a sort of *nostalgie de la boue* ploy that hasn't wanted for lurid allure. It was there, adjacent to the cupboards where Jean stored her sealed Mason jars of bread-and-butter pickles and mincemeat, back in the day where her efforts at preservation weren't necessarily self-directed, that Gary first heard Randy squeal his accustomed *cri de guerre*.

"Oh, jeepers!"

Somewhere in that self-same basement, on a shelf high enough to spare it from flood damage should the sump pump fail, nearby the steamer trunk where the mothball off-gassing fur coat is stored, Jean has a banker's box in which are lovingly preserved birth certificate, report cards, various academic commendations, a sports-day ribbon for "Tried Hardest." Somewhere, wrapped in tissue, tied with raffia twine, is the scroll Gary received for perfect attendance when he graduated from primary to intermediate Sunday School. (The signatory to this document, to whose name he has never paid any mind, nor will he ever, is Superintendent Norman Rover, whose great-grandson is none other than Randy. As it happens.)

Perfect attendance. It seemed to Gary then, it seems still, a strange achievement for which to be rewarded, requiring, as it did, nothing more than turning up. Degree of difficulty: very low. It wasn't as though he'd had a choice. It was Jean who compelled him to be there; by rights, she should have received the acknowledgment.

"I am fifty-nine," thinks Gary, which would be news to Randy, to whom he admitted fifty-four. "I have entered my sixtieth year upon the earth. I have never, not once, for any reason, been anywhere on Christmas Eve other than here, in this cold but warming prairie town, in this unremarkable church, with this maddening woman, the only woman I've ever loved. How can that be? How?"

If one of the officiants were to look down upon him now from their pulpit perch, were to call him forth to acknowledge his singular, his well-nigh saintly, accomplishment – which they might, if they only knew of it – he would take whatever plaudits came his way. If there were a certificate to be had, he would frame it. Now, Reverend Pickle steps to the microphone – another innovation of which Jean disapproves, she feels the word of God does not benefit from artificial amplification – with something similar in mind that doesn't append to Gary, yet also, in the strange way of these things, does. As it happens.

"We give thanks to God for the service and gifts of our brother, Weldon Bedford. As many of you know, Weldon has been a member of the choir here, our leading tenor, for many, many years. How many years? Weldon, I hope you don't mind if I get specific. Fifty-nine. Yes, just one shy of sixty. He's been with the choir since the age of thirty. I'll give you all a second or two of silence to do the math." (Here, in his prepared notes, Reverend Pickle has written, "Pause for chuckle.") "Weldon has never missed a performance. Never a Sunday or holiday service. Never a spring concert or nursing-home performance. Never. Not one. I spoke to him tonight, before our celebration began. I asked him if he'd never wanted to take a holiday or go on vacation. He allowed that yes, he'd thought of that, occasionally. But in the end, he said, there's nothing that makes him feel so refreshed or alive as singing. 'This choir is my vacation,' he told me. 'I'm on holiday all the time.'"

"Hallelujah!" cried a worshipper at the back of the hall.

"Praise the Lord," said someone else, similarly moved.

"Horrible," said Jean, choosing a fortune cookie, holding it to her ear, giving it an experimental shake.

"One of our great traditions, our blessings, in this holy season is Weldon's singing, his matchless rendition, of the carol 'O Holy Night.' I know it's a moment for which we all wait with joyous anticipation. Without further ado, please welcome, for the fifty-ninth consecutive year, the eighty-nine-year-old Weldon Bedford."

Weldon advances, cautiously, nervous of tripping – he has a cane but has chosen not to use it, has set it aside with Lourdes-like assurance – to his position next to the pulpit. The organist plays the familiar opening arpeggios. The world slows in its spinning.

Gary places his hand atop his mother's, out of love, also to prevent her from ripping into the wrapping of the fortune cookie, of ruining the moment with rustling. He is struck by how slender are her fingers, the joints untouched by arthritis, how youthful appear her hands, unlike his own, mottled with liver spots. This is how his father's hands would have looked, perhaps, had he lived. That Gary has lasted this long, that he has almost outlived his own middle age, is nothing he expected. His blood had spoken. Its message was clear, in no way enigmatic or vague. A time bomb circulated in his veins, his arteries, primed to explode sooner rather than later. But the days went by, the weeks, the months, the years. By what dumb luck, what stroke of blind fortune was he spared, was he allowed to become the beneficiary of all the research that had gone on while he went undetonated, all those grasping, experimental forays for which tens of thousands of lab rats had perished, that came too late for so many, so many friends, acquaintances, whom he'd watched sicken, suffer, die, always with the clear sense that this was his path, too, that he would follow in short order. He saw in Philip the same creeping dread, also resentment. This was not what he had signed on for. Was he going to wind up being a nurse? Would he be up to such an assignment? Would he want to, even if he could? Would he be condemned if he jumped ship?

"Are you going to tell your mother?"

"How can I tell my mother?"

Gary never told. He's glad. It would have been for nothing. After all those years of certainty that his time would not, could not, be long, here he is. He is now, he will go on being, what Jean thinks every Christian gentleman should be. At home. Undetectable.

Gary takes a quick census of the cookies arrayed before them, thirteen all told, each of them curled around some fraying, fading nugget of wisdom, who can say what?

Happiness will be yours.

Wisdom will bring you wealth
more surely than wealth will bring you wisdom.

You will take an exciting voyage
to an unknown land.

He's visited by a memory, recently impressed, of a morning drive, just this past August, the 23rd. It was Jean's birthday. She had a hankering to see, perhaps for the last time, the land her grandparents had farmed. She'd spent her girlhood summers there, and that time was still deeply rooted in the folds of her brain, those furrows as yet unsalted. They headed out early, right after breakfast, light traffic, high hopes. Jean was asleep before they'd left the city, her head bowed as though in prayer. It was a peculiar day, weather-wise, unsettling. Smoke was blowing in from the northwest. Once again, all the forests were burning. It was foggy, too, the first of the Brigadoon mists that signal summer's end.

"A real pea-souper," said Gary, unoriginally, to Jean, unresponsive, a dozing bobblehead.

They drove in the direction of Souris, visibility near zero on a two-lane highway that was cratered with potholes. Oncoming cars were metres away when their dazzling brights announced their imminence. Gary, cautious behind the wheel in clement conditions, had adjusted his tempo accordingly, a commonsense protocol scorned by the other southbound drivers of the pickups and SUVs and transport trucks that tailgated before pulling into the northbound lane to pass, at speed, sometimes hooting their annoyance.

Jean slept on, snoring slightly, and Gary remembered the West Coast foghorns, their warning *No-Go, No-Go*. Obscuring mists were not so usual in Vancouver, oddly enough, and the horns were a rare-enough addition to the soundscape that he was always surprised, taken aback, by their cautionary, mournful yawning. They put him on edge with their threatening vernacular, reminded him that he was a foreigner, not fluent, accent detectable, out of his element, washed up on this exotic shore, far from home, hobbled by some congenital defect that rendered him unable to understand the workings of the tides. *No-Go* went the horns, *No-Go*, their baritone adumbrations of danger so different from the more familiar tenor of a far-off train whistle, Dopplering across the wide bowl of the prairies. Foghorns presaged shipwreck, drowning. Train whistles were rich with the promise of distance, escape, and also of return. Gary came back. He came back for good. He said farewell to the deep blue sea. He returned to the devil he knew.

Distracted by fog and by his own musings, Gary missed the turn-off from the highway onto the unpaved road they'd travel to reach the old homestead. He doubled back, located the exit, slowed up to accommodate gravel. Jean never stirred, was dead to the world when a doe emerged from the starboard field. The doe was exactly the colour of whatever grain grew there, ripened, harvest-ready: wheat, probably, maybe rye, Jean would have known; Gary can reliably identify only canola or flax. Corn, on a good day. Nor is he in the know about deer. He couldn't have made an informed guess about whether she was running to or running from or simply running for running's sake, for the joy, for the hell of it. Running because she was able. She was nowhere to be seen. Then she was there, fully gestated, miraculously spawned by the mating of fog and field. The path she followed, whether practised or spontaneous, was cut on the bias. She made no alteration to the angle of her course when she hit the road, didn't scruple to look both ways. Gary pumped the brakes. The Subaru threatened to fishtail, might well have spun out, have landed in the ditch, overturned even, had he been driving any faster. Gary prevailed. Jean slept. The deer, whether protectively or out of curiosity, broke the angle of her run, described, for what couldn't have been more than a couple of seconds but seemed an eternity, a parallel path with the car, kept apace, might even have decelerated, was so close that Gary could have reached out, could have touched her muscular haunch. He looked her in the eye. She fired up her jetpacks, leapt her whole body length, once, twice, a third time, gave a quick over-the-shoulder glance, cut directly in front of the car, resumed her angle of flight, was gone in an instant, swallowed by fog, by field. By smoke.

Jean woke.

"Where are we?"

"Almost there."

"Did I miss anything?"

"No love. I missed you, though."

You will have a close call.

Miracles await those who are ready for them.

Not everything means something.

On Christmas Eve –

O holy night! The stars are brightly shining,
It is the night of the dear Saviour's birth.

On his way to church, Weldon stopped at the letter box outside the Happy Shades Home for Independent Seniors. He's lived there for fifteen years in a tidy apartment; a bachelor apartment, as befits his status.

Long lay the world in sin and error pining –

"Dear Ginny,

I don't know if you remember me. No. That's not true. I know you do, just as much as I remember you. For the same reason, too. There's something I've been thinking about, something I'd like to say …"

(As it happens, Ginny, at the very moment of this mailing, is in a Chinese restaurant in Victoria, not far from the Empress Hotel. She's with her girlfriend, Claudia. Their cumulative age is 163; they like to eat early. They wait for their separate cheques and crack open their fortune cookies.

"'Your lover has a complicated past,'" Ginny reports, with her trademark snort.

"'You will receive an unexpected letter.'"

"Mine's better," Ginny says and Claudia agrees; Ginny's future, like her past, is always more interesting.

Ginny asks, "You want to swap?"

"Isn't that against the rules?"

"There's no playbook, honey."

"Tradesies, then.")

– Till He appear'd and the soul felt its worth.
A thrill of hope –

231

The Reverend Pickle's implied reservations notwithstanding, Weldon feels not much different in his body at almost ninety than he did at eighty, at seventy. He feels good. It's his ambition – secret, there'd be no surer jinx than to speak it aloud – to officially retire from the choir on the occasion of his hundredth birthday. He has a solo recital planned, an afternoon concert since his voice is in its finest fettle before 6 p.m. The program will include all his favourite hymns – "Abide with Me," "The Old Rugged Cross," "Onward, Christian Soldiers" – as well as some popular favourites, even a country tune or two. Sons of the Pioneers. Wilf Carter. Not many know that Weldon is an expert yodeller. It's a card he plays close to his chest. Yodelling is like reading palms: admit to knowing how and everyone wants you to prove it.

Weldon's audience at his one-stop farewell tour – he imagines a full house, standing-room only – will expect him to finish off with "O Holy Night." It will be out of season – his is a May birthday – but you give your fans what they want. Would Anne Murray turn her back on "Snowbird," Frank Sinatra on "New York, New York"? There'll be at least five minutes of cheering, stamping, enough time for Weldon to settle his larynx for the encore, one only. "Danny Boy." Leave them weeping. Leave them wanting more.

Oh, but Ginny. What if Ginny, with whom he's had no contact for so many years – she's never come back to Brandon for one of the occasional choir reunions – decides to dig through memory's fusty hamper, what if she names names? There would be a reckoning, as he's heard in the news. Would he be shunned, booted out of the choir, the church? Oh, lord. Not that. Best to take the high road. Best to write. Best to mail.

☎   ☎   ☎

("Sweet Jesus," Ginny will say, five days later when the Christmas Eve fortune-cookie prophecy is fulfilled, when she reads her unexpected letter. "Oh, sweetheart, come see. This is incredible.")

She'll pass Weldon's plea for pardon over to Claudia; "long-suffering Claudia" is how the members of their circle refer to her. Ginny is a handful, a prankster. Not for nothing does she have the nickname Spike; she was almost kicked out of nursing school for punch tampering. All their friends have heard about that choir shindig, the fumbling in the closet, the toppled hymnals. It's one of Ginny's reliable standbys. She never tires of telling it. If she never mentions Weldon specifically, it's only because she's forgotten his name.

"That poor man," Claudia will say. "That poor, poor man."

"I know. I know."

Ginny will send off a short, sweet note. "Thank you for writing. All is forgiven." She will decline his proposal. She'll fold up his letter, keep it in her bag. She'll show it to everyone she knows.

It will take Weldon three days to steel his nerves before he can open her reply. He'll have a good, long cry. He'll feel considerably relieved, lighter than he has in years.)

On Christmas Eve –

– the weary world rejoices,
For yonder breaks a new and glorious morn.

Weldon's spine is straight. His stance is sturdy. His vibrato oscillates so widely even tone-deaf Gary can tell he's slipping in and out of pitch, like a car, hydroplaning but not quite skidding off the asphalt. Barely hanging on. Whatever the imperfections, there's no questioning his commitment. Commitment, as Weldon understands, as Gary knows, too, is really all you need to get you through; to ensure that the beginning becomes the middle becomes the end.

Gary hears Jean's happy sigh, feels the press of her head as she leans into his arm. He looks down. She gazes back, girlish, dreamy.

"Callum," she says. "Our song."

Or so Gary supposes. The fortune cookie she's worked loose from its wrapper is an impediment to articulation. She's managed to place the whole crescent in her mouth. She savours it with intense, transubstantiative pleasure. Remember my body. Eat my body.

"I love you," Gary thinks. "I will love you to life."

Fall on your knees! O hear the angel voices!
O night divine –

On Christmas Eve –

For nearly sixty years, this is where Gary has been, here in this church. For all that time, for Gary, this is how it's been, what it's been, unchanging, steady: the ritual, measured telling of a story in which he's called to believe, but can't; the company of these strangers; the abiding, guiding beacon of his mother, her lights dimming, dimming. Not to forget Weldon; Weldon, to whom he has never spoken; Weldon, who has never failed him. Surely he won't, not now, not tonight. Gary is not as blithe or as unconcerned as in previous years. The Reverend Pickle's introductory encomium was well intentioned and kindly, yes, but also maladroit. By drawing attention to Weldon's age, by implying infirmity, was he trying to insulate everyone against his probable crumpling? Weldon is not in the most elastic of voice; what could be less likely than that he will manage, once again, to scale his cherished summit? But despite it all, here he is. Despite the predictions, the shaky vectors of triumph, he hasn't stumbled. Not yet. Watching him, listening to him, Gary, along with everyone around him, can only believe that Weldon has faith, faith that he can still pull it off, one more time, at least. If he's going to do so, then that time is now.

Across town, Randy, so young, so mischievous, employs his nimble opposable thumbs to wing off another lubricious emoji. They are accruing on Gary's phone, applying their defibrillating pulses not quite to his heart but to its agent in the external world, his left, his most sensitive, nipple. Later that night, for the first of what will prove to be many times, Randy will call him "Gare Bear."

"What did I say? What did I say?" he'll ask when Gary lies sobbing, uncontrollably, in his lavishly tattooed arms.

For now, Gary's phone vibrates promisingly in his pocket, and Jean's grip tightens on his arm. Hold on. Hold on. He realizes that, for the first time since he began his covert tradition of making a wish upon Weldon's success, he has become a man without requirement, with nothing specific in mind. What to do? This moment is so charged, it's like a fallen wire, live, sparking in the driveway. It can't be ignored.

"Have mercy," he says, not knowing exactly what he means, or quite whom he petitions.

"Watch over us," he adds, just because it sounds right. Complete. The resolving note in that secret chord the lord is said to love.

It can't go on. So Philip said about Frances, and he might just as easily have been talking about Jean or, for that matter, about Gary or Bonnie or about himself, come to that. It can't go on, not much longer. That's true for them all, just as it is for everyone they know, everyone who's been lucky or stubborn enough to last this long in the game. The youngest among them is already old. They are of dubious utility, exert no influence, have relinquished whatever claim they might once have staked on the inherited earth. The debris of all they've squandered is thick on the ground. What do they have to grab onto in the event of a stumble? Not relevance, that's for sure. They've had their kick at the can. Whatever scraps are left to them will be comical, accidental, a series of reprieves, commutations of sentences that will grow ever more dire, less susceptible to leavening, increasingly pathetic. What if there were an album devoted to their lives together, the parties, the dinners, the vacations, the betrayals? Who would write the captions? What would they be?

"Hey there, losers!"

"You were wrong about that, too!"

"I guess the joke was on you!"

It can't go on much longer, it can't, none of it, but Gary is so reluctant to let it go. It can't go on but it can't end yet, not yet, just one more year, one more year, that much mercy, just that much, which is surely not too much to ask. Oh, Lord. Jeans tugs at his sleeve. He looks down. She smiles up, extends her tongue upon which lie the masticated remains of whatever her fortune. Before he can retrieve it, her tongue lizards in. One swallow. Two swallows. There. It's gone. She shakes with silent laughter.

Outside the fragile light of the stars spills down upon the night divine, upon earth as hard as iron, water like a stone. It is a light that is millennia old. Weldon, focused, intent, is heedless of how it seeks him out, begins to fill him, makes a vessel of his orthopaedic shoes, then migrates up through his ankles, tibia, knees, hips: one original, one more recently brought on board. On this holy night he is wholly light, he can feel the thrumming in all his pulse points as it rises, up, up, ascendant through his ribcage, thorax, through all the murky passageways of his able, feeble body, cleansing, annunciatory, penetrating, warming his every cell, he has never felt so steadfast, so furious, so incandescent with the faith, not unfounded, that he'll do it, he'll do it, this is what he was born for, on he blazes, full of purpose, utterly ignorant, mercifully so, of just how much is riding on all of this.

(Strong is your hold O mortal flesh,
Strong is your hold O love.)

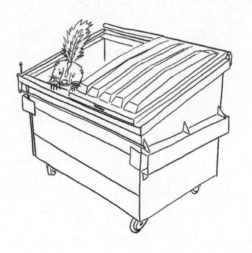

STILL GOODBYING

Story-collection Endnotes – these are those – are even more needless and dubious than forewords. They're symptomatic of a writer who doesn't know when to shut up, let go; who's fretful the reader will overlook the most gilded of his subtleties, or not fully appreciate the best jokes. Perhaps the author is trying to plump up the word count, possibly for kabbalistic reasons. "Just a few more adverbs and we'll get to 77,777 and all my dreams will come true!" My own experience of such appendices suggests that whatever questions or concerns one might have as a reader – usually they amount to "Where are the lifeboats?" – are rarely addressed. That'll surely be so here. Feel free to seek me out if clarifications are required. I can often be found in the No Frills on Denman. I'm the pale, disappointed-looking, elderly gentleman who buttonholes strangers and compels them to listen to my complaints about the outrageous price of prunes. Don't hesitate to stop and chat, if you have an hour to spare.

"Since We've No Place to Go"

"I Saw Three Ships" was the title of the original story, broadcast December 19, 2014, on CBC Radio One's program *North by Northwest*.

The Nina, the Pinta, and the Santa Maria are fictions, but plausible. Such building names – historical or aspirational or baronial – are usual in the West End. Many modest, even creaky and decaying, apartment blocks represent themselves as "Mansions" or "Manors," as "Palaces" or "Estates." Also usual are fanciful meldings, the combined names (as I always imagine) of the children of the building's original owner. The Shaunavon. The Shelmarjay. At 2030 Barclay Street – a block from where I live at this moment of writing, but probably not for long – is a boutique hotel, the Rosellen Residential Suites. I can't say for a dead cert, but I'd guess a Rose and an Ellen are commemorated. I borrowed my character's name – Rosellen Sweete! Get it? – from the hotel. Katharine Hepburn occasionally stayed there; she filmed some of her most forgettable projects in Vancouver. The Katharine Hepburn Penthouse Suite at the Rosellen is, with its vast spaces and generous patios, a much grander affair than the Santa Maria carbuncle in which Bonnie lives for thirty-five years. It's been a popular venue for weddings and receptions and such. Progress is no respecter of reputation or legend, and in the spring of 2018, the Rosellen was slated for demolition. Luxury condos are promised to rise. That's show business, kid.

"Everybody Knows a Turkey"

I don't know who did the title assigning at *Reader's Digest*, where this story, much shorter, appeared in December of 2009 as "Fate, the Yuletide Trickster." I was a bimonthly humour columnist for the *Digest* for a few years – I loved writing for them, they paid well and on time – and when I was told, not long after this story appeared, that my services would no longer be required, the reason provided – not that I asked for one – was that I just wasn't funny. With this I couldn't argue. My experience of being fired, which by now is extensive and varied, is that the employer is always right and is typically doing one a favour. Thank you, editor whose name I've forgotten.

Along with the raccoons and the coyotes, the skunks of the West End are a neighbourhood heritage feature. They're everywhere, going about their skunky business, peaceable and discreet until disturbed. I had dogs for thirty years in the West End and always made sure to have a skunk-stink-removal unguent under the sink. It came in handy once. Anyone who lives in the West End soon learns one of its ancient folk dances, the "Skunk Ahoy." It's easy – a sudden stop, a backward step, a hurried crossing of the street – but devastating in its outcome if you get it wrong.

Late February is mating time for skunks; at least, this is so for the urban examples of the species in the West End. They get quite carried away and have at it in the middle of the laneways, late at night, not caring who sees. Well. Who am I to carp? It was like that for me, in the West End, in the late '70s. Latterly, I'm not quite sure for what reason, the city has taken to naming the lanes in the West End, commemorating various worthies, none of whom is alive and able to take selfies next to the signs that bear their names. I sent a long and eloquent and, I thought, quite persuasive letter to Council asking that the commercial throughway behind my building be christened Skunk Fuck Alley. I'm still waiting for a reply, and yes, I'm still willing to officiate at whatever ceremony might commemorate such an act of civic probity.

Walt Whitman fell grievously ill in the week before Christmas of 1891. The *New York Times* reported his decline and predicted his quick demise. There were daily updates about the Good Gray Poet's deepening frailty. On December 23, readers were told, he'd grown tired of milk punch and had taken no nourishment other than two oysters, one in the morning, one in the afternoon. On Christmas Day, he drank clam juice. Whitman's readers, by contrast, had huge appetites, at least for news of his worsening condition. In the *NYT* of December 18, 2018, Tina Jordan wrote a comprehensive account of how the *Times* kept vigil until Whitman finally gave up the ghost on March 26, 1892. Those were the days.

"Snow on Snow on Snow on Snow"

My suggested title for this story, when it was published in the *Georgia Straight*, December 21–28, 2000, was "Leonard Cohen, Walking Home." They preferred, God knows why, "A Winter's Tale."

Contentious it was born and contentious it has remained; it's the story about which andrea bennett, the editor of this collection and therefore my collaborator, and I had the most back-and-forth. I suspect, given her good instincts and respectful reservations, that it's flawed, by which I mean more flawed than the others. You can make up your own minds and speak to Goodreads about it and then, on some sleepless night when my defences are down, I will read your dunning dismissals and harrumph about pearls and swine and precedence in the privacy of my own apartment, wherever that turns out to be.

I think "Snow on Snow on Snow on Snow" has its origins in an interview I hosted on CBC Radio with Ivan Sayers, a curator who amassed a vast costume collection, mostly of women's historical clothes. I asked him if he'd ever tried them on, and was surprised, possibly incredulous, when he said he had not, would not. Had I access to such treasures, I know what I'd be doing pretty much every night of the week. Around about the same time I was going through a hagiography phase, as one does, and learned about Zita of Lucca. A melding occurred.

Hazel was a show with which I was obsessed as a child. It ran for five seasons, 1961–1966, and when I first read about Saint Zita and her long, troubled tenure with the Fatinelli family, Hazel Burke and the Baxters came immediately to mind. I was sure Zita, who relied on the angels to do her baking, would love the opening credit sequence where Shirley Booth, in the eponymous role, takes cookies from the oven and the family, drawn to the kitchen by the fragrance, gathers round. Shirley Booth (1898–1992) was a brilliant actor who really made something out of Hazel. She's buried in the Mount Hebron Cemetery in Montclair, New Jersey. Look on the Find a Grave website and you'll see she shares a plot and a headstone – a massive boulder – with her second husband, who predeceased her by many years. Writ large on the stone under which they lie is his surname, "BAKER." Zita would love that. I do, too.

"With Man to Dwell"

This is embarrassing for me, and will be a frustration to any historical bibliographers who might be jonesing for the detail, but whatever computer on which the original story was written has long since been decommissioned, and the relevant roll of microfilm has disappeared from the Vancouver Public Library, and no one at the paper has any idea, and I've never been a keeper of hard copies, so I can't tell you what the original title of this story might have been when it was published in the *Georgia Straight* in their Christmas edition of, I think, 1996. It was written so long ago, I hardly recognize myself in it, my own style, I mean. It sounds to me as though I was caught up in someone else's voice, which I might well have been; this happens, in the same way one might wind up saying "y'all" after a day in Texas. Whose voice, though? Some wry dame's, I figure; possibly I was playing parrot to Tama Janowitz's pirate. I admired her *Slaves of New York* when it was published ten years earlier. I think it's possible that the cadences of her stories about Eleanor and Stash made their way into this account of Philip and Gary, much diluted, of course. I know I wouldn't have done this deliberately, certainly didn't see it at the time. But now, a quarter century later, I find myself wondering.

"Sinners, Reconciled"

"It's in the Cards" was the original title when this story was published in the *Georgia Straight*, December 23–30, 1999. It won some prize, I think it was the gold medal in fiction (who knew such a thing existed?) at the National Magazine Awards in 2000, so mother pin a big fat fucking rose on me.

I suspect no one reading this – I have such a clear picture of who you are, dear reader (I use the singular advisedly), and it's plumb amazing how much you look like me, and how nearby you live – will need to be reminded that Peter Gzowski (1934–2002) was the host of CBC Radio's *Morningside* from 1982 through 1997. It was a very popular and influential program and Peter – I knew him, just a little – was venerated, a radio god. The letter segments, where Peter was often joined by Shelagh Rogers, were especially beloved. I was always struck by how those letters represented the authentic voices, urban and rural, of the listeners but also suggested an evolving and particularly Canadian literary style. I observed, as does Bonnie in the story, that they seemed to be written with Peter's, or Shelagh's, voice in mind. I kept an informal tally of the phrase "needless to say," which cropped up in most of them, usually as a signal that the peroration was near to hand. It made me grit my teeth and also rejoice at my own smug perspicacity. I was horrible then. I'm horrible now. More so, really. Oh, well. It's almost over.

"Sinners, Reconciled," in that first iteration, was published twenty years ago. To Bonnie are imputed reflections on changing weather patterns that now seem uninformed or otherwise naive, but "climate change" in 1999 seemed futuristic and speculative; it wasn't yet widely bandied about as a concept or damaging possibility. Let's cut her some slack on that front, at least.

"Bless All the Dear Children"

The *Georgia Straight* was incredibly kind and supportive to me during the years when I was able to stand the sound of my own voice in my head and wrote columns for them, along with occasional longer pieces. They published this story – as always, much shorter – in their December 20–27, 2007, issue. "A Waxy Christmas," it was called, again, not by me. Well. Not to complain. They were brave to take it on.

This is one of two stories in the book that hinge on something dire happening during a vocal performance. Students of my oeuvre, were there any, would know I've used this ploy, also in a Christmastime setting, elsewhere: a rut, I'll be the first to admit. The unnamed narrator's high-school mentor, lydia de'ath, who inserts many editorial comments, favours the lower case for her name. This was a decision made before Kevin Williams from Talonbooks matched me with editor andrea bennett, who also prefers lower case, and whose comments are more enriching and improving than those offered by lydia. This would be a good time to make that libel-quashing disclaimer about how any resemblance to persons living or dead, or to named and recognizable places, is entirely coincidental. Specifically, may I aver there is no building in Vancouver's West End called the Pauline Johnson Mansions and that, while there is a restaurant called Tavola just west of Denman on Robson Street, which is more or less the neighbourhood described in the story, there is no restaurant called Tabula. Let it also be known that while the bar at Tabula (fictional) is much like the bar at Tavola (actual) it is not the same bar. It's just not. Please be advised that while behind the bar at Tavola presides the charming and pulchritudinous Dennis, he does not have a man bun, nor is he named Bjorn. Bjorn is the bartender at Tabula, which is made up, and which is not Tavola, which is dimensional. Tabula is a fiction, utterly. Tavola is real. I eat there, often. At the bar. In the care and keeping of Dennis. Who is not Bjorn. Hi, Dennis.

"In Flesh Revealing"

Another one from the *Georgia Straight,* God bless them. "Della's Hair" was the original title – I think that was my own! – when it appeared in the December 18–25, 2003, edition. Della, of course, is the woman in O. Henry's "Gift of the Magi" who sells her hair to buy her husband, Jim, a watch chain, only to find that he has sold his watch in order to buy her combs for her hair. Oops. Spoiler alert. I wonder if "Gift of the Magi" is still a high-school staple? I hope so. *I Saw Three Ships* is dedicated to Jean McKay whose *Exploded View: Observations on Reading, Writing and Life* should be as celebrated as "Gift of the Magi." Jean – we are only peripherally acquainted, really, but I'm so glad to know her – has a rare, rare mind. She is a brilliant writer. A dedication is a dedication, and I didn't want to seem wavering or indecisive by tossing in other names, willy-nilly. Jean, I know, won't mind if I use this forum to say that in writing this story, and most particularly in revising it, I felt the presence of my own mother, Margaret Frances (1927–2003), and any number of other women, colleagues, friends, acquaintances, stricken and valiant and determined, and most, mercifully, still among the quick. Long may they reign.

"Sin Error Pining"

Originally "O Holy Night," it was broadcast on *Sunday Afternoon in Concert* on CBC Radio 2, December 2007, as part of a special program called *Carols and Legends*, which was recorded at Glenn Gould Studio, at the CBC Broadcasting Centre in Toronto.

The urtext was very short and very quickly written. It was revised and published in *Reader's Digest* the following year. When I looked at the story again, I was struck by how the church-choir alto, with whom Weldon has his one and only fling, and who, in the original story was never accorded the courtesy of a name, is described as "willing." Obviously, the public discourse over the last few years makes so flip an assurance catch in the throat. I always preserve, on principle, a skeptical distance from any social movement that catches fire and fans its own flames, #metoo and #timesup, no more nor less than any other. They are the work of human beings and therefore imperfect and to be feared when they become powerful. That said, it was when I reread that little throwaway, meant-to-be-jokey line, "a willing alto," and found myself doubting it, or, at least, questioning it, that I understood how much I'd been educated by the uprising. (I won't say "woke," because I just won't say "woke.") I wanted the revised story to reflect, however awkwardly, that shift in awareness. Weldon, then, becomes someone who understands that a change is taking place and is studied enough to know he must acknowledge it, even if he doesn't do as so feelingly as might be ideal, even if his contrition is contrived.

The envoi to "Sin Error Pining," and to the collection, is from Walt Whitman's "The Last Invocation." The story's epigraph, from the title song to John K. Samson's 2016 album *Winter Wheat*, is used with the kind permission of John K. Samson. I love this album, in its entirety, and it took on a kind of talismanic importance for me while I was doing the revision work on these stories. That was a bleak time, tainted by loss and discouragement, and I found solace in these songs, which chart their own course of irony and melancholy. The simple, self-evident truth that the world is what we have, that it is necessarily sufficient to our needs, I found reassuring. I waited for that line to come along – buoyed by John's witty quotes from the "Ode to Joy" and Christine Fellows's harmonies – with the same avidity I brought as a child to the closing credits of *The Friendly Giant*, when the sun set on Friendly's castle and the cow jumped over the moon. To that particular moment of crude animation, that enchanting display of bovine agility, I attached huge importance. Occasionally, the credits would be cut short and the cow would be gravity-bound overnight, confined to Earth, and I would be devastated and nervous and good for nothing. Seeing that leap was a sign to me that all would be well; God knows why, because by the time I started school I'd accumulated plenty of evidence to the contrary. Nonetheless, I held onto the certainty. It's exactly the same primitive magical thinking that informs Gary's reliance on Weldon's singing success.

I was interested to learn, from John, that the line in *Winter Wheat* that snagged my attention and so comforted me and that I wanted to allude to here, is, in fact, a borrowing. John based it on this passage from the masterful and much-lauded novel *A Complicated Kindness* by Miriam Toews (Knopf Canada, 2004) who, like John, is an old prairie soul. "I want to be nine again and be told, Nomi: someday you'll be gone, you'll be dust, and then even less than dust. Nothing. There's no good other place to be. This world is good enough for you because it has to be. Go ahead and love it." Thanks to Miriam Toews for permission to quote, and to anyone who paid me the immense compliment of reading these unwholesome stories, in whole or in part. God speed. Goodbye.

BILL RICHARDSON lives in Vancouver's West End neighbourhood, located on xʷməθkʷəẏəm, Sḵwx̱wú7mesh, Stó:lō, and səlilwətaɁɬ unceded Lands, as well as in the Manitoba rural municipality of Louise, located on the Treaty 1 Ancestral and Traditional Lands of the Anishinaabeg (ᐊᓂᔑᓈᐯᐠ), Očhéthi Šakówiŋ (Sioux), and Métis Nations.